For Luke.

TANYA BIRD

THE Captain's Prize

THE COMPANION SERIES

5

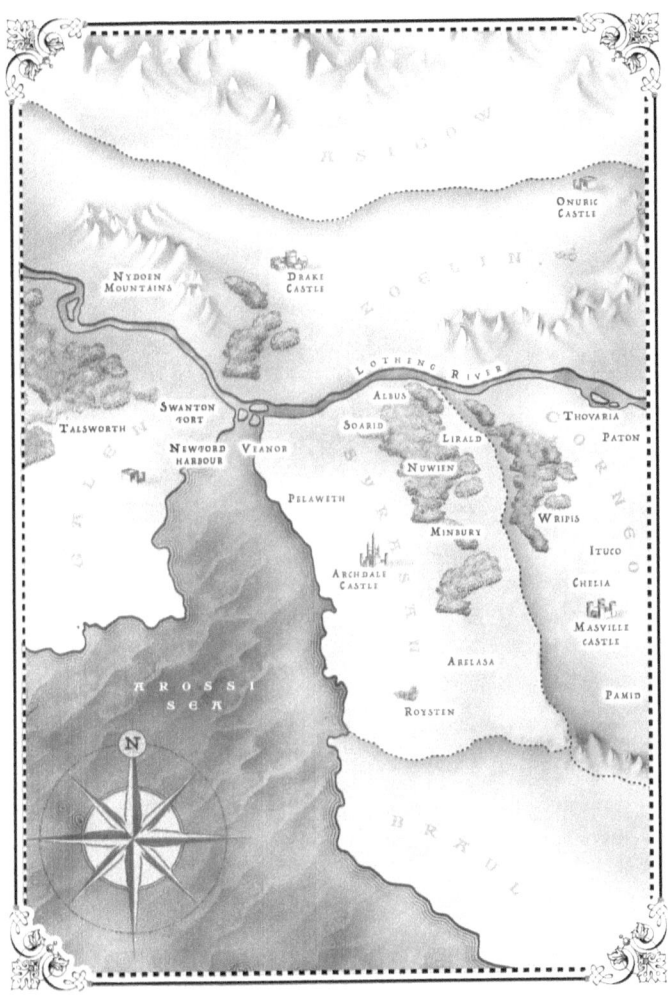

CHAPTER 1

The walk along the north corridor felt painfully long that morning. Astra glanced at the colourful windows as she passed, trying to gauge the time. Soon, the sun would rise, splashing colour across the floor. But for now, she walked in shadows, her head high despite the paint smudged beneath her eyes and bare lips. She had spent so much time perfecting that lip line the night prior.

A maid came towards her, nodding a greeting as she passed. There was no judgement, no pity, just a brief acknowledgement of her existence. More footsteps approached, and Astra held her breath. A servant walked by, frowning in her direction. Definitely some judgement this time. She set her cold eyes on him, and he looked away. Her inner critic was loud enough without the disapproval of those who cleaned the mud off her boots.

For the first time since arriving at Archdale, Astra was *not* returning from King Pandarus's chambers. The evening had not gone to plan—not her plan, anyway. She was supposed to be the star attraction, admired at a distance as she had always been. Sure, Pandarus barely looked in her direction nowa-

1

days, but plenty of others did. Her role was to ensure the guests were at ease, fill their cups, speak to them in their language, pay attention to every word that passed their lips. Smile, laugh in that way that made men feel good about themselves, and play the harp like no one else could. That was her talent, after all, the thing that separated her from the others. No other Companion came close.

It was the first time King Tuyon of Asigow had visited Syrasan, and King Pandarus was eager to make a good impression. The women had joked that he might offer his firstborn son as a welcoming gift. But he had not done that— he had offered Astra instead. What bigger gesture was there than to offer one's prize Companion.

Astra forced her hands open as every muscle in her body grew rigid with the memories. Despite his rather dominating tendencies in bed, she had performed her role perfectly. He had been completely unaware of the repulsion, the disconnect.

She reminded herself to breathe.

'Good girl,' her mentor would say. 'Now go wash off the stench of your vile act.'

Maybe not those exact words.

Now Astra had to face the other Companions, who would be so pleased to witness her fall. She could hardly blame them. Ten years was a lifetime for a Companion.

As she neared their quarters, she could feel a headache starting behind her eyes. They were becoming a regular occurrence.

'That is part of ageing,' Panthea had said with a smirk.

'Likely stress,' the physician had said when Fedora had insisted she be examined.

Astra paused outside the main room, eyes sinking shut for a moment. She could hear Mira, Pandarus's latest purchase, humming inside. God, she was the last person

Astra wanted to see. Taking a few deep breaths, she walked into the room, where she was met with the warmth of the fire and the smell of hot soup.

'Morning' came Mira's sweet voice.

Astra could tell by her smug expression that she knew. 'Good morning.' She made her way over to the fire, rubbing her hands together in front of the flames. The heat made little difference to her icy hands.

Mira resumed humming. It was the song she had sung at the feast the evening prior, the one that had brought kings to their feet. The applause had gone on and on, Astra forced to clap along with them until they finally sank down into their seats. The new Companion was only seventeen, her entire future ahead of her.

'Are the others here?' Astra asked, not looking away from the fire. She might be spared some embarrassment if they were not.

Mira flitted around the large table straightening the cutlery, all fresh-faced and energetic. 'Only Violeta. She is taking a bath.'

Astra tried to remember if she had been the same at that age. Her chest tightened when she realised how many years ago that was.

Fedora entered the room and stopped when she spotted Astra. Her eyebrows rose in surprise. 'I did not know you were back.' She looked Astra over before asking, 'How did it go with King Tuyon?'

Did she really expect an honest answer in front of Mira? 'Very well.'

Fedora's gaze flicked to the new Companion, who had stilled to listen. 'As you were.' Once Mira resumed fiddling with the items on the table, the mentor returned her attention to Astra. 'You go and take a bath. We can speak later.'

Astra blinked, eyes heavy. King Tuyon had fallen asleep

before dismissing her. Trapped beneath one heavily muscled leg, she had been forced to stare at the roof of his bedchamber until he woke. 'Yes, my lady.'

Fedora cleared her throat. 'And do not forget your herbs.'

Astra never forgot her herbs.

'I can assist you if you would like,' Mira offered.

Astra regarded the girl for a moment. Always *so* helpful. On top of that, she could sing, dance, play the flute, already spoke two languages before coming to Archdale, and seemed to pick up everything else at twice the speed of the average Companion. Fedora had always said that some women were born for the role. Mira was one of them.

'That will not be necessary.' Turning, she stepped past Fedora and exited through the door on the other side. She walked down the passageway to the bathing room, relieved to find it empty. Violeta must have gone to dress.

Leaning against the wall, Astra took a moment. That was all she would give herself, one moment. Then no tears, over-thinking, self-pity, or replaying the events of the night in her mind. It was done. It was over. And it was just *one* evening. It was not as though she had been handed over to some random guest. King Tuyon ruled the Asigow empire. In many ways, it was an honour.

Pushing off the wall, Astra walked over to the steaming tub and tugged down her dress. She let it fall to the wet floor, standing on it as she pulled off her undergarments, dumping those also. The maids could burn them for all she cared. She would never wear them again.

Astra climbed into the tub and lowered herself into the water. Her gaze fell to the purple mark on her left breast, and a spark of anger coursed through her. It was bad enough that she had to endure Tuyon's company for an entire evening, but now she would be reminded of it every time she was naked.

Her fingernails turned white as she held the edge of the bath. *Not too much longer*, she told herself. She had performed her role without fault for a decade. She was the longest-serving royal Companion and the obvious next choice for mentor. While Fedora was still beautiful in her forties and able to perform the role, every mentor had an expiration date—as did every Companion. At twenty-six, Astra had all the experience one needed for the role, while encompassing everything it represented. Pandarus owed her that much.

Letting go of the tub, Astra sank beneath the water's surface, washing away her sins. She watched bubbles rise from her mouth.

Just a little longer.

CHAPTER 2

*I*t was Dion's version of hell. Four kings bumping egos for three days on foreign land. It was also the first time in history an Asigow king had ventured farther south than the Zoelin border. Everyone had been on edge since King Tuyon had arrived with his party of warriors, except the unshakable King Jayr of Zoelin, who appeared to thrive on tension.

Dion was playing the role of bodyguard to King Linus. The new Galen king had requested the highly trained captain for the trip. Understandable given the company he would keep during his stay. Thankfully, Stamitos had also been forced to attend. Saviour of his sanity. The young prince managed Syrasan's relations with neighbouring kingdoms, though his main job seemed to be managing his brother's ego. From what Dion had observed, King Pandarus of Syrasan was one of the reasons his wife chose to remain in Galen with their daughters on a more permanent basis.

'Where did you disappear to last night?' Stamitos asked, circling him. The men were sparring in Archdale's training yard, the prince's hair stuck to his sweaty forehead and his shirt untucked. He held a sword in his left hand; the other had been cut off a few years back. All in the name of love, according to Dion's sources.

'Bed. I'm only required to stay as long as my king, and he's not as young as he used to be.' Linus had not taken the throne until his mid-fifties thanks to his father's good health.

'Lucky you.' Stamitos delivered a sequence of blows with his wooden sword, looking rather pleased with himself when Dion was forced to take a step back. There was a small shield strapped to the severed limb, a clever device Stamitos's father-in-law had made for him. 'Pandarus likes to be the last man standing at the end of a feast. Barely standing, mind you.'

Dion stopped, wiping a calloused hand down his face. The frosty air felt good. The snow had melted in Syrasan, but the cold lingered. 'The man can drink. Can't dance to save his own life though.'

Stamitos winced. 'Got a little messy towards the end.'

'Wine and women in excess.'

Stamitos let go of his weapon. 'I noticed you did not dance once.'

'I don't know any Syrasan dances.'

'The Companions know *every* traditional Galen dance, so that is a terrible excuse.'

Of course they did. Dion dropped his sword on the ground. 'They seemed in high demand.'

'You are supposed to get in line with everyone else.' Stamitos unstrapped the shield from his arm and dropped that on the ground also.

'I was content being a spectator.'

A smile played on Stamitos's lips. 'Yes, I noticed that.'

Dion looked at him. 'What?'

'Watching one woman in particular, if my memory serves me correctly.'

Dion handed his weapon to the young boy collecting them. 'What are you going on about?'

'I am referring to the redhead who held your attention for most of the evening.'

Ah. It was true that one woman had caught his eye—a few times. 'Don't know what you mean.'

Stamitos watched him with amusement. 'Her name is Astra, by the way.'

He knew her name. He also knew she belonged to King Pandarus. She was beautifully packaged trouble. 'You Syrasans and your strange traditions.'

The two men turned and began walking back up the hill towards the castle.

'I learned something interesting this morning,' Stamitos said, falling into step with him.

'What's that?'

'Astra left the feast with King Tuyon last night.'

Dion wiped the sweat from his forehead. 'We're still talking about her?'

'Yes.'

He shook his head. 'All right, I'll bite. Why is that so interesting?'

Stamitos drew a long breath, as though preparing to tell an important story of his ancestors. 'She is my brother's longest-standing Companion, a decade at his side.'

Dion rolled his eyes. 'Hasn't your brother had a dozen Companions since coming of age?'

Stamitos waved a finger at him. 'But only one who has stood the test of time.'

Dion could see why. She had one of those smiles that stopped a man in his tracks and bright blue eyes that anchored him there. Then there was that dress with the ridiculous neckline, ensuring every grown man in attendance had looked her way.

He had listened to some of her conversations from a safe distance. She seemed intelligent enough, had a sense of humour, appeared worldly despite her sheltered existence inside the castle walls. And she could *really* play that harp of hers, closing those pretty blue eyes and not opening them until the last note rang out. He had wondered where she disappeared to.

Stamitos stopped walking. 'Are you even listening to me?'

Dion turned and nodded. 'Yes.'

A mischievous smile spread across Stamitos's face as something caught his attention behind Dion. 'What convenient timing.'

The captain turned to see what he was talking about. The Companions were coming towards them, dressed as though they were attending a fancy event. Their gowns did not seem warm enough for the weather. They were holding blankets and carrying books, likely headed to the cherry trees, where Dion had spotted them the day before. He stepped to the side of the path to let them by, but they did not stroll past, instead stopping to greet the men formally.

'My lord. Captain' came a chorus of pretty voices. They all dropped into a curtsy.

Astra was standing within arm's reach, her eyes moving briefly over him before turning her attention to the prince. She was hard to miss with that startling hair and those matching cherry lips. Dion made a point of not looking at her while Stamitos's laughing eyes remained on him.

'Ladies,' the prince said. 'Lovely day to be reading outdoors. Would you not agree, Captain?'

Dion looked tiredly in his direction. 'Yes.' One word. That was all he would give his friend before nodding at the ladies and strolling away.

A few moments later, Stamitos caught up with him. 'Would it have killed you to at least wait for me?'

'Probably.'

'I think you broke a few hearts back there.' Stamitos's eyes shone with mischief.

Dion glanced over his shoulder at the women walking off in the other direction. 'I suspect their hearts are well guarded.'

Stamitos laughed. 'You might be right.' He adjusted the sleeve of his shirt. 'I trust you are coming to the card game tonight?'

He normally loved cards, but he usually played with soldiers, not spoiled kings. 'If King Linus is attending, then I must also.'

'Do not be like that. These great men usually wager something worth playing for.'

"Great men" was a stretch. 'It's always the same—women and horses.'

Stamitos turned to look at him. 'You like women and horses.'

'But I'm rather fussy with both.'

'Fussier with women.'

Dion glanced sideways at him. 'And what will you wager?'

Stamitos thought for a moment. 'I have a crate of rather expensive Galen wine.'

It was Dion's turn to laugh. 'The one my king gifted you on your birthday?'

'That is the one.'

'The one we *drank* on the evening of your birthday?'

Stamitos thought for a moment. 'So we did. In that case, I have *half* a crate of fine wine to wager.'

Dion shook his head.

'Be sure to wear your uniform tonight,' Stamitos said. 'The Companions always flock to the men in uniform.'

'I'm required to wear a uniform.'

'With the green sash, the one that makes all the women go weak at the knees.'

Another shake of his head. 'It's a game of cards, not a royal wedding.'

'And your big sword.'

'Shut up.'

They had reached the bailey. Stamitos turned and clapped him on the shoulder. 'I have to see a man about a horse. See you tonight.'

Dion nodded, watched him leave, then glanced once back down the path. He glimpsed the Companions just before they disappeared beneath the blossoming trees. With a shake of his head, he made his way inside.

CHAPTER 3

*T*he card game was being held in King Pandarus's private rooms. All that self-importance in one cosy space. And Dion was running late. He had ended up accompanying King Linus on a hunt that afternoon and barely had time to wash and change.

Rounding the corner of the south corridor, he glanced out the window to gauge the time. The sun was setting, and the servants would soon light the lamps and torches around the castle. For now, he walked in semidarkness. Ahead, he could see two guards outside Pandarus's quarters. Hopefully he would not draw too much attention when he entered.

His feet stopped when he noticed a woman up ahead. She stood just out of sight of the guards, her back to him, eyes down, and one palm pressing the wall as though balancing herself. He took in her rigid posture, a hand pressed to her stomach. Even bathed in darkness, he knew she was a Companion. Her gown, if you could call it that, opened all the way to her buttocks.

As though feeling his gaze, the woman turned suddenly. It was Astra. Her hand left the wall, and she grew taller. The quick transformation into confident goddess was impressive. She smiled, though it did not quite reach her eyes.

'Sorry.' He spoke quietly so as to not draw the attention of the guards. He had intruded on a moment not meant for his eyes.

Her gaze fell to his green tunic, and then she curtsied. 'Captain Dion.'

She knew his name. Of course she did. Every Companion knew the name of every guest.

She took a step forwards, closing some of the distance between them. That vibrant red hair was unmistakable then.

'I can fetch someone for you if you'd like,' he offered.

'Whatever for?' The words came out like a laugh. 'My shoe was loose,' she lied. 'They are so pretty I thought them worth the hassle.'

He looked down at her silk-covered slippers with jewels along the toes. 'I see.'

She flashed those bright teeth at him. 'I am Astra, Companion to King Pandarus.'

Not *only* King Pandarus. 'I thought maybe you didn't want to go in either.'

Her smile never faltered. 'The invitation is an honour.'

He regarded her for a moment, her demeanour so convincing he might have thought she were telling the truth if she were not a Companion. He shook his head. 'You people.'

'Sorry?'

'It's no wonder you fall apart when you think no one's looking. The act must be exhausting.'

She glanced behind her, checking that the guards were not listening. When she turned back to him, her smile was gone. 'Companions do not fall apart, Captain. That is one luxury we do not have.'

He crossed his arms, amused by the change, the glimpse

of something resembling honesty. Eventually he nodded. 'Time for some new shoes, then.'

She stared at him for the longest moment before stepping to the side. 'It might raise eyebrows if we arrive together. You go in first.'

He glanced down at the neckline of her dress. There was barely any more fabric at the front than the back. 'I suspect if we walked in together, no one would be looking at me.'

She cocked her head. 'That almost sounded like a compliment. Was that your intention?'

One corner of his mouth lifted. 'You can take it as a compliment if you'd like.' He moved to the side also, leaning one shoulder on the wall. 'You go ahead. It seems you're far keener than me.'

Her intelligent eyes remained on him a moment longer; then she gave a small curtsy before turning away. Her slippers clicked on the floor as she glided away, hips swinging. The guards reached for the handles of the double doors, pulling them open as she approached. He watched her pause and draw a breath before going inside. The moment she was out of sight, Dion turned so his back was against the wall, though his eyes remained on the door where she had disappeared. She was something all right, the type of something that made sensible men do stupid things.

He waited another few minutes before following after her. One of the guards announced his arrival as he strode in, looking about. He took in the scene in one clean sweep. Well, almost. His vision snagged on Astra momentarily. She was seated beside King Tuyon, who had one enormous arm slung over the back of her chair as he studied his cards.

'You are late,' King Pandarus said, not looking up from his hand.

The Syrasan king was not a fan of his, probably because the captain had not spent the entire visit kissing his arse. The man also liked to assert himself in front of soldiers. He had never seen battle, and a king reliant on others for protection was always going to feel inadequate.

'I apologise, Your Majesty.' His eyes went to the woman seated beside the king. Another Companion, judging by the way she leaned in with familiarity. It seemed she used the same seamstress as Astra, who was feigning interest in the game. He walked to the opposite side of the table, taking the empty chair between Stamitos and another Companion whose name he had forgotten. He leaned towards the prince. 'What have I missed?'

'A lot of drinking,' Stamitos whispered, 'and that is about it.'

Dion looked over at King Linus, who was intensely studying his cards. The man was possibly the worst bluffer Dion had ever come across. Not ideal given the crowd. Dion looked around the rest of the table, eyes meeting with King Jayr of Zoelin's. The man nodded before returning his attention to his cards. In addition to royalty, there was King Linus's advisor, Philo, and Grandor Pollux, who seemed more interested in watching the Companions than playing cards.

Noticing Dion's wandering gaze, Stamitos said, 'I do not believe you are acquainted with the Companions of Archdale.'

Dion picked up the cards in front of him. If it were just the two of them, he would have shoved the prince off his chair. 'I met most of the ladies at the feast last night.' A lie— and Stamitos knew it.

The prince gestured to the woman seated beside Pandarus. 'That is Mira, royal Companion to our beloved king.'

Mira bowed her head.

'To your right are the noble Companions,' Stamitos

continued. He spoke Zoelin, the only language every guest understood. 'Violeta, Rhea, and Panthea.'

Dion acknowledged the women, who all wore matching smiles and copious amounts of paint on their faces.

'And seated across from you is the talk of Syrasan, Astra.'

Dion looked across the table at her. She stared back at him.

'And which category do you fall under, royal or noble?'

Her expression fell, and he immediately regretted the question.

'Astra is next in line to mentor, which will make her queen of the Companion world,' Stamitos said, saving her. The prince had a talent for putting everyone at ease.

'Are we actually going to play?' Pandarus asked, leaning his elbows on the table.

Dion was still watching Astra, who was keeping a polite distance between herself and King Tuyon. She glanced at him, then away. More of a glare, perhaps.

'What are we playing for tonight, gentlemen?' Stamitos asked. 'I have a dozen bottles of fine Galen wine on offer.'

Pandarus looked up at him. 'Did you steal them from my cellar?'

Everybody laughed.

'Not this time,' Stamitos replied.

'Prince Stamitos won *me* once,' Violeta said. 'Never did claim his winnings.'

'If my memory serves me correctly, the prince lost that evening,' Astra said, 'and you offered yourself as a consolation prize.'

More laughter, though Violeta's was a little stilted.

'Happily married and all that,' Stamitos said.

King Tuyon dragged Astra's chair a little closer. She managed to keep smiling.

'I thought happy marriages were a myth,' he said.

The Asigow king had managed to avoid marriage so far, though soon he would need an heir. There had been rumours of Princess Tasia of Zoelin as a potential match.

'They *are* a myth,' King Jayr said, speaking up for the first time.

It was a bold comment, given he was married to Pandarus and Stamitos's sister. Pandarus said nothing, while Stamitos sat a little straighter in his chair.

'My sister has won the hearts of the Zoelin people.'

Jayr looked up tiredly. 'Yes, she is an excellent performer.'

'She just needs to be pulled into line,' King Tuyon said, running a finger along Astra's cheek.

Dion marvelled at her ability to remain still as he touched her openly in front of the other guests.

'I am prepared to offer up one of my prize fillies,' King Linus said.

King Tuyon glanced at Astra. 'I would take another evening with Astra over any beast, no matter how well bred.'

'Our Astra is well bred,' Panthea said. 'Just look at that flawless confirmation.'

All eyes were on her then. Agitation twitched inside Dion.

'Now I feel a bit like a filly at the sale yards.' Astra kept her tone light.

Pandarus spoke up at that. 'You do realise that fillies are *young* horses?'

Dion's gaze snapped to the king. Had he really just said that? It was a special breed of man who took pleasure in publicly putting down women. As if Dion needed another reason to dislike him. He was tempted to say something but did not want to put himself in the middle of whatever lovers tiff they were having.

'Age is just a number,' Rhea said, joining the conversation.

Astra tore her gaze away from Pandarus to look in the

Companion's direction. Her blue eyes had lost their vibrancy.

'I see a queen,' King Tuyon said, bending to brush his lips over her neck.

She managed another smile. 'You are very kind.'

'Are we playing?' Dion asked, his tone sharper than it should have been in a room filled with kings.

Pandarus glanced at him. 'Somewhere you need to be, Captain?'

Oh, how he wished there were. 'No, but I came to play cards, Your Majesty.'

'You have not told us what you are wagering.' Pandarus leaned back in his chair. 'Does Goldmont House produce anything besides orphans? My kingdom has enough of those.'

Dion's eyes did not leave the king. Every muscle in his body was rigid as he stared at the arrogant pig. 'Apples, Your Majesty.'

A smug grin spread across Pandarus's face. 'I have enough apples.'

'For your people.' He watched the king, knowing he was stepping into dangerous territory. 'Starvation is still the leading cause of death in the south of Syrasan, is it not?'

The smile vanished from Pandarus's face. He leaned forwards again. 'What about rain, Captain? Can you wager that instead?'

Dion glanced at King Linus, whose eyes held a warning for him. He returned his attention to his cards. 'Afraid not, Your Majesty.'

Stamitos cleared his throat. 'Well, the orchard at Goldmont House produces three and a half tonnes of fruit each season, so let us say five hundred pounds for anyone prepared to collect the fruit.'

'I hear the climate in Asigow makes it difficult to grow fruit,' Mira said.

King Tuyon looked in her direction. 'Apples we manage.' He stretched his neck from side to side. 'I will wager five children.'

Everyone stilled, except King Jayr, who continued sorting his cards.

'You're wagering *children*?' Dion asked incredulously.

Stamitos kicked his leg under the table, reminding him that now was not the time.

'They make loyal soldiers if trained from a young age,' Jayr said before turning his attention to King Linus. 'What about you? What does Galen have to offer?'

King Linus cleared his throat. 'I have a brood mare worth a small fortune.'

'Gentlemen,' Stamitos said, 'the game is all fours. We are all familiar with the rules?'

'I am certainly familiar with the position,' Jayr said, making King Tuyon laugh.

Dion caught Astra's eye briefly before looking down at his cards.

'What is the matter, Captain?' Pandarus asked. 'Is the humour too crude for your sensibilities?'

'I'm a soldier, Your Majesty. I've heard far worse.'

Stamitos cleared his throat. 'What are you wagering, brother?'

Pandarus lowered his cards, looking around the table. 'Since everyone else is being half arsed, I guess it is up to me to offer a *real* incentive.' He looked at King Linus. 'Since you are offering your prize mare, I will wager a prize of my own.'

'Another horse?' Mira asked.

Pandarus emptied the cup she had just refilled for him. 'A Companion.'

King Jayr looked up at that, settling back in his chair to take in everyone's reaction. 'Which one?'

Dion could not help a glance at Astra. She was ashen, her fingertips pressing into the arms of the chair.

'Astra,' Pandarus said.

Dion looked down. Mira stiffened in her chair beside him. There was a collective intake of breath to his right, the noble Companions unable to hide their shock. Stamitos dropped his cards face down on the table.

'Pandarus—'

'You do not have to play, brother. I know how protective you are of the women.' His gaze fell to Stamitos's missing hand. 'Who is ready to play?'

Violeta leaned forwards, seeming confused. 'Do you mean one night with Astra, Your Majesty?'

'No.'

Grandor Pollux suddenly looked far more interested in the game. Philo stood, excusing himself from the table. King Linus looked unsure of what to do. Stamitos rose, scraping his chair against the floor.

'You cannot be serious,' he said.

Pandarus looked up at him tiredly. 'You are the one who is always telling me I should cull my collection.'

'Those comments were more along the lines of *"stop buying new ones"*.'

Astra sat white-faced with her hands folded in her lap. She looked ready to fall off her chair. Dion could not help but feel sorry for her.

Stamitos left without another word. The other Companions all sat in stunned silence. King Tuyon was looking at Astra like he had already won.

Pandarus looked around at the remaining players. 'Anyone else want to leave?'

Dion considered it. He could get up and leave like the others. Easy. But he could also win if he tried. Then he could collect his new horses, keep his apples, and he and Stamitos could drink the rest of the birthday wine the moment they returned to Goldmont House. He could spare the children and the Companion a much worse fate.

'Captain?' Pandarus asked.

Dion focused on his cards. 'Ready to play, Your Majesty.'

The king patted Mira's leg, then leaned forwards. 'Let us begin.'

CHAPTER 4

'Shall I sing something?' Mira was trying to ease the tension in the room, the only one able to think through the fog of it. Astra meant to reply, but her voice seemed to be failing her.

'Lovely idea,' Rhea said, nodding encouragingly at Mira.

That was when Astra realised that her harp had never even been brought in. Pandarus wanted no part of her. She did not know where to look. Not at Mira, who had replaced her so easily. Not at the other Companions, who stared at her with pitiful expressions. Not King Tuyon or King Jayr, who were positively predatory in that moment.

Tuyon's hand found her leg beneath the table. Was that to be her life? A silent plaything at his side in the land of ice and snow?

She looked across at Captain Dion, finding him watching her over the top of his cards. He looked down when their eyes met. What did she know of him? That admittedly handsome face was completely unreadable. Fedora had told them only that his father had been a captain in the army also, beheaded for treason four years earlier.

Tuyon's hand left her leg, reaching for his empty cup and waving it in the air. A servant stepped forwards to fill it. Astra should have taken care of that, should have ensured the guests' cups were always full, every need taken care of. Failure was breeding failure.

Mira's voice was too large for the small room. She was using up all the air.

The hand returned to Astra's leg, causing her to jump. Dion glanced up at that. She did not look at him this time. Perhaps it was a test. Maybe Pandarus wanted to see how she would perform her role under pressure. She was more than capable, just needed to focus on one thing at a time. Chin up, relax the jaw, some slow breaths. That was better.

She wet her lips, feeling returning to them. A smile. Almost there.

She leaned towards King Tuyon and rested a hand on his large arm. Pandarus looked over at that, and she paid him no attention. She needed to take back some of the power he had snatched away. Never mind her wildly beating heart and dry mouth. Pandarus was *very* good at cards, and there was every chance he would win. That was probably why he had offered her up, to impress his guests while knowing that nothing would come of it.

Cards were going down, and Astra struggled to keep track of the game. A four, a two, a seven. Who had put down the seven?

'Stand,' Dion said, his face giving nothing away.

Pollux dealt three more cards each, and the game continued.

Astra shifted in her chair, fearing her rigid bones would fuse if she did not move. When it came time for King Tuyon to deal, he turned up a jack. That was not good—for her. Tuyon emptied his cup, and this time Astra took it from his hand, smiled up at him, and gestured to the servant. The guests were leaving the next day. Just one more night of this insanity; then they would all be gone, and Pandarus would be in a good mood after the win. The man loved to win.

More cards went down.

Astra swallowed, but her tongue would not move in her mouth. She looked behind her to the table of refreshments, thinking about asking the servant to bring her something, but did not trust herself to speak. She was about to slip away from the table and get it herself, but Tuyon's hand tightened on her leg.

'Stay,' he said. 'You're my good luck.'

She nodded and faced forwards again. A minute later, the captain slid his full cup across the table in her direction. Astra looked from the cup to him, but he was staring at his cards. Her gaze instinctively flicked to Pandarus who was so engrossed in the game he had not noticed. She hesitated before picking it up and taking a sip, resisting the urge to empty it in a few greedy gulps. Her gaze returned to Dion, finding him watching her this time. She gave a small nod of thanks before he looked away. He placed another card on the table.

Pollux placed his cards down. 'King Tuyon and Captain Dion are both on six points.'

Pandarus tossed his cards on the table, gesturing for Mira to stop singing and fill his drink. He glanced briefly at Astra as Mira returned to his side. Astra's fingers whitened around the stem of the cup. He was out of the game.

'Tell you what,' King Tuyon said, leaning back in his chair and looking at Dion. 'How about we divide the winnings and both walk away with what we want?'

Dion watched him from across the table. 'And what is it you want?'

'Astra. You can have the rest.'

If Dion was surprised by the suggestion, he hid it well.

His gaze drifted to Astra, who was trying very hard to relax and failing. She could not go to Asigow, could not belong to Tuyon and be his plaything. She did not dare look back at Dion, because she did not want him to see all the fear she was barely containing.

'I appreciate the offer, Your Majesty,' Dion said, 'but I'd prefer to see the game through.'

Tuyon shook his head. 'You might leave with nothing.'

'I might.'

Tuyon looked down at his cards, considering his options for a moment before placing one down, following suit. Astra watched as Dion did the same. A few more cards were dropped onto the table, and then King Tuyon cursed under his breath and tossed his cards, leaning back in his chair to regard Dion.

'Very lucky hand, Captain.'

Astra stared at the mess of cards on the table as she processed what had just happened.

'Congratulations,' Pandarus said, emptying his cup again.

Dion straightened his remaining cards and placed them neatly on the table. 'Good game, gentlemen.'

Normally the Companions would congratulate the winner, make a fuss, pour him a celebratory drink, smile. At the very least, smile. Panthea and Violeta sat stunned, while Rhea watched Astra through tear-filled eyes. Mira stared at her lap, looking far from triumphant.

Astra let go of her cup and looked at Dion, wondering what a captain in the Galen army would do with a Companion. Sell her? Yes, she was valuable enough. King Tuyon would make him a private offer. She knew because one of his hands remained like a vice over her leg. Pushing her chair back, she rose, thankful when her legs did the job required of them. She was even more thankful when Tuyon's hand fell away.

'I will give Fedora instructions,' Pandarus slurred, well past drunk now.

Astra's chest tightened as her entire future fell apart. 'Congratulations, Captain,' she said without looking at him. 'Excuse me. I need some air.' She just needed to make it to the door.

Violeta stood also, walking around the table to her. 'Shall we go together?' She offered her arm to Astra.

Astra straightened. She would walk out of that room the same way she always did, with her head high and in complete control of herself. Lowering into a small curtsy, she turned and left with Violeta following closely behind her.

CHAPTER 5

'Stay calm,' Fedora said, hand on her brow, 'while I think through this.'

Astra was pacing from one end of the room to the other, reminding herself to breathe. 'He drank too much. Thought he could win, perhaps.'

Fedora watched her pass. 'I am sure that is part of it.'

'But not all of it?' Astra stopped. 'He has tired of me. Say it.'

'Ten years is a long time—'

'Yes, yes, I know. But you have been mentor for longer than that.' She resumed pacing. 'I do not see him wagering *you* at a game of cards.'

'Lower your voice.'

Astra shook her head. 'Your days of telling me what to do are over.' She was barely aware of the words spilling from her mouth. 'Who knows what plans those men are making for me.' She glanced at the door on the other side of the room, where the other Companions were likely listening.

'The captain has shown very little interest in the women during his visit,' Fedora said.

Astra thought back to their conversation in the corridor. He had seen straight through her lies. 'He will take the first offer made.'

'Let us not get ahead of ourselves. We wait for the king's instructions before panicking.'

Astra stopped walking and faced her mentor again. 'His exact words were "I will give Fedora instructions".'

Mira entered the room, and Fedora looked at her in surprise.

'Why are you not with the king?'

The young girl tried to appear stoic. 'He was not in the mood for company.'

'Did he say why?'

Mira shook her head. 'No, my lady.'

'Has he retired for the evening?' Astra asked, a plan forming.

'I believe so.'

Fedora and Astra looked at each other.

'I will go speak with him,' Fedora said. 'Perhaps I can convince him to make the captain an offer.'

Astra swallowed. 'Ten years I have been his Companion. If there is one thing I know for certain, it is when he is done with a woman, he is done.'

A knock came at the door, and the three women turned to see a messenger standing there.

'A note from the king, my lady.' He held it out and waited for Fedora to collect it, knowing better than to enter the Companions' quarters. Fedora viewed their section of the castle as a sacred space.

Dismissing the messenger, Fedora unfolded the note and read it to herself as she always did. When she was done, she folded it and looked at Astra. Her expression only confirmed what Astra already knew.

'You will depart Archdale in the morning,' Fedora said.

She was gripping the paper too tightly. 'I am to pack you a bag.'

Astra blinked. 'With whom?'

'With the captain, it seems.'

'To Goldmont House?' Her voice rose slightly. 'But it is a *farm*.'

'It is a profitable manor.'

'Known for its sheep and apples.' Astra's eyes widened. 'Is that where Sapphira resides?'

'*Princess* Sapphira. And yes, her charity work is based there.'

'Of course it is.' Astra glared at Mira. 'Is there a reason you are still standing here?'

The girl fled the room.

Astra's gaze returned to Fedora. 'What else does the letter say?'

Fedora drew a breath. 'It contains a list of items you are permitted to take with you.'

'Which are?'

Fedora opened the letter again and read from it. 'Gowns, footwear and any other necessities required for the journey.'

Astra stared at the parchment. 'Ten years I have been at his beck and call. I have stayed silent through every demeaning comment and bad mood, laughed at his terrible jokes, cried out in his bed despite feeling nothing.' She stopped when her eyes began to sting, waiting for the sensation to subside. 'And all I will have to show for it is a handful of gowns and a few pairs of shoes.' Turning slowly, she walked off in the direction of the door.

'Where are you going?' Fedora called to her back.

'To speak with the king,' she replied before disappearing through the door.

Unsurprisingly, footsteps followed after her.

'Astra, stop.'

Her pace quickened. 'No.'

'Do not make me fetch the guards.'

Astra turned on her heel, forcing Fedora to pull up quickly. 'What is it you are afraid of? That my lack of self-control will reflect badly on you? It seems your position here is secure.'

Fedora took a firm grip of Astra's arms. 'I am trying to prevent you from making things worse for *yourself*.'

Astra searched her mentor's eyes. 'How much worse can it get?'

~

The guards on either side of King Pandarus's door made no move to open it.

'I need to speak with His Majesty.' She was calm, courteous, but playful enough to hold their attention. It was an art form—one she was good at.

'He's asked not to be disturbed,' one of the guards said.

She smiled deviously. 'Do I look like a disturbance?'

She watched as his weight moved from one foot to the other.

He sighed. 'Wait here.'

She did as she was told, aware of the other guard watching her. When the man reappeared, he gestured for her to go through. She drew a long, deep breath and walked in. Pandarus was slouched in a chair with his feet resting on a footstool, staring into the open fireplace. A half-filled cup hung in his hand, fresh stains on the rug beneath it. His lips were tinted red from the wine. She knew how bad his breath would be, even with five feet between them. Yes, she knew him so well.

'Let me guess,' he said, not bothering to look at her. 'You just wanted to thank me for housing you, dressing you, spoiling you with gifts you could not have fathomed as a peasant.' He laughed as though it were a joke. 'No. You are here because you want something.' He let his head fall back on the chair. 'You women. It is never enough.' He rolled his head to look at her. 'Go on, then. Say what you have come to say.'

At least she knew what sort of mood he was in. 'I cannot believe it has been a decade.' She took a few steps closer to the fireplace. 'You were twenty-four when I met you—and smitten.'

He studied her face in the poor light. 'And you had just come of age. You were so naive.'

'And you took full advantage.' She smiled when she said that part.

He continued to regard her. 'You want to reminisce about the past? Is that why you are here?'

Her time was running out. 'I just want to know why you did it.'

Pandarus drained his cup before replying. Rather than placing the empty goblet on the nearby table, he dropped it onto the rug. Astra watched it roll as she waited for his reply.

'Can you not feel it?' he said. 'It is over.'

She swallowed. 'So make me mentor.'

He breathed out through his nose. 'Fedora performs her role to an exemplary standard. She is widely respected, despite my dislike for her.'

Astra remained composed. 'I would perform the role to the same standard. That is how it works. Fedora cannot mentor forever. There will come a time when you will need to replace her.'

'And when that time comes, I will do what I must.' He looked at the fire.

'I have fulfilled my role to the highest standard. I am

without question the most highly trained in social etiquette, music—'

'Do you think I give a shit about your musical abilities?'

Astra felt her heart thudding in her ears. 'What?'

'I never cared for the harp.'

She was at a loss for words for a moment. 'You have always enjoyed my playing.'

'I have always enjoyed seeing *others* enjoy your playing.' His gaze returned to the fire. 'I was the envy of every man.'

She had to look away. 'So it was not that I grew stale with you but with your acquaintances. Is that it?'

He thought on the matter. 'I gave you to King Tuyon last night because I wanted to feel that rush of jealousy that has been absent for so long.'

'And what did you feel?'

'Nothing.' The word came out as a whisper.

Astra blinked, went to speak, then closed her mouth. She tried again. 'My mother warned me this day would come.'

'Do not be so dramatic.' He stifled a yawn. 'You are not going to a brothel. The captain should be easy prey for a woman with your skills.'

It was time to leave. 'Goodbye, Your Majesty.' She lowered into a graceful curtsy, hands loosely at her sides, then strode away.

'It could have been worse,' Pandarus called out. 'King Tuyon could have won.'

She closed her eyes as the doors opened in front of her, then exited the room.

CHAPTER 6

*D*ion needed to leave at first light if he stood any chance of making it to Veanor by high tide. When he arrived at the mounting yard, he found Stamitos fiddling with a strap on his saddle. King Linus's horse was also saddled, though there was no sign of him yet.

'I thought you were staying in Syrasan a few extra days,' Dion said.

Stamitos turned to look at him. 'Change of plans.'

'Not avoiding your brother by any chance?'

The prince walked around to the other side of his horse. 'Never.' A smile played on his lips. 'Congratulations, by the way. Heard all about your big win.'

Dion's horse was brought to him, and he thanked the groom. 'Before you go getting any ideas, I'm not keeping all of the prizes.'

Stamitos eyed him. 'Specifics?'

'I'm not taking Astra to Galen. I have no use for a Companion.'

'What exactly is your plan, then? Sell her like a brood mare?'

Dion looked around to ensure no one was listening. 'I had her legally freed this morning.'

Stamitos only looked more confused. 'Freed? You cannot just wipe your hands of her and leave her on the side of the road.'

'She's free to go where she pleases. Home, I imagine.'

Stamitos laughed at that. 'Captain, Captain, Captain.'

'What?'

'*Archdale* is her home.'

'I'm referring to her home before Archdale.'

'There is no before Archdale.'

That made no sense. 'She must've had a home, a family. Ship doesn't leave until this evening. I'll take her there myself.'

Stamitos mounted, shaking his head. 'Let me know how that goes.'

Dion watched him gather the reins. Before he could ask any more questions, he spotted Astra walking towards them, dressed like she were on her way to a social gathering with royalty.

'Good morning,' she said before turning to thank the young servant who had carried her bag down. The boy placed it at her feet before leaving.

'Morning,' Dion replied, picking it up. 'Is that everything?'

She nodded. 'Yes.'

'Do you have a horse?' he asked, realising he had not thought about transport.

Her gaze settled on him. 'Everything I own is in that bag, Captain.'

He tried to read her expression, but she was not giving much away. 'Well, then I guess you'll ride with me.'

'On horseback?'

He began strapping the bag to the horse. 'How do you normally travel?'

'Wagon.'

Dion glanced past her at a smiling Stamitos, who was pretending not to listen. 'Well, I'm afraid you're on horseback this time.' He looked down at her dress, which was far from practical. At least she was wearing boots instead of slippers. 'Do you have another dress?'

She looked down. 'What's wrong with this one?'

'It's... missing parts.'

Stamitos coughed. More of a choke, really.

'All my gowns are rather similar in style,' Astra replied. 'I was not expecting to leave on horseback.'

'And I wasn't expecting to leave with additional people.'

She glanced at the gelding, clearing her throat. 'I can ride a horse if necessary.'

He nodded. 'Good.' When the bag was secure, he turned back to her. 'Listen. I'm not taking you to Galen with me. Neither of us wants that.'

She stared hard at him for a moment. 'Did you sell me to someone else?'

'No, nothing like that. I'm just going to take you home.' He watched the delicate skin between her eyebrows pinch. 'Tell me where you live, and I'll take you there.'

'I do not understand.'

He glanced at Stamitos, who wore a smug expression. 'Where does your family live?' He gestured towards the castle. 'Before all of this.'

'Forgive me, but you plan on... dropping me home?'

Was she angry? Laughing at him? He really could not tell. 'Yes.'

'There is no *before*. That person no longer exists.'

He was very confused. 'You came from somewhere. You must have parents.'

'I did once. I do not know if they remain in the same house, or even the same village for that matter.'

He could barely comprehend it. 'Is that another Companion rule? Cutting all ties with your past?'

'Yes.'

He took the reins from the groom and mounted. 'Well, I guess we'll find out. Which village did you grow up in?' He guessed somewhere in the south, where the hungry did desperate things.

She hesitated before replying. 'Pelaweth.'

Pelaweth was north. If she had been raised there, she was no pauper. 'That's on the way, which makes things easier still.' He offered his hand and steadied the stirrup with his foot, not bothering to wait for the groom to fetch the stool. She stared at his hand for a moment before slipping hers into it. He pulled her up behind him, then looked over at Stamitos.

'Tell King Linus I'll meet him at the port.'

Stamitos looked from him to Astra, then nodded. 'Very well. And good luck.'

'Ready?' Dion asked over his shoulder. She nodded, and he continued to wait. 'I'm not moving until you hold on. Or are Companions incapable of falling from horses?'

Exhaling, she took hold of the back of the saddle. Dion pushed the horse into a walk and nodded at Stamitos, who gave him a playful salute. A few minutes later, the portcullis was opening in front of them. He saw Astra look back at the castle as they passed beneath the arch.

'You all right?' he asked.

'Yes.'

Her tone gave little away. He glanced over his shoulder at her. 'Are you leaving anyone important behind?'

She drew a long, slow breath. 'If it is all the same to you, Captain, I will enjoy the quiet for a while.'

'What a classy way to tell a man to shut up.' He faced forwards again. 'And you can call me Dion. We're not big on titles where I come from, though you probably already knew that. You would know more about Galen culture than I do.'

'Very likely,' she said tiredly.

'Or call me Captain if you prefer. Doesn't really bother me.'

'Will the *silence* bother you, Captain?'

He bit back a smile and pushed his horse into a trot. 'Not at all.'

*A*stra took in the small houses and bustling marketplace from her youth. Children played on the roads, as she had once done with her brother. They stopped to watch the horse pass. Dion saluted them, which made them turn to each other and laugh. Astra figured he liked children, given that Goldmont House was home to a small clan of orphans.

Everything in Pelaweth felt familiar, yet nothing looked the same. Astra had returned every year for the flag tournament, but she had only ever seen the village overrun with people and horses. Without them, the experience was more nostalgic. 'Take a right up here.' She pointed to a road ahead.

A few moments later, Dion turned the gelding onto the narrow road, and they headed towards a tidy wattle and daub house at the end. Astra's heart beat so wildly in her chest that she feared Dion would hear it.

'When was the last time you saw your family?' he asked.

Did he not realise she had no family? She gave them up when she chose the Companion life.

'*If you leave, there's no coming back,*' her father had told her.

The next day she had put herself in Pandarus's way at the flag tournament, knowing it was her one chance to capture his attention.

'Not since I left,' she replied.

'Not one visit?'

'No.'

'What about letters?'

She shook her head, wishing he would stop asking her questions. 'It is just ahead.'

Dion rode right up to the small fence made of sticks, pulling up the horse and looking around. He offered his arm, and she took hold of it as she slid down to the ground. She was surprised how much control and strength he had from that difficult angle. It was strangely reassuring in a moment when she felt ready to fall down. She kept hold of his hand until she was sure her legs were steady.

Chickens roamed in the front garden, looking for insects among the vegetables and flowers. Purple milkweed, snap-dragons, pansies and irises. Flowers of her childhood. She knew at a glance that her family still lived there.

Family.

A chicken flew atop the fence, startling her. She had been responsible for their care as a child, had given them all names. She had even taught one of them tricks.

'*Stop crying into your food,*' her brother had said every time one of the birds appeared on the dinner table. Her mother had scolded her for becoming too attached to them.

'Want me to come in with you?' Dion asked, pulling her from her thoughts.

She shook her head. 'No, thank you.' She smoothed down her dress, tucking loose pieces of hair back into her braid before looking up at him. 'If you have to go—'

'I have some time.' He rested his hands on the front of the saddle, making no move to untie her bag.

Nodding, Astra made her way along the fence. She had barely made it to the gate when a woman stepped out of the house, a hand going over her brow to block the sun. Astra recognised an older version of her mother. Same face, just a few more lines and grey around her hairline. Every year Astra had looked for her at the flag tournament, but she had never shown up. No one had, despite living only a short ride from the venue.

Her mother's hand fell away from her face, her shock evident. 'Astra.'

Even at that distance, she could feel the awkwardness. 'Hello, Mother.' She stepped through the narrow gate, trying to get out of earshot of Dion, but her mother came out to meet her. They stopped a few feet from each other. Astra found a smile because she had no idea what else to do. 'You look well.'

Her mother smiled, but it wavered. 'And you look... just as beautiful as the day you left.' She opened her arms. 'Come on, then. Give your mother a hug.'

Astra stepped into the embrace, patting her lightly on the shoulder before stepping back. Her mother took a step back also.

'Who's that with you?'

Astra looked over her shoulder. 'That is Captain Dion. He is on his way back to Galen.' She faced her mother again. 'He was kind enough to bring me here.'

Her mother frowned as she looked Astra over. 'The king permitting visits nowadays?'

'No.'

Her mother's expression hardened as the pieces fell into place. 'He doesn't want you anymore. Is that it?'

Astra's cheeks heated. 'It is more complicated than that.'

Her mother laughed. 'He's finally tired of you and turned you out.' She tutted. 'If you need money—'

'I am not here for money.' She saw Dion shift atop the horse. 'Is Father here?' Perhaps she would have more success speaking with him.

'At the church.' Her mother wiped her hands on her apron, which was stained with lard.

'He is still the caretaker?'

'It's a very respectable position, and the pay is fair. Rowan works there now.' That was her brother. 'He married Father Rulf's niece.'

Of course he did. He had been the one who paid attention in church. And particular attention to the priest's niece, apparently. 'I am not here to make trouble for anyone.'

'Then why *are* you here?'

Astra pressed her lips together. Because she was an unwanted prize and had nowhere else to go. Yet she could not bring herself to ask her mother for help, the woman who had raised her, warned her against her choices. The woman now using herself as a blockade between Astra and the house.

'Astra,' Dion called out.

She turned.

'Don't keep your mother in suspense. Tell her about the role in Galen, how you'll be helping Princess Sapphira with her charity work.'

Astra was confused at first, then realised he was saving her from the humiliation.

Her mother's eyebrows rose. 'Charity work?'

Dion nodded. 'Astra is going to help Princess Sapphira teach.'

'Orphans,' Astra said, turning back to her mother.

Her mother was speechless for a moment. 'Like a governess?'

She had no idea. 'Exactly like a governess.'

'We should go,' Dion told her. 'Ship leaves at high tide.'

Astra stepped forwards and embraced her mother again. 'I just wanted to see you before I left.' She smiled as she pulled away.

'Well, don't keep the captain waiting.' Her mother ushered her towards the horse.

Astra stepped back through the gate and walked towards the gelding. She took hold of the outstretched hand and was lifted and placed on the back of the horse once again. Dion said nothing as he nodded in the direction of her mother before swinging the horse around and trotting off down the road.

Astra closed her eyes, gripping the saddle tighter. Dion noticed.

'You're not going to fall off, are you?'

'No.' She opened her eyes. 'You did not have to do that.'

'I know.'

'You can just drop me in the village.'

'What for?'

Her mind was racing, and she could not come up with a plan on the spot. 'I will figure this out.'

'I thought we just did.'

She looked at him. 'I do not need your pity, Captain.'

'It's not pity. I'm offering you employment. There's plenty of work to be done at the manor. Princess Sapphira is to give birth to her third child soon. You can teach reading and writing, can't you?'

She studied his face, trying to gauge his sincerity. 'You said you did not want to take me to Galen.'

'I said I have no need for a Companion, but you have other skills, don't you?'

She nodded. 'History, languages, the arts.'

He did not look impressed. 'The arts? Like painting?'

'That is one form, yes.'

'Can you cook?'

'A little.'

'A little?'

She bit her lip. 'I cooked before going to Archdale.'

He turned his body to look at her. 'You haven't made a meal in ten years?'

'I have not needed to.'

'But you can paint a landscape.'

'Yes.'

Dion faced forwards again. 'You'd think they would teach the Companions useful skills.'

'My skills are useful.'

'If I needed some colours mixed or a harp tuned, sure.'

She cleared her throat. 'I am a fast learner, Captain.'

They rode in silence until Dion said, 'I'm offering you a job if you want it. Princess Sapphira will be focused on the baby for at least a few months. That should give you some time to come up with a plan.'

She watched him for a moment. 'This feels a lot like a pity offer.'

'Maybe,' he admitted. 'But I think we can help each other for a few months. Assuming you can teach children.'

She had no idea, had not been around them since she was one herself. 'Of course I can teach children.'

'Though I might need you to be more practical in your approach. Princess Sapphira will guide you.'

Astra winced at that last part. 'To be clear, what will our relationship be?'

'You and I?'

'Yes.'

'Employer and employee.'

She looked around. 'Except that you have a piece of parchment that states I am your property.' She knew he had been given a legal document transferring ownership—just like one did for an expensive horse.

'I had a different document drawn up. I've no interest in owning anyone. That includes the children King Tuyon so generously offered up.'

Her hands went limp around the saddle. 'You could have sold me if you did not want me, you know.'

'I know. King Tuyon made me an offer.'

No surprises there. 'And you just told him no.'

'I told him you could choose for yourself once you were free.' He paused. 'Do you want to go to Asigow?'

'No.'

He nodded. 'Then would you like to come to Goldmont House and help out for a few months while you sort through offers?'

'Very funny.' She looked past him to the village ahead, thinking. 'Can I teach music?'

He nodded. 'As long as you teach the important things first.'

'Music is important. Children need it most of all.'

'Might also be a good chance for you to learn how to cook.'

Astra resisted the urge to roll her eyes. 'I am not afraid of work, Captain.'

'Good.'

She let go of the saddle and took hold of his tunic. 'Thank you, by the way.'

He simply nodded.

CHAPTER 8

$\mathcal{D}$ion had meant to leave her there. Her mother might have come around. But that was not what he did. Instead, he remained in front of the house, listening, watching Astra struggle. It was in her body language, her inability to get the words out. It was clear her mother did not want her quiet life disrupted by the scandal of her daughter's return.

So he took her with him.

They made it to Veanor with an hour to spare, finding the ship already loaded with supplies and ready to leave with the tide. The village reminded Dion of home, the friendly atmosphere, busy shopfronts, the music and laughter spilling out of the taverns. The port itself was alive with men, horses and carts that would carry shipments of supplies to their buyers.

'Hope you don't get seasick,' Dion said as they climbed the gangplank to the ship. She was walking ahead of him, looking at the water below them.

'I have a very strong stomach.'

He smiled to himself. She was the kind of woman who

was too proud to give in to sickness. 'Well, let me know if you do. There are some things that might help.'

'Focusing on objects in the distance, light meals, avoiding wine, and if that fails, wormwood or mint.'

He watched the back of her head. 'You did your research.'

The moment they stepped down onto the deck, he handed Astra her own bag to carry. She would need to get used to a life without servants and maids running about the place. She took it without complaint.

'There's usually a supply of wormwood on the ship if needed,' he said.

'I have some in my bag.'

Of course she did.

Dion spotted Stamitos and King Linus walking in their direction. The moment Stamitos spotted them, he excused himself and came over.

'I thought you were leaving us,' he said to Astra while glancing sideways at Dion.

'Change of plans,' Dion said. 'Astra's coming to help out for a few months so your wife can focus on the baby.'

Stamitos nodded. 'Sounds very sensible. Has he warned you that you will be the only female travelling on a ship full of men?'

Dion gave Stamitos a tired look. 'You'll be quite safe.'

The prince clapped Dion on the back. 'Our fierce captain will protect you.'

Astra did not appear worried. 'Where will I be sleeping?'

Stamitos's eyes shone with amusement. 'Excellent question.'

'Stamitos's cabin has a bed. You can sleep there.' Dion squeezed the prince's shoulder before walking off in the direction of the ladder. 'He can bunk with me.'

'You know I hate hammocks,' the prince called after him.

Dion ignored him, and Astra cast an apologetic look at Stamitos before hurrying to catch up.

'I cannot take the prince's cabin.'

'He doesn't mind.'

She moved her bag from one hand to the other, stretching her fingers. He took it from her.

'I can carry it,' she said.

'Not while climbing down the ladder.'

'Oh.'

As they neared it, they crossed paths with King Linus. He looked Astra up and down as she curtsied before him. 'Joining us in Galen, I see.'

'Yes, Your Majesty,' she replied, smiling. 'Looking forward to seeing what all the fuss is about.'

King Linus's chest expanded. 'If you need anything at all during the voyage, come and see me. My cabin door is always open to you.'

Dion waited politely for the king to finish embarrassing himself.

'You are in good hands with the captain.'

Astra glanced sideways at him. 'So everyone keeps telling me.'

'You can dine with me this evening,' the king said, rocking on his feet. 'In my cabin.'

Dion brushed a finger over his nose in place of shaking his head.

'That is very kind of you, Your Majesty.' Astra gave a small curtsy.

King Linus nodded. 'I am sure the captain will escort you when you are ready.'

They both looked at Dion.

'Of course.'

'Very good,' King Linus said, hands coming together. 'Until then.' He strode off across the deck.

Dion looked back at Astra. 'You've only been on the ship three minutes. That's fast work, even for a Companion.'

She tilted her head. 'It is just dinner.'

Dion gestured to the ladder. 'I see. After you.'

She turned, gathered the skirt of her dress and carefully descended. When they reached the bottom, Dion handed her the bag and walked ahead.

'You'll need to be careful going up and down the ladder. There's still frost in the evenings and early morning. The steps get slippery.' He spoke over his shoulder as they walked along the narrow passageway.

'I do not plan on wandering about on my own.'

'If you need to leave your cabin, come and get me.' He had not thought through the inconvenience of having to supervise her on board. He could vouch for the king's men, but he could not count on the crew to be so well behaved. One woman among two hundred men was a challenge. One beautiful, unattached Companion among two hundred men was trouble.

Men stepped aside as they passed, their eyes trained on Astra. The occasional whistle followed them. She ignored them.

'This one's yours,' Dion said, pushing the small door open. He glanced in the direction of the men still watching Astra, and they immediately resumed walking. 'Watch your step.'

She entered and looked around, her expression giving little away. Bleak light filtered into the small space. 'Where will you be?'

He jerked his head right. 'Next door.'

She nodded. 'Are you sure it is not too much of an inconvenience for the two of you to share?'

His eyes searched her painted face, wondering if she would try and keep up the facade of perfection while at sea.

The ocean had a way of stripping a person bare. It was man against the elements, and usually the elements won.

'It's just one night.' He pointed to the door. 'There's a lock. Use it.' With that, he tugged the door shut.

When Astra opened the door of her cabin that evening, she was met with a stern expression. Dion's hands went to his hips, his head shaking.

'What is the matter?' she asked.

'What the hell are you wearing?'

She looked down at her green velvet gown. 'A dress.'

'Do you have a cloak to put over it? It's freezing.'

She lifted her arm where a cloak hung. 'One would think I was wearing a jester's costume by the look on your face.'

His eyes travelled up, taking in the fresh paint. She had made her lips a softer shade of pink. 'You looked fine as you were.'

She frowned. '*Fine*? Better rein in the compliments, Captain, before you embarrass yourself.'

He gestured for her to start walking. 'Just surprised at the effort is all.'

She looked over her shoulder. 'I am dining with the king. If I were joining you in the galley, I would have dressed very differently.'

When they arrived at King Linus's cabin, Astra turned to Dion. 'You will collect me on your way back?' She did not want to be alone with King Linus longer than she had to. While she knew him to be harmless, a family man at heart, she knew better than to be too comfortable with any man.

Dion crossed his arms. 'You don't have to go. Just tell him you're seasick.'

She glanced at the closed door. 'I need to be in favour

with at least *one* king right now.' She gave him a resigned smile.

'Send for me if you're done early, and I'll come collect you.' He knocked on the door, waiting for her to be received before leaving.

The evening went as predicted. She picked at her food, never really eating anything. She drank the wine, slowly. She asked interesting questions. She paid close attention to his answers, laughing and leaning in at all the right times while remaining a lady in every sense of the word. They were habits she had spent ten years perfecting. She won him over, and that was smart given her situation.

'The meal was lovely, Your Majesty. I am afraid I have grown too tired to be suitable company any longer.'

'You are free to rest here. The shipmaster informed me earlier that we are heading into bad weather. Seas might get a little rough overnight. No point you sitting frightened in your cabin.'

And there it was. The classic overstep. The inevitable proposition. She had spent the entire evening inflating his ego and now had to let him down gently without undoing all her hard work. It was important to keep him onside in case she needed something from him at a later date. 'So kind of you to be concerned, but I assure you, I do not scare easily, Your Majesty.' Turning to the servant standing by the door, she said, 'Please send word to the captain that I am ready. I cannot possibly intrude any longer.'

'I will not hear of it,' Linus said, standing and stepping around the table. He held his hand out for her.

She took it and rose, her mind ticking over. It was a situation she had been in more times than she cared to count—and there was usually always a graceful exit.

A knock sounded at the door, and they both looked over as the servant opened it to see who was there. It was Dion.

'Forgive the interruption, Your Majesty. I thought I would see if the lady is ready to return to her cabin.' His gaze fell to their joined hands. 'But I see she is not.'

Astra gently pulled her hand from Linus's. 'Actually, your timing is perfect, Captain.'

The king exhaled, stepping back with a slightly disappointed expression. 'Well, I thank you for your invigorating company.'

She curtsied. 'Your Majesty.' She turned and walked over to where Dion was watching her with those steel-grey eyes of his. The salty air had turned his hair into a scruffy mess that was less soldier and more farmer. As she neared him, he stepped back from the door, offering a small bow of his head that was more patronising than polite. She walked off down the passageway, listening as he wished the king a pleasant evening before closing the door. His footsteps drew closer, not because he was walking fast but because one of his strides equalled two of her own.

'Pleasant evening?' he asked.

'Very, thank you.' She rounded the corner, not wanting him to see the lie.

He kept up with her. 'Looked like I interrupted.'

'Not at all.'

They had reached her cabin, but when she opened the door, he caught her arm. She turned, looking down at his hand before meeting his gaze.

'You don't have to do that anymore.'

She searched his eyes. 'Do what?'

'Appease him. Next time, just tell him no.'

She tugged her arm free, not liking being handled. 'Just tell him no?' She leaned closer. 'Tell a *king* no?'

'It's good practise.'

'For what?'

'For the rest of your life.'

51

She regarded him coolly. 'Do you think I have a problem saying no to men, Captain?'

'I didn't mean it like that.' He leaned on the door frame. 'I'm only pointing out that you're not obligated to lift your skirts just because he's a king. You're not in Syrasan anymore.'

He was so close she could smell the ale on his breath. That explained why he was being so brazen. 'Are you speaking as a concerned friend or as my employer?'

'As an impartial observer.'

She let her cold stare remain on him a moment longer. 'Thank you for escorting me to my cabin, Captain.'

He pushed off the door frame. 'Don't forget to lock your door.'

CHAPTER 9

$\mathscr{A}$stra's eyes snapped open the moment her body hit the floor. It took her a few breaths to get her bearings. Lifting her head, she stared down at the wet ground, then pushed herself up onto her knees. Water everywhere. The sound of footsteps pounding overhead caused her heart to beat a little harder in her chest. She tried to stand up, but the floor tilted suddenly, tipping her onto her side and sending her rolling into the wall. Her mind raced with all the terrible possibilities. When the floor began to lean in the other direction, she rose to her feet and snatched her cloak, wrapping it around herself before going to the door. Unlocking it, she tugged it open and paused as two sailors ran past.

'Are we sinking?' she called after them.

They did not even look in her direction.

The walls groaned around her as the ship tipped once more, forcing Astra to take hold of the door frame. She waited a moment, then stepped out into the passageway and looked in the direction of Dion's cabin. His door was closed.

When another man went to run past her, she grabbed his arm, stopping him.

'What is going on up there?'

The man glanced in the direction of the ladder. 'Foremast's broken, and she's taking on a lot of water.'

Astra released his arm and looked down at the water sloshing at her feet. She did not want to die in the sea.

'Safest place for you's in the aftercastle.'

She immediately edged in the other direction. 'Where is Captain Dion?'

'He's helping on deck.'

Astra blinked. 'Oh.'

'Come,' he said, grabbing her arm and pulling her towards the ladder. 'I'll take you to the aftercastle.'

She looked over her shoulder. 'Are you sure I should not wait in my cabin?' She was shouting to compete with the noise.

'Bed might be afloat soon,' he shouted back.

When they reached the ladder, he began climbing, pulling her up behind him. She slipped a few times because there was water running down it, but he kept hold of her. The moment her head emerged, a spray of seawater hit her face. She gasped and looked around at the chaotic scene. Men ran in all directions, shouting and tossing ropes to one another, all the while being pelted by water.

'Where is Captain Dion?' Astra yelled, but the wind snatched her words away.

The young man was pulling on her arm before she had even set foot on deck. She held her cloak closed with her free hand, squinting into the wind and rain. Her eyes went to the swells of water all around them. *Dear God.* Her stomach dropped with every rise and fall, her bare feet slipping with each step.

As they hurried beneath the main mast, a loud crack

sounded above them. They both looked up as the sail began to lean. The man tugged on her arm, trying to get her to move faster, but she pulled up, knowing they could not make it through in time.

'Move!' he shouted.

She tore her hand free of his just as something hard slammed into her. The next moment, she was lying on the deck.

'Stay down!' It was Dion. His warm body cradled hers.

The mast swung overhead, collecting the other man who had tried to outrun it. Astra heard the air leave his lungs as it slammed into his middle and carried him away. The tip of the mast smashed through the taffrail before finally coming to a stop. Only then did the weight of Dion's grip on her ease. She drew a greedy breath.

'Are you hurt?' he shouted over the howling wind.

She stared up at him, trying to figure out if she was. She did not think so. Water poured off Dion's face as his eyes moved frantically over her, checking for injury. Male screams made them both look back at the mast. Dion pushed himself up into a crouch beside her. 'Go,' she said, rising into a seated position and taking hold of one of the ropes attached to the mast. 'I will wait right here until you get back.'

He looked in the direction of the incessant screams and finally nodded. 'All right. Don't move from that spot, and don't let go of the rope.' He waited for confirmation that she had heard him before standing. A hand went up to shield his face from the water pelting him from one side, and then he disappeared behind a swirl of sailcloth.

Astra did exactly as she had promised, holding tightly to the rope. She sat frozen, shivering, eyes glued to the spot where Dion had disappeared. The crew continued to run around her, their boots pounding the deck as they attempted to gain control of the situation. She doubted anyone saw her amid the chaos.

Then the ship began to tilt again, and Astra watched as the mast moved. She sucked in a breath when it swung back towards her suddenly. Tossing the rope aside, she threw herself down onto the deck, feeling the change in the air as it passed overhead once more. She looked around for Dion as she felt herself begin to slide. Fingernails scraped timber as she tried to anchor herself. More shouts from all directions, none of them Dion. The ship corrected itself for a moment, and she breathed deeply while one cheek rested on the frigid wood.

Boots stomped past her head, then stopped. 'Incoming!'

Astra raised her head, her eyes widening when she caught sight of a twenty-foot wave coming at the port side of the ship. She was pulled to her feet by the stranger.

'Get below deck!' he shouted in her face, shoving her in the direction of the ladder.

He barely got the words out before the wave crashed into the ship, sending it rearing up. The busted mast flew back in their direction, narrowly missing her head as she tumbled towards the taffrail. A rope snagged her leg, dragging her for a moment before she managed to kick free of it. She tried to focus, but her vision was failing her. All sense of direction was lost as water rained down from every possible angle. Then she was sliding again, the stranger alongside her. She grabbed hold of what felt like a rope, but it moved with her. In a moment, she would hit the taffrail. Except there was no taffrail, only a splintered gap where it had once stood.

Astra gripped the rope with both hands, closed her eyes, and prayed.

~

After dragging the injured man to the aftercastle, Dion's only thought was to get back to Astra. He took off at a run in her direction, but he almost stopped when he caught sight of the wave approaching port side.

'Incoming!' he shouted to the few men who might hear him.

They looked in the direction of the wave before dashing to take hold of something, and Dion took off at a run. He knew she would not stand a chance against a wave that size. Of course, he fell when it hit, landing on his side and rolling a few times. A moment later he was back on his feet, running again. There were so many things moving on deck that he almost missed her as she tumbled past him. She was holding a piece of rope that was not attached to anything, eyes squeezed shut as she headed for the side of the boat. He dived after her, his weight helping to close the distance between them. Catching her by the arm, he reached up and grabbed a handful of sailcloth, bringing them both to a sudden halt. She opened her eyes, looking like a drowned cat minus the claws. He did not wait around for another wave to hit; he was on his feet a beat later, pulling her along with him. He ran for the ladder, tugging her up whenever she slipped, his hand wrapped so tightly around hers that he feared her bones would turn to dust beneath his grip.

'Go,' he shouted. He waited until she was on the ladder before letting go of her hand. At least if she fell at that point it would not be overboard. The moment he stepped off the ladder, he took her by the shoulders and looked at her. Hair clung to her forehead and cheeks. He had never seen her face unpainted before and was surprised by a spray of freckles across her nose and cheeks. 'Anything hurt?'

She shook her head. 'Are we sinking?'

She did well to rein in her panic. He shook his head despite his thoughts heading in the same direction. 'No.' The ship tilted once more, and he turned her in the direction of her cabin. 'Inside. Quickly now.' They were forced to hold onto the walls as they walked. When they arrived at her door, Dion reached past her and pushed it open. 'In you go.'

Astra went to step through but was thrown back into him as the ship leaned once more. He caught her about the waist and lifted her inside, closing the door behind them and locking it.

'The sailor said the safest place was the aftercastle,' she said, looking around at the water on the floor.

'It's damaged. Still safer for you in here than up there right now.' He placed her down on the ground.

'Where are you going?' Her hands were like tiny vices on his arm.

He turned her so he could see her face. 'Nowhere. I'll stay with you until the storm passes.' He leaned his back against the door as the ship tilted again. Her heart drummed wildly against his ribs as she pressed into him. The moment the ship was horizontal, he gestured to the bed. 'Sit.'

She stepped out of his arms and looked down at her soggy nightdress and cloak. 'I... I should change.'

'What?' His eyebrows formed an angry line. 'Are you going to paint your face too? Sit down.'

She backed away to the bed and sank down onto it. The floor began to lean again, and Dion climbed up to the bed and sat beside her.

'How long should we expect it to last?' Astra was gripping the mattress, shivering.

'As long as it lasts.' He grabbed the damp blanket from beneath them. 'Take off the wet cloak and put this around you.'

Astra did as she was told while the ship continued to shift and groan. At one point, her feet slid out from beneath her, and she almost tumbled forwards off the bed. Dion pulled her to him, tucking the blanket tighter around her. She held on to his arm, her eyes closing every time the ship leaned.

'Breathe,' he reminded her.

They remained that way for another half hour, swaying back and forth until they were both nauseous. Dion watched her skin turn greyer and greyer.

'Are you going to be sick?'

She shook her head.

'Anything in that fancy bag of yours to catch vomit?' Her tired eyes came up to meet his, and he almost felt bad for teasing her. 'Lie down.'

'I will just roll off.' Her voice was raw, exhausted.

He laid her down, then shuffled along the bed so his hip was blocking her torso. 'No you won't.' He pressed a hand to the wall, the side of his body hovering over hers. He blinked a few times, praying the nausea would not win. She must have had the same thought, because she covered her face with her hands.

'I do not think I have ever felt this ill,' she breathed.

Dion wiped a hand down his clammy face. 'Focus on objects in the distance, eat light meals—'

'Not funny.'

The bed tilted again, and Astra's back lifted off it. Dion dropped his elbow down, and the weight of him held her in place. 'Don't be sick on me,' he whispered.

Astra sucked in a breath as the full weight of her pressed against him. She looked around the cabin as though expecting the ocean to swallow them. Eventually the ship righted, and she released the breath she had been holding. 'What a horrible way to die.'

He let his forehead drop to the bed while his stomach settled. 'We're not going to die.' When the ship moved in the other direction, he lifted his head and reached for the bulkhead. 'What are you most afraid of? Drowning or dying in your nightdress with your lips unpainted?' He felt her stomach contract beneath him as she braced for the next wave.

'Drowning in this compromising position with dead rats floating around me.'

He smiled despite the nausea rolling through him. 'I assure you I've not had one inappropriate thought since entering your cabin.'

A hand landed on his shoulder.

'Thank you for staying,' Astra said.

The roof creaked above them. More footsteps drummed overhead. The ship levelled, and Dion dropped his forehead to the bed again.

CHAPTER 10

When Astra peeled her eyes open, she felt as though someone had poured sand in them while she slept. The ship rocked gently. The wind had died. She was aware of a heavy weight pinning her to the bed. Her gaze slid down to a sleeping Dion. His body lay across her hips, his arm tucked beneath her. His breaths were even, every exhale a soft snore. It was not the first time she had woken trapped beneath a man, but it was the first time she had woken *calmly* trapped beneath one. She had not done anything wrong, and he had most certainly not done anything wrong. He had stayed to protect her.

She looked around the cabin, trying to gauge the time. Daylight seeped through the cracks in the walls. Above her, she could hear conversation and the footsteps of men going about their work. She moved her arm, her muscles aching after hours of being flung left and right. Dion had done most of the work, holding and pushing, before eventually collapsing into an exhausted heap on top of her. She did not remember that part, had likely fallen asleep before the storm had even passed.

She wondered at the best way to wake him. It was hardly appropriate for her to just lie there while he continued to sleep, even if he had earned the rest. Should she tap his shoulder? Clear her throat?

As she pondered this, something caught her vision. Her head snapped left, and she spotted a rat standing on its hind legs, looking at her. That moved her decision along. She shook Dion's shoulder. His eyes snapped open and he pushed himself upright, blinking a few times before focusing on her.

'Rat,' she whispered, gesturing with her head.

He rubbed one eye. 'What?'

She pointed this time. '*Rat.*'

'Ah.' He sat up properly, turning away and leaning his elbows on his knees. 'He won't hurt you. The ship's taken on water. Rodents naturally seek higher ground when their homes are flooded.'

Astra pushed herself up into a sitting position. As she did so, the rat scurried off, disappearing through an impossibly small crevice. 'Great. Shall I prepare for the Black Death?'

Dion pressed his palms to his eyes. 'If you'd like. I'm sure you have a book on the subject.' He patted her leg before standing.

'Where are you going?'

He looked back. 'To check on the king and help with the clean-up. You go back to sleep. You'll only get in the way.'

She felt her irritation returning. 'Do you think I can get some clean water from somewhere?'

He moved his head from side to side, stretching out his stiff neck. 'Assuming some barrels survived.'

She had not thought of that.

'I'll have some sent down.' Walking over to the door, he tugged it open. 'Lock it behind me.' As he stepped through, he added, 'And don't let the rats bite you.'

An hour after Dion's departure, a crew member knocked on Astra's door, handing her a waterskin. 'Captain says he'll have some food sent down after the clean-up.'

'How bad is it up there?'

'All three masts were damaged.'

She frowned. 'Does that mean all three sails are down?'

'That's right.'

'Then how are we moving?'

'Right now, we're drifting. Expect to be up and running soon though. But we won't reach Newford Harbour until tomorrow.'

She nodded. 'Thank you.'

'Captain also said to lock your door.'

Of course he did.

Once alone, she took a long drink and used the rest of the water to clean herself up as best she could. She was thankful her bag had kept most of her things dry, selecting a gown appropriate for helping on deck. After applying a little paint to disguise her tiredness, she combed her hair back into a slick knot and spent the next half hour cleaning and straightening her cabin, jumping at anything that slightly resembled a rat. Once done, she made her way above deck to see what she could do to help.

Astra ignored the whistles from men mopping the floors that followed her along the passageway, continuing to the ladder at the end. A crew member was already descending. He stopped when he saw her, extending a hand.

'I've got you.'

She sighed inwardly. 'I am quite capable, thank you.'

Another man appeared behind, taking her elbow. 'Allow me to help ya.'

Before she could object, she was hoisted up the ladder.

'We've got you. Mind your step,' they said, passing her along.

She emerged into blinding sunlight, blinking against it for a moment. When her vision cleared, she found a smiling Stamitos watching her, clearly entertained by what he had just witnessed. Astra thanked the men before turning to the prince.

'My lord,' she said, curtsying.

'Those poor men have no idea what to do with themselves.'

'I suspect they were trying to be helpful.'

He laughed. 'How do you manage to look so fresh-faced when the rest of us are staggering around trying to figure out which way is up?'

'You know a Companion never reveals her secrets.'

He pulled a face. 'Not true. Sapphira revealed all of hers.'

Astra tilted her head. 'Well, you and I both know that the princess was not very good at her role.'

Another laugh. 'One of the reasons you never got along, I suppose.' He stepped past her. 'Dion is up front. Do you need a few men to help you get there?'

She gave him a dry smile. 'I think I will manage.' She watched him a moment. 'Were you one of the smart ones who remained in their cabin last night?'

'Dion practically locked me in there.' He raised his severed arm, studying it for a moment. 'Perhaps I should get a hook or something added so I can be of some use during a crisis.'

'And give your daughters nightmares?'

He lowered his arm. 'Fair point. Better make myself useful while I can.'

She watched him leave, then looked around at the men walking back and forth carrying crates, ropes and various tools she did not recognise. Drawing a breath, she set off towards the foremast, where Dion was talking with the ship-master. The men working in the area looked in her direction. Some of them stopped working altogether. Noticing their distracted state, Dion looked around for the source and spotted Astra. He said something to the shipmaster before making his way over to her.

'All right. Back to work,' he said as he passed the men. They reluctantly returned to their duties. 'What's wrong?' he asked the moment he reached her.

'Nothing.' She looked past him. 'The man who delivered the water said there was significant damage.'

'Every able-bodied man's helping with repairs, so we'll be done in no time.' He glanced over his shoulder, then back at her. 'Why are you up here?'

She was taken aback by his tone. 'I thought I might be able to help.'

'With what?'

She looked around. 'Well, what needs to be done?'

'Nothing that you can help with. I told you you'd get in the way.'

She watched him for a moment. 'What condition are the sails in? I can sew.'

'You got all dressed up to come mend sails?'

'This is not dressed up. This is the simplest gown I own.'

His gaze dropped. '*That* is your simplest dress?'

She folded her arms in front of her. 'Is there a dress code I am unaware of?'

'You're distracting the men.'

She felt her face twitch with irritation. 'Would you feel better if I put a flour sack on my head?'

His eyes narrowed on her face. 'Did you... colour your cheeks?'

'You must be looking very closely to notice such a thing.'

He looked away. 'The sails have already been mended.'

What was his problem? 'Have I offended you in some way? Or is this just how you behave with people when you have not had adequate sleep?'

His eyes returned to her, and he studied her face before saying, 'Perhaps I am tired.'

She tried again. 'Everyone is tired. Now, what can I do to help?'

His expression softened a little. 'You can go to the galley and get yourself some food.'

'Have you eaten?'

He shook his head. 'Not yet.'

She was about to offer to bring him something when one of the king's servants marched up to them.

'Pardon the interruption, but His Majesty the King wishes to see you.'

Dion exhaled. 'I'll be right there.'

The man looked between them. 'Actually, he wishes to see the lady, Captain.'

Astra looked away. Surely the king had more important things to worry about. When she looked back at Dion, she found him watching her with those unreadable eyes. 'Excuse me, Captain.'

Dion stepped back from her. 'Ensure the lady is accompanied at all times.'

'Yes, sir.'

She wanted to smile, but it did not come. 'Shall I come find you after?'

He was already walking away. 'Don't wander about by yourself again.'

She watched him leave, his broad shoulders shifting with each stride. The servant cleared his throat, and her head snapped in his direction.

'Let us not keep His Majesty waiting.'

That evening, the crew caught fish and cooked them on deck. They ate it with biscuits beneath a clear sky, stars blazing overhead. It was washed down with the surviving ale. When everyone's stomach was full, someone fetched a lute, another his fiddle, and the men sang and danced despite their fatigue.

Instead of joining in, Dion filled his cup and went over to the taffrail, looking out at the still water. It was black and glistening. He stifled a yawn, exhausted after no sleep and having laboured all day. He thought about collecting Astra from the king's cabin but knew he needed to take a step back. She was starting to get under his skin, and if he was not careful, pretty soon he would be just another moth to the flame.

He was annoyed at himself. Not only for waking up in her bed but the irrational urge to bury his face in her warm stomach once more. He liked to think he was smarter than that, but when she had appeared on deck that morning, his reaction had been no better than the rest of the crew who all stood there ogling her. To make matters worse, he had been struck with jealousy he had no right to feel. Damn that velvet dress.

She must have known. Every Companion knew.

If she had just remained in her cabin with the door locked during the storm, he would not have been forced to save her goddamn life and drag her back below deck. If she had just been able to stay on that bed, he would not have remained there with her using his body as an anchor to keep her safe. If he had never held her that close, experienced the heat of her, seen those freckles, he could have remained oblivious. Except he had never been oblivious to her, simply too proud to admit otherwise.

Stamitos wandered over to him, ale sloshing in his cup. 'Why are you hiding in the shadows? Come dance.'

'Too tired.'

Stamitos slid down beside him and looked over at the men. 'You are not *pining*, are you?'

'What are you talking about?'

'Astra is dining with the king again.'

'So?' Dion pushed himself up to a stand. 'Just because you fell in love with a Companion doesn't mean I'm destined to.'

'She's not technically a Companion anymore.' Stamitos stood with great effort. 'And you did spend the night in her cabin last night.'

'They were extraordinary circumstances.'

Stamitos leaned against the taffrail, grinning. 'Tell me more of your chivalric act. My skin is tingling all over.'

'Shut up.'

The prince chuckled. The fiddle player started a new song, replacing the traditional lyrics with funny ones. The men laughed, the lute player joined in, and everyone cheered and clapped in semi-time with the music.

'How are you going to survive living under the same roof?'

'I'm rarely there anyway. I'll admit I'm second-guessing my decision though. She's very... distracting.'

Stamitos took a long drink. 'That is how attraction works.'

'Attraction I can handle, distraction I can't. Perhaps King Linus will make her a better offer.' Yet the thought of her as King Linus's mistress was too much in his tired state.

'It will do her good to have some time away from court, experience the real world. It sure did *me* some good.' Stamitos emptied his cup.

Dion was too tired to continue the conversation. 'I'm going to bed.'

'Are you going to collect Astra on your way?'

'No.'

Stamitos regarded him. 'All right.' He patted Dion's shoulder. 'I will try not to wake you.'

Dion tipped the rest of his ale into the sea. 'Don't fall overboard.'

The promise of more was generally enough for men like King Linus. He was also at an age where his body was softening and his hair was thinning at an alarming pace, so he wanted to feel like a young man, if only for a few fleeting moments. She could give him that without giving him *her*.

'I have so enjoyed our dinners together,' she said, withdrawing her hand from his at the door. 'There is nothing more satisfying than intelligent conversation.'

'You are really not going to stay?' he asked as she prepared to leave.

No, she would not stay. 'And start rumours? You are a better man than that.'

She did not send for Dion. He deserved a night of fun after staying with her throughout the storm only to work the entirety of the next day. Everyone was on deck anyway, enjoying themselves.

'You are welcome at Reave Castle any time,' the king reminded her as she curtsied before him.

'I appreciate that, Your Majesty.'

Astra was exhausted by the time she reached her cabin, but the music drifting down from the deck made her pause. Men sang, feet stamped. All out of tune and out of time, but with plenty of heart. She stepped back from the door and leaned against the wall, listening. The sound of unbridled fun usually spelt disaster for a Companion. All it took was a little too much wine, one person, one thoughtless comment, one misplaced hand, and an evening could be turned on its head.

But as Fedora had pointed out many times, it was not her job to have fun, it was her role to ensure everyone else had fun. That was why she held the same cup of wine for an entire evening, giving the illusion of joining in and letting go while doing neither of those things. The control was what set a Companion apart from other women.

'What are you doing out here?'

Astra gasped and straightened. She had been so lost in her thoughts and fatigue that she had not even heard Dion approach.

'Sorry,' he said. 'I thought you heard me coming.'

She leaned back against the wall because it was him, and he did not expect her to play Companion. 'I was listening to the music.'

'Is that what we're calling it?'

She smiled. 'How drunk is the prince?'

'Very.' He leaned against the wall opposite her. 'They're just letting off some steam after last night.'

'That is the only reason I am not up there giving the fiddler tips.'

Dion studied her in the dark. 'Do you play the fiddle?'

'I play all instruments, but the harp is my gift.'

He nodded. 'I watched you at the feast. You were very good.'

'You are not supposed to watch, you are supposed to listen.' She closed her eyes for a moment. 'If you let it, the music will take you away.' Her eyes opened again. 'Maybe not this music.' When she looked back at Dion, she was met with a serious expression.

'Where does it take you?'

She thought for a moment. 'Depends on the song and who I am with. Sometimes escaping the room is enough.'

'Escaping the people, you mean?'

'Certain people.'

He looked up at the roof. 'How was your dinner with the king?'

'Fine.'

'I would've collected you if I'd known you were ready to leave.'

'I figured Stamitos needed you more than I did.'

He looked back at her. 'Are you still coming to Goldmont House?'

She frowned. 'Of course. Why would you ask that?'

He shrugged. 'Perhaps the king made you a better offer.'

'What kind of offer exactly?'

Another shrug.

She pushed off the wall and stepped up to the cabin door. 'Perhaps you think I just roll from the bed of one king to another?'

'Like King Pandarus to King Tuyon?'

Her chest pinched, and she saw his immediate regret at speaking those words.

'What I meant is—'

'I know what you meant, Captain.' She was not interested in his explanation. 'Good night.'

'Astra....'

She pushed the door open, stepped inside and closed it quickly. Securing the lock, she leaned her forehead against the back of the door. Footsteps faded on the other side until she heard his cabin door click shut.

CHAPTER 11

*a*stra held the taffrail, taking in the sights of Newford Harbour. Merchant ships and fishing boats were anchored nearby. Horses and carts moved in all directions along the dock. Women stood talking, baskets in hand. They were a stark contrast to the women loitering at the docks in Veanor. These ladies wore long-sleeve cotton dresses buttoned to their chins, the kind who kept tidy houses and well-mannered children. Passers-by nodded polite greetings at them.

The crew were shouting instructions behind her, tossing ropes in all directions before the gangplank finally landed on the dock with a thud. It was time to disembark.

'Do you have everything?' Dion asked, stepping up beside her.

She gave him a small smile and bent to pick up her bag, pretending it was not heavy. 'Yes.' It was as if the awkward exchange the night prior had never happened.

Dion leaned his elbows on the taffrail and drew a heavy breath. 'About last night….'

Or not. 'I would rather hear about the plan for today.'

He regarded her for a moment, then nodded, straightening once more. 'We'll travel to Talsworth on horseback. It'll be a long day in the saddle.'

'Talsworth. A full day's ride northeast at a steady pace. Located at the foot of the Bolltree Hills.'

He looked down at the dock. 'I suppose I shouldn't be surprised that you know your geography.'

'Not just a pretty face, Captain. Despite strong opinions to the contrary.' Perhaps she had not moved on from their awkward conversation after all.

Dion took the bag from her without a word and strolled off. She had no choice but to follow after him. He stopped at the gangplank and gestured for her to go ahead. Always the gentleman, when not calling her a big whore. The plank swayed beneath her, but she managed her descent with grace —right up until the moment she stepped foot on the dock. The ground seemed to come at her suddenly. Every muscle in her feet and legs tightened, waiting for the sensation to pass. But it did not pass, and she found herself tilting left suddenly.

God, what is happening?

A hand caught her elbow, righting her. 'You all right?' Dion asked.

'Fine.'

He let go of her. 'Horses are just ahead.'

She saw them, but when she took a step in their direction, she felt the ground shift beneath her again. 'Is this… are we afloat?' She was falling backwards.

Dion dropped the bags and caught her properly this time. 'Are you dizzy?'

Was she? 'I am not sure what I am.' Nauseous, perhaps.

He guided her out of the way of the people trying to disembark. 'Sometimes it takes a while to find your land legs if you're not used to the sea.'

'Land legs?' She had never read anything about land legs.

Stamitos stepped down onto the dock, looking a little worse for wear after a late evening.

'Can you grab some water?' Dion called to him before coming around to stand in front of Astra. 'Do you need to sit for a minute?'

'No, I am fine.' She had managed three days at sea with perfectly functioning legs. She was not going to have them fail her on solid land. If he would just keep still, she might get her bearings. 'Can you... can you please stop moving?'

'I'm not moving.'

She was too embarrassed to look at him then.

Stamitos arrived with a waterskin, handing it to her. 'Happened to me the first time I travelled by sea. Only lasted a few minutes.'

Astra drank and took a few deep breaths, feeling her temperature lower and vision improve. Dion's hand rested lightly on her back, as though expecting her to topple at any moment. 'I am feeling better.'

Dion finally moved back, his hand falling away. 'Good. There's no rush. I won't put you on a horse until I know you can stay on it.'

She looked up at him, knowing her face was likely a mess. 'Is there somewhere I can clean up before we leave?'

Dion frowned. 'Clean up what? You look fine.'

'You will be rewarded with a hot bath at the end of all this,' Stamitos said, 'but we need to get to Goldmont House for that.'

'I'll have your horse brought to you,' Dion told her.

She tested her legs, relieved when the ground did not move this time. 'That will not be necessary. I can walk.'

Dion watched her for a moment. 'You're sure?'

'Yes.'

Clearing his throat, Stamitos walked ahead of them. Dion

stayed beside her, eyes on her legs the entire time—but not for the reasons men usually watched them.

'Tell me if you don't feel well at any stage during the journey,' he said as they reached the horses.

She nodded.

'And stay close to me.'

He placed her atop a grey gelding before mounting his own horse.

The journey was like a Galen baptism. Astra was immersed in the landscape, from the quaint houses to the vibrant green hills dotted with sheep. She removed her cloak, letting her arms soak up the sun. The clouds seemed to pass at just the right time, bringing instant relief.

They stopped only once for a brief rest and some food, arriving in Talsworth a few hours before sunset. The village was much smaller than the others they had passed through, with one main road and a handful of shopfronts.

Dion brought his horse in step with Astra's. 'Named after Merek Talsworth. His family own most of the land here.'

'And almost every shop you see,' Stamitos added. 'Savvy merchants who like to be treated like their bloodlines are royal.'

'And are their bloodlines royal?'

Dion shook his head. 'They're as common as the rest of us.'

'Bit of a sore point for our captain,' Stamitos said, pretending to whisper.

Dion rolled his eyes. 'All right. That's enough.'

But Astra's curiosity was piqued. 'Did you have a run-in with them?'

'No.'

Stamitos brought his horse closer to Astra's. 'Dion was engaged to Elenor Talsworth for a period.'

Astra eyed the captain. 'Until she saw sense?'

Dion glanced sideways at her, saying nothing.

Stamitos answered on his behalf. 'The family severed ties when Dion's father was sentenced.'

Astra immediately felt bad for her comment.

'Must we?' Dion said. 'It was a bad match to begin with and a long time ago.'

Astra swallowed. 'I gather the family wished to avoid potential scandal?'

Stamitos leaned closer to Astra. 'Or perhaps Elenor was too frightened to live at Goldmont House. Some say his ghost remains there.'

'No one says that,' Dion said tiredly. 'And my father was executed at Reave Castle.'

Astra tutted at the prince. 'Really, my lord.'

Stamitos continued as if they had not spoken. 'But Elenor remains forever hopeful. Still unwed all these years later.'

'The captain is also unwed,' Astra pointed out.

Dion pushed his horse into a trot. 'Let's move. We're almost there.'

Stamitos laughed, and they followed after him, heading out of the village and turning onto the narrow road lined with tall oak trees. At the end sat a large house, similar in appearance to the ones found throughout Syrasan. Bluestone, two storeys. To the left was a modest vineyard, to the right stables with a mounting yard and small training area. Sheep grazed around the property; chickens roamed freely. With that colourful Galen sunset, the scene was breathtaking.

Dion glanced sideways at her, taking in her expression. 'What do you think?

'I think you were very lucky to grow up here.'

Stamitos cantered ahead, no doubt eager to see his wife and daughters.

'It is bigger than I was expecting,' she said.

'The boundary fence runs along the Bolltree Hills. We have sheep, oxen and horses at the back.'

'And apples.'

He nodded. 'And apples.'

An old groom wandered out of the stables and took Stamitos's horse. The front door of the house opened and a young girl ran out, not quite of age by the looks of her. She descended the steps two at a time then waved at Stamitos as she flew straight past him.

'Dion!' Her face was lit with excitement.

The captain pushed his horse into a trot. When he was closer, he pulled up and jumped down, catching the girl in his arms. 'Told you I'd only be gone a week.' He placed her back on the ground.

'Usually you lie.'

'I misjudge. That's not the same thing.'

The groom came forwards to help Astra dismount. He had deep wrinkles and a kind face.

'Thank you...'

'Hann, my lady.'

'Thank you, Hann.' She went to join Dion and the girl as her horse was led away. 'And who do we have here?'

'This is my sister, Helena,' Dion said, hooking an arm around the young girl's neck.

Astra tried to hide her surprise. 'Your sister?' She looked between them. 'It is lovely to meet you.'

'Don't worry,' the girl said. 'Everyone's confused at first. We have different mothers.'

'Helena's mother was from Asigow,' Dion explained.

Astra smiled at the girl. 'I was wondering how you were so much better-looking than your brother.'

Helena grinned.

'She never believes me when I tell her that,' Dion said.

Astra looked in the direction of the house. 'How many girls live here?'

'Fourteen including the princesses,' Helena said. 'And eight boys.'

Astra blinked. 'You have twenty-two children living here?'

Helena nodded. 'All orphans like me, except for the princesses, of course.'

Dion pulled his sister closer. 'You're not an orphan because you have me.'

'But you're never here, and now Sapphira is having a baby.'

'*Princess* Sapphira, and yes, having a baby, not abandoning you.' Dion gestured to Astra. 'And I've brought Astra to help. She's going to take over lessons for a few months and will also be introducing music.'

Helena played with the end of her plait, a habit that would have Fedora reeling. 'Can you shoot a bow?'

Sapphira's influence, no doubt. 'I am afraid not.'

'You should see Sapphira shoot. She's better than any man. Except maybe Dion.'

'*Princess* Sapphira,' Dion prompted once more.

'She doesn't like to be called that,' Helena whispered back.

As if on cue, Sapphira emerged from the house, barefoot and big-bellied. The two women looked at one another for a moment, all that history there between them. Two Companions who had barely tolerated each other in that life. She and the prince had fled to Galen soon after marrying to avoid scrutiny. Astra watched as she came down the steps and waddled in their direction, her daughters in tow.

'Dion says she's everything a princess ought to be,' Helena said, 'that living in the real world makes her better equipped for the role.'

Astra glanced at him. 'Does he now?'

He cleared his throat. 'Better to be helping people than wasting away in a castle.'

It felt like a dig at her. 'There are many ways to help a kingdom, such as carrying on its traditions.'

'Only if those traditions are beneficial,' Dion quipped, 'or else what's the point of them?'

The two young princesses broke into a run when they spotted Dion. He ruffled their hair when they reached him like one does a dog.

'These are Princess Sapphira's daughters,' Dion said as they waited for Sapphira to catch up. 'Edith and Aimee.'

Astra's gaze fell to their grass-stained feet. They were Sapphira's daughters all right. The only thing missing was a bow slung over their shoulders. 'Which one of you is Princess Edith?'

'Me,' said the eldest.

Astra nodded and looked to the other girl. 'And you must be Princess Aimee.'

Aimee eyed her curiously. 'Where did you fall from?'

'What do you mean?'

'Mother said "how the mighty have fallen". Fallen from where?'

Dion coughed, and Helena covered the girl's mouth with her hand.

'You can't say that,' she whispered.

Astra looked at Sapphira, who had finally joined them, slightly out of breath.

'That was a private conversation between your father and me.' Sapphira looked suitably embarrassed. 'The comment was taken out of context.'

'Of course,' Astra said, lowering into a curtsy. 'I imagine you are surprised to see me here.'

Sapphira placed both hands on her stomach. 'I honestly

thought Stamitos was joking.' She cleared her throat. 'Why don't you come inside and get settled?'

Astra felt a pang of remorse at the way she had treated Sapphira when she had first arrived at Archdale Castle. She had been envious of the younger woman's carefree spirit and the way she had captured the attention of a prince with only her archery skills. He had not cared that she did not speak more than one language or was hopeless with every musical instrument. He had been besotted—still was. 'I could certainly do with a wash.'

Sapphira ushered the girls in the direction of the house. 'Stamitos tells me you hit bad weather.'

'Yes.' Astra glanced at Dion. 'It got a little rough onboard.'

'Excuse me,' Dion said, making a move towards his horse. 'I'll be in shortly.'

'We'll come with you,' Helena said, going after him. The princesses followed after them also.

The two women watched them leave.

'He's a good man,' Sapphira said the moment they were alone.

Astra looked at her. It almost felt like a warning. 'He won me in a game of cards.'

They turned towards the house.

'Stamitos told me. Can't believe Pandarus wagered you in a game of cards, and yet I can.'

Astra's gaze drifted to Dion. 'So here I am, until I figure out a way back into his good graces.'

Sapphira glanced sideways at her. 'I gather your family was not very welcoming.'

'My mother practically shoved me back towards the horse.'

Sapphira drew a slow breath. 'Well, it's a good thing Companions don't have feelings.'

Astra took in her mischievous expression. 'We have feelings. We just keep them turned off.'

Sapphira smiled, but it faded quickly. 'Please don't hurt him. He's already been through hell and doesn't stand a chance against you.'

'I have no intention of hurting him. I need a roof over my head, and he needs a tutor. Problem solved. Now I just need to figure out a way back to Archdale where I belong.'

Sapphira's eyebrows rose. 'That is a terrible plan.'

'I am next in line to mentor.'

'You *were* next in line.' Sapphira's expression softened. 'Is that really what you want? To go back and inflict the Companion life on others?'

'Oh, you mean a life of privilege.'

Sapphira groaned. 'You sound just like Fedora.'

'You do realise that is a compliment.'

The princess stopped at the bottom of the steps. 'I'm one large sneeze away from giving birth, and there are twenty-two children inside. Despite our history, I'm actually thankful for the help. How do you think you'll cope with that many children?'

'Probably better than I coped with one of you.'

Sapphira shook her head. 'God help those poor children.'

'Now off you go,' Eda said, ushering the children away from Astra. 'Save all of your questions for the morning. Poor dear has just stepped foot inside.'

Not only did Eda manage the household, she was also the main cook. Her only help was two young girls; a laundry and kitchen maid. She was everything one would expect of a person in her position: assertive, capable, and utterly over-worked. And soon there would be a baby to care for.

Astra followed her along the landing, noticing her short stride and uneven shoulders. Signs of a tough life.

'I assure you I am quite self-sufficient,' Astra said when they arrived at the door at the end.

Eda gave her a tired smile, her face creasing with the action. Judging by her silver hair, Astra guessed her to be around fifty years old. 'A welcome change.' She pushed the door open and gestured for Astra to go in. 'It's small but comfortable. We don't have a lot of spare rooms, as you can imagine.'

Astra stepped inside and looked around. A bed sat against one wall, a dresser with three drawers on the other side.

There was a small glass window up high for light. It might have been the same size as the dressing room of the Companions' quarters, but it was a private haven compared to her previous arrangement.

'I'll have a chair sent up,' Eda said as she smoothed down the blanket on the bed. She winced when she straightened. 'I don't know what your last position was like, but I imagine it was easier than this one. How many children did you have in your care?'

So, Dion had not told her everything. 'I have not worked with children before.'

Eda hid her surprise well. 'Baptism by fire, then?'

Astra smiled. 'I was preparing to move into a mentoring role at Archdale Castle but ended up here instead.'

Eda did not seem too surprised by the revelation. 'A Companion. My, my. From what I've heard, this might be a refreshing pace for you.'

Astra smiled. 'We shall find out soon enough.' Looking around, she added, 'This is perfect.'

'Easily pleased. I like you all ready.' Eda patted Astra's arm as she passed on her way out. 'Come downstairs for that bath when you're ready.' With that, she left the room, closing the door behind her.

Astra looked around. Yes, she would have more privacy than she could have ever dreamed of, but she was also completely alone. If Sapphira was the closest thing she had to a friend, she was in trouble.

Having said that, she was not entirely sure she had many friends at Archdale either. Not since Idalia.

No, she could not let her mind go there. If she thought about Idalia for too long, she might fall down on the bed and never get up again.

Walking over to the dresser, she opened the top drawer, finding a few wooden hangers inside. She looked about the room for somewhere to hang her gowns, discovering they hooked nicely on the bottom of the window sill. She spent a few moments unpacking her belongings, then looked around to see if her surroundings were beginning to feel more like home.

'*Relax*,' Idalia would have said, taking her hand and squeezing. '*You are Pandarus's little prize, untouchable.*'

Astra blinked and tugged a clean dress from a hanger.

Sapphira was right. The mighty had fallen.

Dion was seated and impatiently waiting to eat when Astra finally decided to join them. He almost fell off his chair when he caught sight of her. She wore a short-sleeve silk dress and her hair swept up in a bun, revealing a long, polished neck. Everyone watched her take her seat, even Eda, who had just arrived with a basket of rolls.

Sapphira glared across the table at her. 'Really, Astra. It's just us this evening. No one's expecting a surprise appearance from the king.'

Astra slid into her seat so gracefully that Dion did not even see it move. 'I hope the addition of footwear is not too formal for the occasion, my lady.'

Sapphira returned her attention to her food. 'You joke, but given how swollen my feet are at the moment, you're lucky I got them into shoes.'

Astra draped a napkin over her lap. 'Oh, I was not joking.'

Stamitos placed a hand over Sapphira's, trying to hide his own smirk. 'Just like old times.'

Dion focused on his plate. 'Sapphira's right. There's no need to dress up on our account.'

'I only have what was packed for me, Captain.'

Sapphira's fork scraped her plate. 'I'm sure Eda has something you can borrow.' She glanced over at Astra, looking rather pleased with herself.

They ate the rest of their meal in silence. When everyone had finished, Eda began clearing away the table. Dion thanked her, and she waved the gratitude off.

'I thought I might take a walk before retiring,' Astra announced. 'Get my bearings of the place, if you do not mind?' She directed the question at Dion.

'I can go with you if you'd like,' he offered.

She eyed him as she stood. 'Only if you are not too tired.'

'Good,' Sapphira said, standing with great effort. 'Can you lock up the chickens?'

Dion nodded. 'Good chance to show Astra the palace.'

Astra waited for him to reach her before asking, 'The palace?'

'Chicken palace.'

Sapphira yawned. 'I'll see you both in the morning.'

'My lord, my lady,' Astra said, lowering into a curtsy.

'Please do not bother with all the formalities here at Goldmont,' Stamitos said.

Sapphira nodded in agreement. 'Heavens no. I'm agitated enough as it is.'

'Very well,' Astra said. 'Then have a pleasant evening.'

As soon as they were alone, Astra turned back to Dion. 'Is there a midwife in Talsworth when the time comes?'

'Yes.' He marvelled at her ability to eat an entire meal without disrupting the colour on her lips. 'Did your mentor teach you how to eat with your lips painted?'

She brushed a finger over the corner of her mouth. 'Yes, actually.'

Dion gestured for her to start walking. 'Let's go.'

He took her to the stables first, where they strolled amid the stalls. Hann was feeding the horses; he nodded a greeting before returning to his work. As they were leaving, Dion thought Astra seemed distracted. 'Spit it out. I can hear your mind ticking away.'

She looked at him. 'Fair enough. I was just wondering what happened to Helena's mother.'

'Ah.' The inevitable question. She would find out eventually one way or another. 'She was supposed to return to Asigow after my father's death, but the loss of him, the separation from her daughter, the uncertainty of what awaited her there, it was too much. She took her own life.'

Astra inhaled. 'How awful. It is no wonder Helena is attached to you. How old was she when all this happened?'

'Nine.'

Astra hesitated before asking, 'And how old were you?'

'Eighteen. I had just joined the king's army.'

'Following in your father's footsteps?' The moment she said that, her face changed. 'I mean becoming a soldier.'

His mouth stretched into a smile. 'I know what you meant.'

She opened her mouth to ask a question but was distracted by the sight of the chicken house ahead of them. 'What in heaven's name...'

The enclosure was almost as big as the stables if you included the large run attached to the front of it. The house itself was made of timber and painted the same shade of blue as her eyes. Astra stood in awe, taking in the sight. He watched her. She was something else when her eyes shone like that.

'I think *why* is probably a good place to start,' Astra said.

Dion unlatched the gate and held it open for her. She stepped inside, moving carefully around the messy areas. 'The children built it. Carpentry's a valued and well-paid skill in Galen. They designed it too.'

'Those clever little things.' Astra looked around. The chickens were unfazed by their arrival. Most were already settled inside the house. 'I am genuinely impressed—and that does not happen very often.'

He watched her face, strangely pleased by her statement. 'Come see inside.' He entered the house ahead of her, waiting for her to join him. She looked around at the boxes filled with straw lining all four walls.

'You must get a lot of eggs from these smug hens.'

'We do, but we also eat a lot, as you've probably figured out.'

She was smiling as she took it all in. He had seen her smile plenty of times, but this was different. The sound of peeping chicks caught her attention, and she wandered over towards the noise, peering into the box where the fluffy chicks were huddled with a hen.

'Hello,' she whispered.

Dion's eyebrows came together. She was talking to them.

'I suspect your rooster is living his best life.' She stroked the hen's back before straightening.

'He does all right for himself.'

Astra's hand went over her nose and mouth. 'Pity about the smell. A design flaw perhaps. Needs more ventilation.'

'I'm not sure more ventilation would help much.' He gestured for her to go ahead of him. Outside, the air was more breathable. 'It's important that gate is locked every evening once the chickens have come to roost. If you don't want to do it yourself, you can send one of the children.'

'Oh, I do not mind. I love chickens.'

She never failed to surprise him. 'You mean roasted with lemons?'

'Alive, preferably.' She gave him a coy look, bringing her hands up to rub her arms. Small bumps had broken out all over her skin.

'Let's go back inside,' he said.

She did not object, waiting while he secured the gate behind them. 'Are wolves the main threat in these parts?'

Of course she knew about Galen's habitat. It had once been her job to know those things. 'Yes. There are no wolves in Syrasan, if my memory serves me.'

'No.'

'But I bet you know everything about them.'

She moved closer as they walked. 'The wolf is the largest member of the *canis* family, with males averaging ninety-five to ninety-nine pounds and females seventy-nine to eighty-five pounds. They are distinguished from other species by their size and features. Mostly grey in colour, but brown, white and red are not uncommon. Attacks are rare, as they are generally fearful due to hunting.'

Dion let out a long whistle. 'My fault for asking.' He glanced again at her bare arms. 'You're cold.'

She looked down at them also. 'A gentleman would offer his tunic.'

'I'm not wearing a tunic, and I have no intention of giving you my shirt.'

'Pity. I would have liked to have seen Sapphira's face when I returned wearing it.' She wore a playful expression.

'Hard to believe she doesn't like you.' When Astra laughed, he could not resist another glance at her. 'I do believe the chickens put you in a good mood.'

'It is that crazy coop.'

'Palace.'

'Sorry, palace.' She shook her head. 'Thank you for showing me.'

He watched his feet press into the grass. 'Any time.'

CHAPTER 13

*L*arkin, Mack, Hamo, Elis, Gosse, Randel, Wilmot, Taki, Dye, Princess Edith, Meggy, two Molles, Aalis, Stace, Diot, Joyce, Jocosa, Royse, Johanne, Princess Aimee, and Helena. It was a good thing Companions had a failsafe technique for remembering names. Forgetting the name of a guest was one of the worst sins a Companion could commit.

The children sat on the floor in one of the upstairs rooms, their ages ranging from three to fourteen. Astra noticed that the older children took care of the younger ones. Now they were all watching her, no doubt trying to figure out what they would be able to get away with.

Not much.

'Does the princess usually teach them as a group?' Astra asked Dion. Sapphira had gone for a lie-down.

He nodded. 'For most lessons. We have volunteers who come to teach specific skills: a swordsmith, shoemaker, artisan, seamstress. Of course, a swordsmith is not going to employ a woman, so we separate them for those types of activities. They all learn the life skills though. The boys know how to cook, and the girls can chop firewood. They all contributed to the chicken palace.'

'Impressive.'

'And Princess Sapphira was adamant the girls learn how to use weapons also.'

'Have to keep those hunting skills sharp,' Astra said dryly.

Dion turned to address the children. 'Astra will be taking over teaching reading, writing, history and geography.'

'And the arts,' she added.

He glanced sideways at her. 'And the arts.'

'Like painting?' Royse asked.

Astra looked at her. 'Painting, dancing, music.'

'But we don't have any instruments for music,' Larkin replied.

Astra turned to Dion for confirmation. 'None at all?' She could not imagine a house without it, a *life* without music.

'It's not something we've allocated money to in the past.'

'What about in the future?'

His eyes moved over her face. 'We were hoping to receive some additional funds from the church.'

'Who controls those funds?'

'Father Agnar decides how donations are allocated.' He paused. 'But a large portion of the donations come from the Talsworth family, who have their own agenda.'

Ah. She had not given much thought as to how they paid for the upkeep and education of the children on his salary. She guessed the manor produced enough apples and live-stock to help with expenses. 'Perhaps we just need to show Father Agnar that music is worth supporting. I could help with that.'

Dion tilted his head. 'Your job is to teach.'

She was not going to argue with him in front of the children. If she stood any chance of winning them over, it needed to at least look like Dion was onside. 'I can still teach music with the instruments we already have.'

The children looked confused.

'Do you mean our voices?' Helena asked.

'Yes, that is one instrument.'

'But only some of us can sing,' Meggy said in her concerned eight-year-old voice.

Astra smiled. 'We can make music without our voices.' She raised her hands. 'Here is another instrument.'

'They already know how to clap,' Dion said. A whisper of laughter travelled around the room.

Astra turned to him, still smiling. 'Might I have a word with you outside?'

He nodded and headed for the door.

Astra looked over at Helena, who had Aimee in her lap. 'Could you take over for a moment, please?' She followed after Dion and pulled the door closed behind her. 'I would appreciate it if you spoke respectfully to me in front of the children,' she said, turning to him.

'It was a joke.'

'It was not funny.'

He sighed. 'I apologise if I hurt your feelings—'

She raised a hand, cutting him off. 'This is not about feelings, Captain. This is about respect.' She pointed to the door. 'Those boys will be looking to you as they grow into men, absorbing everything they witness. If they see you belittling women, they will grow to do the same.'

'Belittling?' Reading her expression, he exhaled. 'I apologise.'

She had no idea if the apology was sincere or not. 'I appreciate that. I would also appreciate the opportunity to meet Father Agnar. Perhaps we could invite him to dinner?'

'He won't come.'

'Why not?'

'I already told you why. He's a good man caught in the real world.'

'I see.' She nodded, thinking on that for a moment.

'Whatever you're scheming in that clever head of yours, forget it. He won't come.'

'When was the last time you invited him?'

'Please just leave it.' He looked off down the landing. 'I need to get going.'

Her eyes widened. 'You are leaving?' It came out in a tone she wished she could snatch back. 'But you just arrived home.'

His eyes moved between hers. 'Most of my time is spent at Swanton Fort. I return here as often as I can, mostly to avoid Helena's wrath.'

Astra realised they were standing too close to one another. There was no need for them to be speaking in hushed voices anymore. She took a small step back. 'And who runs the household in your absence?'

'Everyone, but see Stamitos if you have any difficulties settling in.'

'When will you be back?'

He was watching her carefully. 'A week or two.' His eyes slid down her gown. 'I've asked Hann to take you into Talsworth this week so you can have some new dresses made. The house has a line of credit with the seamstress there. Order whatever you think you'll need to get you through the next few months.'

She crossed her arms. 'Oh, you mean peasant dresses?'

'Order whatever you like, so long as it's practical and comfortable.'

She tilted her head. 'Comfortable for whom?'

He stepped closer, and she was surprised by the nervous

hum in her chest. She did not look away. Reaching around her, he took hold of the door handle and pushed it open before stepping back. The children fell silent inside the room.

'See you in a few weeks,' he said before turning and striding away.

CHAPTER 14

'Still no Captain Dion?' Astra asked Sapphira at the end of her first week. The time had flown by in a flurry of lessons and chores.

The princess looked up from the letter she was writing and regarded Astra with open suspicion. 'No. Why? Do you need something?'

'No.'

Sapphira returned to her letter.

'The children are freshest in the mornings,' Astra continued, 'so I think we should get the heavy learning out of the way early, leaving the afternoons for more physical activities.'

Sapphira nodded and continued writing. 'All right.'

And that was the end of that conversation.

In the second week, Astra introduced music. The children showed little interest in the traditional Galen song she had been certain they would love, so she was forced to rethink her approach. Since they generally preferred to be outdoors, she started there. The tactic had worked well enough on the women at Archdale whenever the monotony of routine became too much.

'All right,' Astra said, gaining everyone's attention. 'We are going to create our own song.'

The children settled themselves on the grass, looking between each other. Astra had assumed she would tire of their constant company, instead finding their unpredictability and curious minds a constant source of amusement.

'You mean write our own song?' Helena asked, sitting herself closest to Astra and pulling Aimee into her lap.

'Yes.' Seeing their confusion, she added, 'Do not look so panicked. I am here to help you. Songs are just another way of telling stories, and we all have stories.'

Wilmot scoffed. 'Sad stories.'

Astra took in his brazen expression. 'Everyone has sad stories, but we do not have to tell sad ones. Let us tell a happy one—the story of Goldmont House.' She handed one of the older girls, Stace, a piece of parchment and a pot of ink, then gestured to the quill. 'I want you to write down everything we talk about.'

'Everything?'

Astra nodded.

'Will they be the lyrics in our song?' Helena asked.

'Maybe.' Astra looked around at the intrigued faces. 'Now, who would like to share something about being here at this house that makes them really happy?' When no one said anything, she cleared her throat. 'How about I go first?'

The children waited.

'At the end of each day, I walk down to the chicken house—'

'You mean the palace?' Molle asked in a quiet voice.

'Yes, sorry, the palace. I go to lock up the chickens—'

'But that's so boring,' Edith said.

Astra gave the princess a disapproving look. 'You need to let me at least finish.' She looked around at the others. 'The house is quiet behind me, the sun low in the sky, painting colourful light all over the… palace.' She crouched down, lowering her voice. 'The hens are settled and safe.' She paused. 'All but one.'

'Which one?' Meggy asked.

Astra looked over at her. 'A freckled black-and-white hen named Primrose.'

'You named her?' the older Molle asked.

'Yes. I knew I had to give her a name when she ran out to greet me a few days ago.'

'Is she your friend?' Hamo asked, leaning forwards to be heard.

Jocosa snorted. 'You can't be friends with a hen.'

Astra rose. 'Of course you can. That is like saying to be family you must share blood. Look around you. Look at the size of your family.'

The children looked around.

'Well, I'm happiest when Dion is here,' Helena said.

Astra nodded. 'Write it down.'

'Eda's cooking makes me happy,' Gosse, one of the older boys, said.

Astra nodded in agreement. 'Oh, her pies are to die for.'

'I was happy when we finished the chicken palace,' Elis said, looking shyly around at the others. 'When we finished painting that day, everyone was smiling.'

Astra pointed at him. 'Good.'

'What about the storms?' Diot asked, trying to sound older than his ten years. 'We all like those. In the warm season, the thunder gets so loud it shakes the house. Everybody screams, but then we laugh.'

'Because it's fun,' Randel said.

'I hate the storms,' Aimee said. 'They scare me.'

Helena hugged her closer. 'Yes, but you love sleeping in my bed, and storms are the only time I let you.' She tickled the girl.

'Good,' Astra said, an idea forming. She looked down at Stace, who was frantically writing. 'Get it all down. This is our story.'

CHAPTER 15

'Where are all my good spoons?' Eda asked Astra.

It had been three weeks since Dion's departure, and Astra found herself growing impatient for his return. She had so much to tell him, to *show* him. 'There are plenty more spoons in the drawer.'

'Yes, but where are they disappearing to?'

Astra focused very hard on the plates she was drying. 'They are being used as musical instruments.'

Eda appeared confused. 'The children are playing... spoons?'

'Yes.'

Eda closed the drawer and turned to face her. 'I don't suppose two of my serving bowls are with them?'

'That is quite probable.'

Eda shook her head. 'What about the shovel that went missing from the stables yesterday? Hann said it disappeared before his very eyes.'

'I told the children to return the shovel at the end of the lesson.'

Eda wiped her hands on her apron. 'What on earth could you want with a shovel? Music must be very different where you come from.'

'Improvisation is universal.'

Eda laughed at that. 'I can't wait to hear what the captain thinks of your *improvisation* when he returns.'

Astra stacked the plate on top of the others. 'And when might that be?'

Eda walked over to the bench and picked up a piece of parchment. She held it far away from her in order to read it. 'All going well, Friday, according to his letter.'

It was only Monday. Astra removed her apron and hung it by the door. 'I wonder if Hann would mind taking me into the village this afternoon to see the seamstress.'

Eda dragged a bowl towards her and poked at the dough. Pleased with the result, she upturned it onto the floured benchtop. 'He won't mind. He has errands he can run while he's there.'

Astra tried to keep her voice casual for the next part. 'And I thought I might drop in and introduce myself to Father Agnar.'

Eda stopped kneading, peering up at her for a moment. 'You mean the Father Agnar I heard the captain telling you to stay away from?'

'Did he? I barely recall.'

Eda smiled down at the dough. 'He used to come to Goldmont for dinner. Every month. Then he started declining the invitations, making excuses. Eventually the captain stopped asking.'

'Does the captain attend church?'

'There's a chapel at Swanton.'

'I see.' Astra drew a line through the floured area with her finger. 'Perhaps I could invite the priest to dinner on Friday.'

Eda looked up again but continued working. 'He won't come. Hasn't stepped foot in Goldmont House since...'

'Since the captain's father was sentenced?'

'Since the Talsworths got in his ear. Control everything, they do. Dion was hurting enough, and then they call off the wedding.'

'Seems awfully harsh to judge Dion based on his father's crime.'

Eda shook her head. 'It's because Dion defended his father's actions. People saw him as an accomplice.'

Astra watched Eda for a moment. If there was ever a chance to learn more, it was now. 'Treason is a rather broad term. What exactly was his crime?'

'Depends who you ask. As far as I'm concerned, his only crime was helping people on the wrong side of the border.'

His father's relationship with an Asigow woman began to make more sense. 'What people?'

Eda threw the dough about a little harder than necessary. 'The Nydoen tribes mostly.'

'Zoelin rebels?'

'Don't let the captain hear you call them that.'

Astra wanted to understand. 'They have separated themselves from their king. What else am I to call them?'

'Heroes, if you ask the captain. Prince Brom stands for something, not like that brother of his.'

'Brom is no longer a prince. He was stripped of his title when King Jayr took the throne.'

'Those loyal to him don't care about titles. The man is a king in the eyes of the Nydoen people.'

Astra thought on that for a moment. 'Does Dion see him as a king?'

Eda fell quiet. 'Not my place to speak for him.'

Hann entered the kitchen and held up a skinned lamb. 'Where do you want this?'

Eda nodded to the space on the other bench. 'Good timing. Astra is wanting to go into the village and see the seamstress.'

Hann smiled warmly at her. 'Happy to take you.'

'And by the church, if it is not too much trouble,' Astra said, ignoring the look from Eda.

'Captain won't be happy,' the old woman sang.

'It is only dinner. And he has not even said yes yet.' Astra looked back at Hann. 'I just need to change. I will be down shortly.'

Hann drove Astra into Talsworth that afternoon, pulling up directly outside the seamstress's shop. A wooden plaque on the front door said Open. Astra waited for Hann to help her down, then stepped up onto the wooden veranda.

'I'll wait here for you,' Hann said.

She gave him an appreciative smile before pushing the door open and stepping inside. Two women stood to one side, one holding a roll of fabric, the other rubbing it between her fingers. They stopped talking when she entered and looked in her direction. One wore a pleasant expression, the other not so much.

'I'll be right with you,' said the friendly one.

Astra waved a hand. 'Take your time.'

The other woman let go of the fabric, eyes raking up and down Astra. 'You can go ahead and serve her. I need some time to consider.'

The woman seemed unsure at first, then eventually stepped away and walked over to where Astra was waiting. 'Right,' she said, all business. 'I'm the seamstress, Isolda. What can I help you with?'

Astra looked around at the rolls of fabric stacked against one wall. 'I was hoping to have some dresses made.'

The woman's eyes widened with recognition. 'Oh. Are you the Companion Dion brought back from Syrasan?'

Astra was not prepared for that question. 'Yes.'

The other woman wandered over to them. 'The castle girl?' Her eyes moved up and down Astra once more.

The term "castle girl" was a demeaning one. 'Actually, I am the new governess.' Astra stood tall beneath her gaze. 'Sorry, I did not catch your name.'

'Elenor Talsworth.'

Astra remained perfectly composed. So, this was the woman who Dion was meant to marry, the infamous Talsworth daughter. Astra's eyes moved over her briefly. She was well presented, dressed in a very expensive but sensible gown, her dark hair braided neatly. There was not a spot of paint on her pretty face. Exactly the sort of woman Astra could see Dion marrying. She seemed threatened by Astra's presence, which was interesting. Perhaps Stamitos was right and she had not moved on.

Turning her attention back to Isolda, Astra said, 'Perhaps you could recommend something?'

The short woman immediately walked over to the fabric wall, looking very serious. 'What colours did you have in mind?'

'Blue is always a safe choice for me.'

Isolda turned with a knowing nod. 'Brings out the colour of your eyes. Startling shade, they are.'

Elenor sauntered closer still. 'I am afraid you will have to wait for the next order of fabric to arrive, as I have my heart set on blue also.'

Isolda looked at Elenor in surprise, and Astra turned tiredly in her direction.

'You need *all* the blue fabric in the store?' Astra asked.

Elenor walked over to the reams, fingers gliding over them. 'We are having some new curtains made.'

Isolda cleared her throat. 'I am sure there is plenty—'

'My father owns the shop.' Elenor cut her off. 'Naturally my family's orders are fulfilled first.'

Perhaps not Dion's type after all. 'Naturally,' Astra said, turning back to Isolda. 'Perhaps we can decide on a pattern and go from there?'

Elenor stepped closer still. 'You know, Isolda does not really make the type of gowns you are looking for.'

Astra turned to face her square on. 'And how do you know what I am looking for?'

'I can guess by what you are wearing.' She scrunched up her face. 'Tight and showy.'

Isolda's face flushed. 'I think it's rather pretty. Compliments your lovely figure.'

Astra pointed to the roll of plain cream cotton. 'What about that?'

'I am afraid that has been put aside for another customer,' Elenor said, as if it pained her to say it.

'The entire roll?'

Elenor raised her chin. 'Yes.'

Isolda did not appear to know where to look.

'Shame,' Astra said, tracing a finger over it. 'Neutral tones also bring out the blue in my eyes.' She looked straight at Elenor. 'Or so Dion tells me when I am wrapped in his bedsheet.'

Isolda turned her smiling face to the floor while Elenor pressed her lips into a thin line, nostrils flaring.

'I think you should leave.'

Astra let her eyes remain on Elenor a moment longer before turning to Isolda. 'Perhaps I will return another day when you are not so busy.'

The seamstress gave her an apologetic smile. 'Yes, please do.'

She left without so much as a glance in Elenor Talsworth's direction.

'That was quick,' Hann said when she stepped outside.

Astra looked down the road as she climbed up into the cart. 'Is there really no other seamstress in this village?'

Hann wandered back to the other side and climbed in. 'Afraid not. Isolda is very good. Nothing take your fancy?'

She faced forwards. 'It seems they are low on stock. Do you mind taking me to the church?'

He nodded and flicked the reins. A minute later, they pulled up outside a small, well-kept chapel with a high steeple and double wooden doors. Astra stared at it for a moment, recalling the compulsory mass at Archdale. The long sermons had often put the women to sleep.

Hann helped her down again and asked if she wanted him to accompany her inside.

'That will not be necessary, thank you. I will not be long.'

Inside was a fairly standard layout as far as churches went. Long wooden pews, stained-glass windows, an altar at the front. The main difference was the brass statue of the Galen god they called Etia. A young boy stood polishing it, turning when he heard her enter.

'Is Father Agnar here?'

The boy nodded and went to fetch him. A few moments later, a man dressed in robes appeared. He had long, wiry eyebrows and smile lines on his face. She noticed his gaze did not drop to the neckline of her dress. She had worn the gown specifically to figure out the type of man she was dealing with.

'Father Agnar,' she said, curtsying. 'My name is Astra, the new governess at Goldmont House. I wanted to come and introduce myself.'

He studied her face for a moment before speaking. 'I heard the captain had employed a Companion.'

This was not a man who could be won over with a flash of skin and a pretty smile. She would need to get creative. 'Yes. I was King Pandarus's Companion for ten years.' And honest.

'So I hear. You've picked a pretty location to retire, though hardly restful with all those children running about.'

She thought his eyes seemed kind. 'The children are the beating heart of that house. I cannot imagine it would be the same without them.'

He tilted his head, watching her a moment. 'I'm guessing you didn't come to confess your sins?'

It seemed he wanted her to get to the point. 'Neither of us has that much time. I actually came to extend an invitation to you.'

'Oh? What kind of invitation?'

'Dinner. At Goldmont House this coming Friday.'

He looked down. 'I'm afraid I don't have much time for social visits nowadays.'

She waited for him to look up. 'I introduced music lessons recently, and the children have prepared something that I would love for you to see.'

'A performance?'

'Yes.'

He nodded. 'I'm afraid I cannot accept the invitation.'

She drew a breath. 'May I be frank?'

'Please.'

'The children need funds to pay for musical instruments.'

He smiled. 'So you want money from the church.'

'Honestly, right now I just want you to come to dinner and witness how amazing these little people are. If you choose to hand over money after that, so be it.' She smiled when she said that last part.

'I heard rumours that Companions are a force to be reckoned with.'

'And I heard that you are a good man caught in the real world.' She paused. 'It has been four years. Please come eat with us. Those children need reminding that God has not forgotten about them.'

He appeared torn. 'Will Captain Dion be attending the dinner?'

'Yes, of course. He is very much looking forward to it.' Only a *small* lie in God's house.

He thought for a moment. 'If my memory serves me correctly, Eda makes excellent pie.'

'If you come, I shall put in a special request.'

He gave a resigned nod. 'Then I guess I will see you Friday.'

'Excellent. Thank you for seeing me, Father.' Astra turned to leave.

'Astra.'

She turned back, waiting.

'I have plenty of time to hear your confessions.'

A smile spread across her face. 'I shall keep that in mind.'

CHAPTER 16

The following Friday, Dion returned to Goldmont House. It was Eda who broke the news that Father Agnar would be joining them for dinner that evening. His agitation grew.

'Where is she?' he asked, already walking away.

Eda did not need to ask who. 'Upstairs with the children, but go easy on her. She means well.'

He marched upstairs and entered the room without knocking, finding Astra on the floor helping the younger children with their writing. She looked up and smiled, but it faded when she registered his expression. 'Welcome home, Captain.' She got up off the floor.

Helena and some of the younger children jumped up and went to him, the smaller ones wrapping themselves around his legs and middle. He greeted them all individually and kissed his sister before returning his attention to Astra once more. She looked different. More relaxed, perhaps—but no less beautiful. He could feel his anger dissolving at the sight of her, and he had to remind himself of why he was mad. 'A word,' he said once the children had released him.

Astra nodded. 'Helena, could you take over for a moment?' She followed Dion out of the room. 'How have you been?' she asked, closing the door.

'Not as busy as you, it seems.'

Her expression did not change.

'Eda tells me Father Agnar is coming to dinner this evening.'

'Yes, I invited him.'

'Why?'

'The children have something to show him.'

He brushed a finger down his nose, determined to remain calm. 'I told you to leave it alone.'

'I know.'

'And yet you went to him for money.'

Astra glanced at the door. 'No, I invited him to dinner.'

He stared at her. 'Does he know I'll be there?'

'Yes, he is very much looking forward to it.'

'And how did you persuade him?' Unfortunately, his gaze fell to her chest when he asked that question.

She must have noticed, because her face hardened. 'What was that?'

'What?'

'That glance down. If I did not know any better, I would think you are implying that I seduced a priest.'

'Did you?'

She looked away, taking a moment to calm herself. 'If you must know, I gave him *exactly* what he wanted from me in that moment.'

Dion had not been expecting that response. 'What?'

'Right there, in the middle of the church.' She paused before looking at him and adding, 'I am referring to honest conversation.'

Dion shifted his weight. 'Not funny.'

She sighed. 'You know, I was actually pleased to see you for about three seconds.'

He stepped back, waiting for his heart to recover. 'He's not just going to hand over money because you laugh at his jokes and serve him pie.'

'That is rather offensive.'

'You're a Companion. You're manipulative by nature.'

'Even more offensive. Why are you so angry over a dinner invitation?'

It was not just the dinner invitation. He had called in on his cousin on the way home. She had told him about the encounter with Elenor at her shop. 'I ran into Isolda on my way here.'

Astra looked confused. 'The seamstress?'

'And my cousin.'

Her expression fell. 'Isolda is your cousin?'

He nodded. 'Yes. She told me what happened when you went to her shop.'

Astra folded her hands in front of her. 'Oh.'

He searched her eyes for a moment. 'I hear you and Elenor did not get along.'

'I can get along with anyone, but she was quite determined not to get along with *me*.'

'I'm sorry she was rude.'

'I can handle rude people. I am trained to keep a level head in those situations, to be the better person.'

'Is that why you told her I like the colour of your eyes when you're wrapped in my bedsheet?'

He watched the colour drain from her face.

'I might have said something vaguely along those lines, but only after being provoked.' She released a breath. 'She was very jealous, by the way, clearly still in love with you. I gather the decision to end the engagement was her parents', not hers.'

Dion rested his hands on his hips. 'Actually, it was mine in the end.'

'What do you mean?'

'They wanted me to jump through hoops in order for the wedding to go ahead, and it all felt like a betrayal to my father.'

'Oh.' Astra sat with that information for a moment.

'I let everyone believe it was their decision to spare Elenor further embarrassment.'

'Well, I suppose that explains the family's grudge against you.' She exhaled. 'I am sorry for going behind your back.'

His expression softened. 'It's done now. Do the children actually have something to perform?'

'Yes, of course. I am really excited for you to see it.'

'Why's that?'

'Because it is the story of Goldmont House.'

There was pride in her voice. She was adorable. 'Well, don't get your hopes up about tonight. You may get nothing but polite applause.'

'Oh, ye of little faith.' Her eyes shone at him for a moment before she turned and went back into the room, leaving him on the landing staring at the closed door.

That afternoon, Astra asked for Eda's help fixing up one of her dresses while Dion played a ball game with the children outside. The old woman agreed on the condition that Astra help her in the kitchen when they were done.

'What exactly do you expect me to do with this?' Eda asked, holding up the silk gown.

Astra chewed her lower lip. She could do things like that now without fear of Fedora catching her. 'I was hoping you could help me make it a little more... modest for our guest.'

Eda turned it around, eyebrows rising as she inspected the back.

'I thought we could fill some of the gaps with the lace off a shawl. Maybe give it sleeves.'

'That could work.' Eda nodded. 'Bring me the scissors.'

Once the altered gown was hanging from Astra's windowsill, the two women headed downstairs to start on the evening meal. Since arriving, Astra had only helped with the cleaning side of things.

'I should warn you,' she said, 'I have not cooked since I left home, unless you count buttering bread.'

Eda did not seem surprised. 'I have trouble fathoming a woman as smart as you not being able to do basics like getting stains out of clothes and making a loaf of bread. What good is speaking five languages when you've no idea how to prepare a chicken?'

'Well, I do not eat chicken, so that is a skill I can survive without.'

Eda stopped working and looked at her. 'What do you mean, you do not eat chicken? Since when?'

'Since I was little.'

'But I have been serving you chicken most days.'

'It is fine. I just eat the other things.' It had been the same at Archdale, a constant source of confusion and jokes among the women.

At that exact moment, Dion and Randel strolled into the kitchen. Randel was holding four headless hens tied in a bundle by their legs. He dropped them onto the bench between the women.

'Killed and cleaned all four of them himself,' Dion said, squeezing the boy's shoulder.

Eda smiled like a proud grandparent. 'Well done, you.'

Astra looked away from the birds, afraid she might recognise one of them.

Dion must have noticed, because he asked, 'What's the matter?' His gaze fell to where she was holding the edge of the bench. 'Are you unwell?'

Eda picked up the birds and took them away, saying nothing.

Astra forced herself to let go of the bench. 'I am fine.'

'Why don't you go collect the fruit for the pies while I prepare the chickens?' Eda suggested when she returned.

Astra nodded and stepped away from the group. 'Good idea.'

Dion's eyes followed her. 'Randel can help you if you'd like.'

'I can handle a few apples.' She was past them and out the door before anyone could object.

CHAPTER 17

*D*ion was walking across the landing towards the staircase when he saw Astra coming out of her room at the end. She was wearing the silk dress she had worn her first night at Goldmont, but lace sleeves had been added, the fabric extending across the previously open back. She had altered it for the occasion—or, more likely, the company. Her hair was smoothed back so she was all beautiful cheekbones and perfectly groomed brows. The jewellery was minimal. She knew her audience.

'The dress looks good,' he called out.

She looked in his direction, a smile on her lips as she came towards him. '"Good" is an enormous compliment coming from you.'

He was out of practice.

Astra stopped when she reached him. 'My dress thanks you for the compliment.'

He smiled at that smart mouth of hers. 'The rest of you looks great too.'

'*Great*? Careful, I may blush.' Her eyes were laughing at

him. 'Are you going to offer me your arm like a gentleman, or have you more compliments to pay?'

He offered his arm, and she placed her hand through it. As they descended the steps, he noticed her distinct scent, not soap but a perfume of some kind, a flower he could not place. It was subtle enough that one would have to be close to notice. It made him want to bury his face in her skin. Not the most helpful of thoughts.

As they crossed the hall, he snuck a glance at her. She walked like a queen. He knew she had been a queen of sorts at Archdale, so it was fitting.

When they reached the dining room, she let go of his arm. Father Agnar was already seated with Sapphira, who looked ready for bed. Stamitos had gone to Reave Castle for meetings.

'So sorry to keep you waiting,' Astra said, going over to greet their guest.

Father Agnar might have been a priest, but he was still a man. He noticed her arrival as any other would, only never letting his gaze drop below the face the way Dion's always did.

'Good to see you again,' he said, standing.

Dion felt some misplaced jealousy as the man pulled out a chair for her and settled her at the table. He took the spare seat opposite them, next to Sapphira.

Agnar and Dion looked at one another.

'It's been a long time,' Agnar said, seeming uncomfortable.

Dion nodded. 'It has.'

'How many years has it been since you pied at Goldmont House, Father?' Astra asked.

'Since I *pied* here?'

'Yes.'

'I believe that is the official term for eating pie at Goldmont,' Sapphira said, joining in.

Dion eyed Astra. He had to admit, she was good at entertaining. 'I believe Sapphira pied just before you arrived, Father.'

Sapphira's mouth fell open. 'How do you know that?'

'I could hear you from out back.'

The priest laughed. 'Well, she has the perfect excuse.'

The evening moved along in much the same fashion thanks to the women. There were no awkward silences or uncomfortable moments. Dion watched as Astra kept the priest's plate full and the wine flowing. At one point he noticed her own plate sat empty. Picking up the chicken, he held it out for her.

'You need to eat something besides carrots,' he said.

Astra glanced down at the plate. 'Thank you, but I am saving room for the main event.'

Dion put it back down on the table, and Astra and Father Agnar continued their conversation.

'She doesn't eat chicken,' Sapphira whispered.

Dion turned to her. 'Why not?'

Sapphira shrugged. 'No idea. Hasn't eaten it for as long as I've known her.'

Dion looked across the table, watching Astra as she nodded thoughtfully, paying careful attention to everything the priest was saying. He liked knowing that little quirk about her. It made her more real somehow. Perhaps because it was the closest thing she had to a flaw. She met his eyes again, a question in them, likely wondering what he was staring at. Thankfully, Eda arrived with the pies.

Half an hour later, Father Agnar leaned back in his chair, hands resting on his stomach. 'That was as good as I remember it being, if not better.'

Eda smiled at him as she cleared away the table. 'Actually, Astra did most of the work.'

'I was carefully managed through the entire process,' she added.

Always the modest Companion. 'I'm still impressed,' Dion said, and her smile softened at the compliment.

Sapphira covered her mouth, stifling a yawn. 'Shall we see if the children are ready?'

'Yes,' Father Agnar said. 'Before you fall asleep on us.'

Sapphira stood, her belly brushing the edge of the table as she rose.

Astra brought her hands together. 'If you would all like to follow me outside.'

'Outside?' Dion asked.

Father Agnar stepped away from the table. 'Now I'm intrigued.'

Astra continued to chat away as they walked. 'We do not have any instruments you will recognise as such, but that does not stop us from making music.'

Agnar nodded. 'The voice can be a beautiful instrument.'

'It can be,' Astra agreed, 'but not everyone is blessed with a good voice. I am certainly not.'

Outside, there was a campfire with three rows of children on one side and chairs for their audience on the other. The older children stood at the back, the youngest seated in front. Dion noted their excited faces as he sank into one of the chairs. His gaze fell to the various dishes and utensils they were holding, narrowing on what appeared to be a shovel. His eyes met with Helena's, and he winked at her. Her smile grew. He had not seen her that happy for some time.

'Goodness.' Father Agnar chuckled, taking his seat. 'Pots, pans, spoons. Are you singing a song or making us supper?'

The children giggled, but not Astra. She turned her back to him and said something to the children in a hushed voice. Dion watched as their smiles were replaced with looks of concentration, their eyes locked on their teacher. Astra made a gesture with her hand, and the children straightened, their instruments still on the ground in front of them, which confused Dion. Astra nodded at Meggy, who stepped forwards, saying in her biggest voice, 'This is the story of our home.'

Dion winked at the normally shy girl, and she pressed her lips together to stop from smiling—all business.

Silence fell over the group, the only noise the crackle of fire and distant chirp of a cicada. Astra swooped a finger up, and Dion had to admit he was curious as to what would unfold. She looked left, nodding again. The children at the end began rubbing their hands together, creating a *shushing* noise. As Astra's gaze moved along the rows, more children joined in, then a few more, until the entire group was doing the same action. The noise whispered across the fire. It sounded like the wind picking up. Astra turned left again, the smallest gesture of her hand sending fingers clicking. Just a few, then more, building into... he laughed.

Rain.

The younger children at the front began patting their legs, like the rain was growing louder. Dion glanced over at Father Agnar, who sat in utter fascination. A nod from Astra, and Larkin brought his foot down on what appeared to be a long piece of timber, Hamo and Ellis echoed the action, creating thunder. A mirror flashed, reflecting the fire, then another, giving the illusion of lightning. The pats turned to clicks, and then the clicking ceased, replaced with the rubbing of hands once more.

The rain had stopped.

Astra looked over at Meggy and Gosse, who stepped forwards, emitting a single note, hers high, his low. A single pure sound. Helena joined in, and soon there was a hum of voices. Astra controlled everything with just a simple move-ment of her hand or a look here and there. Some of the children reached for their... instruments? Spoons circled bowls; forks scraped plates.

The sounds of mealtime.

A shovel scraped gravel, and an axe fell in a steady rhythm. A hammer joined the chorus of tools.

The sound of work.

Dion's eyes moved over the children's faces. A flick of Astra's hand brought complete silence. He waited. Laughter, Stace's familiar giggle. The girl was always laughing. It grew louder, and more children joined in. Dion's gaze was drawn to the sound of water being poured and splashed, somehow creating a beat. It was the sound of bath day. It was also the sound of happy children, not re-enacted but real. He could *feel* it.

More voices joined, Wilmot's deeper than Dion had known he could go. Then Helena began to sing.

'Amid the blossoming trees,
Sheep graze and whisper with the bees.
The oxen watch in the ruddy light,
Hungry owls preparing to take flight...'

Dion smiled because he had not known how good his sister's voice was. He glanced sideways at the beaming priest. Even Sapphira was smiling, proudly watching her girls, who played their parts perfectly despite their young age.

Dion's gaze returned to Astra. He could have sat there all night watching her. She had not closed her eyes and disappeared like she had when playing the harp. She was experiencing the joy with them. He had underestimated her.

. . .

'Around the hearths at night they gather,
In wooden tubs they splash and lather.
Laughter surges, and then it dies,
Home is a vibrant light in their eyes...'

Astra pinched her forefinger and thumb together and the singing stopped, instruments laid down. A flick of her wrist and the clicking of fingers started once more, not building this time but fading to wind. Dion could almost feel the breeze.

Then silence.

Astra looked around at the children, pure pride on her face. She turned back to her audience of three and gestured for the children to bow. They moved in one clean line, their smiles as wide as dinner plates. Father Agnar sat forwards in his seat, applauding. Sapphira cheered. Dion got to his feet and began clapping. His eyes met Astra's over the fire, and he nodded his approval. She had, without question, won the evening.

'Bravo,' Father Agnar shouted, still applauding.

Dion held Astra's gaze. *Bravo indeed.*

Dion glanced in Astra's direction. He was seated with his elbows resting on his knees in front of the fire. 'You're rather pleased with yourself, aren't you?'

She leaned back in her chair, moving her feet closer to the flames. The warmth was heavenly. 'Quite pleased, actually. Father Agnar seems confident he can source some second-hand instruments to get us started.'

He watched her, his eyes reflecting the flames. 'What you did was amazing.'

'You mean what the children did.' She waved her feet from side to side. 'I am glad you enjoyed it though. I think it is nice for you to see this place through their eyes.'

'I wasn't sure how you'd go teaching children.'

'Because I am a cold-hearted Companion?'

'Because it's a big change from your old world.'

She watched the flames for a moment. 'Turns out the children are better company than many adults I know.'

'I agree.' He was watching her again. 'You know, I had no idea Helena could sing that well.'

'Her natural talent is extraordinary.' She met his gaze. 'Do you know what else is extraordinary?'

'What?'

'That you have basically given up your house for these children.'

He looked back at the fire. 'My father took in Gosse when he was four. It just grew from there. Can't tell you how many times I've said no more. I blame Sapphira for the last six. She comes to me with these sad stories...'

Astra smiled at that. 'Do you ever think about what would have happened to them if they had not come here?'

'I like to think other people would have taken them in. Though their lives might have been a bit tougher.'

'I doubt they would have learned to read and write.'

Dion relaxed back in his chair. 'No.'

'Can I ask you something?'

His gaze drifted back to her. 'That depends.'

She hesitated, knowing her question would ruin the mood. 'Were you there the day your father was executed?'

He blinked. 'Yes. Helena stayed here. I went to Reave Castle, mainly to ask the old king to release Helena's mother.'

'But he did not.'

He shook his head. 'He was under a lot of pressure from the northern kings. King Tuyon was still a myth back then, and King Jayr was new to the throne. Everyone seemed to lose their minds to their fear.'

'With good reason.'

Dion laughed through his nose. 'Companions can't say things like that. You're supposed to be neutral.'

She took in his teasing expression. 'And you are supposed to be loyal to your king.'

'I am loyal to my king.'

'But you think him weak.'

'I think him unable to help. There's a difference.'

'But your father helped?'

Dion nodded. 'Yes.'

'And that is how he met Helena's mother?'

Another nod.

She was silent a moment. 'Have you continued your father's work?'

He watched her carefully. 'What are you doing?'

'Getting to know you.'

'By putting me on trial? You want to know if I'm a traitor like my father, is that it?'

She swallowed. 'No.'

He looked away. 'I believe in everything he did. I suppose that makes me a traitor of sorts.'

She leaned forwards. 'The children would be devastated to lose you. Helena might never get over it.'

He sighed. 'I think that's enough questions for one night. I thought Companions were supposed to be discreet when they bleed a man dry.'

She sat back again. 'You made it very clear you did not want a Companion.'

'I prefer something a little more honest.'

'Because you are such a beacon of light to all us liars?'

'I never said you were a liar.'

'Just dishonest.'

He shook his head. 'You're exhausting.'

'And you are a big hypocrite. I am open about who I am, have been from the beginning. You are as shady as a forest.'

Before Dion could retaliate, Eda came running down the lawn towards them. He turned at the sound of her approaching steps and stood when he saw her expression. 'What's the matter?'

She was out of breath as she came to a stop. 'The baby is coming. Hann has gone to get the midwife, but the princess says something feels wrong.'

'What does that mean?' Astra asked, coming off her chair and moving in the direction of the house.

Eda and Dion were moving also. 'The pains are strong for so early in the labour.'

Dion glanced at the house. 'It's her third child. Perhaps things are moving a little faster this time round.'

Eda did not look convinced. 'You should fetch Prince Stamitos.'

Dion turned to Astra. 'Are you able to help?'

She nodded. 'Of course. The midwife will be here soon enough.' Though she did not feel as confident as she sounded. She had sat at Idalia's side during a number of terminations but never for the birth of a living baby.

'You're sure?' Dion's hand was on her back, waiting for her reply.

She could not have him wasting time when he needed to get Stamitos. 'Of course. Go.'

His hand fell away, and then he was gone.

CHAPTER 18

Sapphira was perched on the edge of the bed with her knees pressed together, holding her stomach with both hands. She looked at Astra, who stood frozen in the doorway. 'Something's wrong.'

Idalia's pale face flashed in Astra's mind, sweat beading on her forehead while the so-called midwife finished the job. Blinking, Astra rushed forwards and knelt in front of Sapphira. 'The midwife will be here soon.'

'What about Stamitos?'

'Dion has gone to fetch him. It will be at least three or four hours, even at a gallop.'

Sapphira nodded, a few tears escaping.

Astra reached out and took her hand. 'Eda is here, and I am not going anywhere. Just tell me what you need.'

Sapphira searched her eyes for a moment. 'I want my baby to live.'

Astra attempted a smile. 'Your baby will be fine.'

Tears fell down Sapphira's face. She brushed them away with her spare hand. Another contraction arrived. Sapphira tried to breathe through it, but then her head tipped back and she cried out. Panic pounded Astra's insides.

'I hear the cart pulling up,' Eda said. 'That'll be Suetta.' She left the room.

Sapphira wiped her damp hands on her nightdress. 'They're coming closer together.'

'Do you want some water?'

Sapphira shook her head, eyes trained on Astra. 'Do you remember the night Idalia died?'

At first Astra was not sure if she had heard correctly, but the fear on Sapphira's face confirmed she had. 'You cannot think about that now.'

Sapphira gripped her arm. 'I think about it all the time. One moment she was sitting beneath the cherry trees with us, the next she was dead in her bed covered in her own sick.'

Astra fought the urge to tear her hand away and cover Sapphira's mouth. 'They were completely different circumstances. The pregnancy was terminated, then infection.' She forced a smile. 'Your baby was kicking through dinner.'

Sapphira's shoulders relaxed a little. 'Maybe it's a boy.' She stiffened again as another contraction arrived.

'Deep breaths,' Astra said.

'This is not the time for Companion tips,' Sapphira said through gritted teeth. When the pain passed, she hung her head in her hands. 'Sorry.'

Astra rubbed her leg. 'Do not apologise. Remember how mean I was to you at Archdale?'

Sapphira leaned back on her hands, eyes closed. 'You were awful to everyone.'

Everyone except for Idalia.

'Well, now is your chance to unleash all that resentment and blame it on childbirth.'

The door swung open, and Eda walked in followed by the midwife, a tall woman in her fifties with a round face and deep frown lines across her brow. She glanced at Astra, smiling.

'I'm Suetta.'

'Astra.'

The woman turned her attention to Sapphira. 'Here we are again. Another royal baby.' She walked over to the bed and placed her bag down. 'I need you to lie back so I can have a proper look at you.'

Astra rose, helping Sapphira lie down before stepping back. The midwife poked and prodded, finishing with an internal examination.

'The good news is you are almost ready to go.'

'What is the bad news?' Astra asked before Sapphira had a chance.

'Baby's the wrong way up.'

Astra looked down at Sapphira, who was staring at the midwife, obviously wanting a different answer.

'The baby didn't turn?' Sapphira's voice was small.

Suetta shook her head. 'I'm afraid not.'

Panic passed over Sapphira's face. 'Can't you... turn it? I've read about babies being turned before delivery.' She tensed up as another contraction arrived.

'How far apart are they?' Suetta asked Astra.

She tried to think. 'Barely a minute since the last one.'

Suetta observed Sapphira throughout the contraction. She was starting to bear down. 'This baby is coming whether we like it or not.' She walked around the other side of the bed and took Sapphira's arm. 'I'm going to need you on your hands and knees. It's the best position to get the baby out safely.'

Sapphira moaned as she got on all fours. 'It's not supposed to happen like this. I've heard stories—'

'We've all heard the stories,' Eda said, not letting her

finish. 'But those women weren't you, and they didn't have Suetta.'

'Have you delivered many breech babies?' Astra asked.

Suetta smiled across the bed at her. 'A few in my time. I have some tricks, don't worry. Pass the bag, would you?'

Astra slid it across the bed to Suetta, who opened it and began taking out instruments that looked like the ones used for Idalia's second termination. She had been further along that time. Astra pressed a leg to the bed to steady herself.

'Your job is to keep the princess nice and calm. Give her water if she wants it. Clean up any sick.'

A vision of Idalia lying in blood-soaked sheets covered in her own vomit flashed in Astra's mind. She pressed her leg harder into the bed, needing to keep it together for Sapphira. 'I can do that.'

'Don't worry about what I'm doing this end. You stay up there and remind her of how well she's doing.'

Sapphira cried out as another contraction tore through her. Astra bent forwards, brushing hair off Sapphira's sweaty face. 'I need to confess something.'

'Now?' Sapphira asked, collapsing onto her elbows.

Astra leaned closer. 'You were always so much stronger than me. You still are. I guarantee you I would be a sobbing mess by now.'

'You never cry.'

Not true. She had cried the day Idalia had passed. It was like someone had torn her beating heart from her chest. 'I am going to remind you of that strength until you are holding your baby.'

'And then put it in writing?'

Astra knelt down beside the bed again. 'If you like.' She covered Sapphira's hand with her own. 'I have complete faith in you.'

Sapphira's stomach tightened, and she roared through gritted teeth as the pain took hold once more.

Two hours later, all Sapphira had to show for her efforts was the tiny backside of a baby and one leg. 'It hurts.' She half shouted, half cried the words, her jaw clenched tightly. Her bottom lip was swollen and bloodied from biting down on it.

Astra had given her a belt to bite down on only to have it spat back at her. She had no idea how else to help, so she continued wiping Sapphira's face with a cool cloth.

'Is the other leg out?' Sapphira asked, letting her head collapse onto the pillows for a moment. Suetta gave her a pat on the leg. 'I need to turn the baby to get the other leg out.'

A sob escaped Sapphira. 'I don't think I can keep going.'

Astra reached forwards, covering Sapphira's hand with her own. 'Of course you can.'

'I can't.'

'One thing at a time,' Suetta said, her tone demanding calm. 'Let's get the baby turned. I'll tell you when it's time to push.'

Silent tears fell down Sapphira's face for a moment, but then she pushed herself up onto all fours once more. Astra held her breath, watching the discomfort play out on her face. *God, please don't let them die.*

'All right,' Suetta said. 'I need a little push with the next pain.'

Sapphira cooperated, and Astra released the breath she had been holding when the second leg came out. 'Just two arms and a head to go.'

Sapphira turned her red face to Astra. 'Just two arms and the head? You mean the head that's supposed to come first?'

'You're doing splendidly,' Eda said.

Suetta took charge again. 'All right, I need another push.'

Sapphira pressed her fingers into the bed. 'Just get it out.'

Astra leaned right to see the baby's gender. Returning to Sapphira's head, she whispered, 'You were right. It is a boy.'

Sapphira looked at her. 'A boy?'

Astra smiled and rubbed her hand. 'Just a little longer, and then you will get to hold your son.'

'And sleep?'

'And sleep.' Astra wiped her face with the cloth. 'He has ten perfect toes and the sweetest feet.'

'Push,' Suetta said, her tone firm. Sapphira cried out. 'That's one arm. Now don't push again until I've turned him.' Everyone held their breath. 'All right. Little push now. That's it.'

A smile broke out on Eda's face. 'And ten perfect fingers.'

Sapphira rested her forehead on her fisted hands for a moment.

Astra wiped her face again. 'Good girl.'

'I'm not going to lie,' Suetta said, her expression serious. 'This part is going to be very uncomfortable.'

Sapphira pushed herself up on her hands again. 'Uncomfortable? This is *torture*.'

Astra rubbed her hand. 'You are almost there. I know it hurts, but—'

'You know?' Sapphira shouted. 'How do you know? Have you ever had a baby's head and an adult's hand wedged inside you at the same time?'

Astra let her shout. In some ways it was easier than tears.

'I need some pressure on her stomach,' Suetta told Eda. 'And I need one long, even push from you, Sapphira.'

'I don't think I can.' Sapphira's entire body shook, perspiration dripping on the linen below faster than Astra could wipe it away. 'I'm so tired.'

Astra took a firm grip of her hand. 'No you do not. The

Sapphira I know does not give up. Come on. You were always the one with something to prove, so prove it.'

Sapphira's head lifted, a roar tearing from her throat like a warrior going into battle.

'That's it,' Suetta said. 'Nice and steady. Keep going.'

Finally, the baby was free. Sapphira collapsed onto the bed, her eyes closing with exhaustion. Astra's gaze was fixed on the child, limp in the midwife's hands, not making a sound. Eda handed Suetta a towel, and the midwife wrapped the baby with it, rubbing his little body. When he did not cry, she placed him on the bed with a determined expression, working away on him.

'Is he all right?' Sapphira asked, eyes still closed.

No one answered. Astra stroked Sapphira's hair, feeling the sting of tears. She would not let them fall. Another minute went by. The prince's colour was not the usual pink of a baby but a pasty colour that made Astra's stomach knot. She reminded herself to breathe.

After a terrifying amount of time, a tiny cry finally came from the prince. Sapphira's eyes blinked open at the sound. Eda let out a breath as Suetta wrapped the little boy tightly. She gave Astra a look that suggested she had been as scared as everyone else, then brought the baby to Sapphira.

'Look at that fighting spirit.'

'Just like his mother,' Astra said, finding a smile. She squeezed the princess's arm. 'You are truly amazing.'

Sapphira smiled weakly. 'I want that in writing also.'

Astra laughed, expelling some of the built-up tension. Suetta laid the baby beside his mother, and Sapphira placed a hand over him, pressing her lips to his face.

'Oh, you are perfect.' Her eyes sank shut again.

'Suetta,' Eda called, her relieved expression gone.

The midwife returned to the end of the bed, examining Sapphira, then the placenta.

'What's wrong?' Sapphira asked without opening her eyes.

Astra did not wait for an answer, just stood and went to look. There was blood on the sheets. *So much blood.* Astra sucked in a breath, unable to help her reaction.

'What's the matter?' Sapphira asked again.

Suetta looked up. 'Just a little bleeding. No need to panic.' She directed that last part at Astra, but Astra could barely hear what she was saying over the drumming of her heart. It was too much like Idalia. She took a step back.

Eda walked over to her. 'It's fine. Placenta's all there, and the bleeding's slowing.'

'To be expected with a breech delivery,' Suetta said.

The room was turning, and Astra drew a lungful of air. She was supposed to be helping, not panicking. 'Good. Everything is fine.' She said it more for her own benefit.

'Perhaps you should sit,' Eda suggested.

Astra waved her off with one numb hand. 'Do not worry about me. Tend the princess. Please.'

Eda hesitated before turning back to the bed. 'Perhaps you can take the linen down to the laundry, get some air.'

'What about Sapphira?

'We'll let her rest a bit. She's exhausted.'

Astra nodded. Everything was fine. No one was going to die. She returned to the bed, helping the women move Sapphira and the baby so they could strip away the linen and put a clean sheet down. Sapphira barely woke, letting the women rock her from side to side.

'She's fine?' Astra asked, a bundle of bloodied sheets in her arms.

Suetta checked her pulse, temperature. 'She'll be fine.'

'Don't be scared,' Sapphira said, her voice barely above a whisper. 'I just need to rest a moment.' Even in her exhausted state, Sapphira knew what Astra was thinking, what she was remembering and feeling. She opened one eye, managing a slight smile. 'Thank you.'

Astra forced herself to relax.

Footsteps pounded on the landing, and a moment later, Stamitos burst through the door. His eyes narrowed on the bed before he let out a relieved breath. He held one of his knees for a moment.

Saphirra opened her eyes and smiled at him. 'He's perfect.'

Stamitos straightened and walked over to her. 'A boy?'

'Ten fingers, ten toes, and the heart of a lion.'

Astra closed her eyes for a moment, still clutching the bloodied sheets to her. She needed to take them away before Stamitos saw them. She also needed some air. Turning away, she headed for the open door, almost colliding with Dion as she stepped out onto the landing. The sheets fell to the ground between them. Instead of stepping back from him, she stayed where she was, her face just inches from his chest. Her breathing was fast. Dion reached around her, pulling the door closed. Her forehead brushed against his chest as he did so.

'Is Sapphira all right?' he asked, his voice a low rumble.

She did not look up at him. 'I think so.' She had no way to escape and no desire to move anyway. 'Syrasan has a new prince.' His earthy scent was familiar to her now, and she wanted to fall into it.

Without saying anything, Dion pulled her gently to him. She let her head tip forwards against his chest, the instant warmth a bandage on her tired mind. Eyes closed, she breathed him in, trying to remember the last time she had found comfort in another person. Nothing came.

A Companion in need of comfort was a woman failing at her role.

His arms went around her, the weight of them bringing air back into her lungs. She sank into the sensation of him, giving no thought to the mess on the ground between them. He did not seem to care. When was the last time someone had put their arms around her outside of a bed? Idalia? What about before her? She had cut her finger, and her father had tended the wound. She had been eight, maybe. Not one tear shed through the entire ordeal.

'*Good girl*,' he had said. '*Tears never help anybody.*'

He was right, of course. They had not helped when Idalia died, when grief had torn through her like a rabid wolf.

'What do you need?' Dion asked.

She could hear the steady thud of his heart through his tunic. It was everything. 'Nothing.' She should have straightened, explained herself, blamed fatigue and exhaustion. Instead, she placed a hand to his chest to feel the vibration. He must have thought her mad, but his arms tightened around her anyway. The crushing weight of them was bliss.

'Was it that bad?' he asked.

'Yes.' It had brought every memory of Idalia's death to the surface. 'But everyone is fine.' That was closer to what a Companion ought to say. Always the optimist in the room.

His hand went to her head, cradling it gently. She gave herself three more breaths to indulge before withdrawing from him. The second he felt her pull away, he took a small step back.

'Sorry,' she breathed, bending to collect the sheets. 'Long night.' She looked up at him for the first time. His face was filled with understanding. It was almost enough to make her look down again, but she was too well trained. 'It was a breech birth. Sapphira was amazing.'

He searched her face for a moment. 'I'm certain she was a warrior in another life.'

'I think you might be right.'

His eyes moved over her face again. 'You're sure you're all right?'

She looked down at the linen in her arms. 'I should get these to the laundry, then get some sleep.'

He took another slow step back, moving out of her way. 'Goodnight, Astra.'

'Goodnight, Captain.'

CHAPTER 19

*T*he following morning, Dion was woken by the sound of a horse out front. He threw on his clothes and wandered downstairs just as Eda was closing the front door. She held a letter up, and even at that distance, he could tell the parchment was foreign. No seal either. A bad feeling coiled inside of him. His father had received similar letters when he had been alive.

'Thank you,' he said to Eda, taking it from her and returning to his bedchamber to read it. His gaze went straight to the name at the bottom of the page.

It was from Brom—leader of the Nydoen people, former Crown Prince of Zoelin, King Jayr's brother, rebel, and a path to trouble.

He wanted to meet Dion in person, suggesting a location and time with no explanation offered. Probably smart. Dion closed the letter and sat on the edge of his bed, thinking. The smart thing to do was burn the letter and forget he had ever received it. But his father would not have done that. He would have shown up and heard him out. If Brom was reaching out, he needed something. The question was not what but *if* Dion was prepared to open that door again. He had the king's trust, and even a meeting would jeopardise that.

After a wash, Dion made his way to the dining room to eat. The letter was not the only reason his mind was in a spin. The intimate moment he had shared with Astra the night prior kept replaying in his mind. He had known something was wrong from the moment she exited the bedchamber. At first, he had assumed it had to do with Sapphira or the baby, but they were fine—and she was not. He saw cracks, scars maybe, and he had not known how to help her. It was difficult watching someone normally so resilient come undone in front of him. He had wanted to fix her. For a moment, she had appeared human. For a moment, he had forgotten what she was.

'All done?' Eda asked, clearing away his bowl.

He rose. 'Yes, thank you. I'll be returning to Swanton Fort this morning.'

She looked up in surprise. 'So soon?'

He was going to hear Brom out. It was possible he had lost the ability to make sensible decisions with Astra around. She splintered his mind. Three weeks away had not been enough, so best to leave before he did something foolish, like offer up his beating heart to a *Companion*, of all women. It did not help that her intoxicating scent lingered in every room of the house. What the hell was it? Definitely a flower. It had clung to his tunic the night before, filling his bedchamber until he eventually went downstairs and dumped it alongside the bloodied linen.

He realised Eda was still waiting for an answer. 'Afraid so. Stamitos will be here for a few days, at least.'

Dion patted her arm before turning and walking away, feeling her eyes on him all the way to the door. When he rounded the corner, he almost collided with Astra. He reached out to steady her before stepping back. She looked as fresh as ever, despite the lack of sleep, her lips painted and hair swept up into a high knot. He could still see those freckles peppering her nose and the tops of her cheeks though. He really needed to stop noticing them. 'Morning,' he said. 'Did you get some sleep?'

She nodded. 'Yes. You?'

Why on earth was he nervous? He never got nervous around women. 'Barely remember my head hitting the pillow.' And now he was lying.

She looked past him to where Eda was clearing the table. 'Have you already eaten?'

He nodded. 'I needed to get an early start. I'm returning to Swanton Fort this morning.'

Her eyes snapped back to meet his. 'But you only got here yesterday.'

It sounded like she wanted him to stay. All the more reason to leave, before his mind ran with those thoughts.

Too late.

'The new recruits won't train themselves.' Possibly the worst excuse for leaving he had ever given. He breathed in, her scent already taking over the air.

'Listen. I hope you are not leaving on my account.'

'Not at all.'

'I hope I did not make you feel uncomfortable.'

The problem was more that he had never felt more comfortable in his life. 'As long as you're all right.'

She looked behind her. 'Would you like to come let the hens out?'

He should have said no, but she was looking up at him with those blue eyes of hers, waiting for his answer. 'Are the children slacking off?'

She smiled and began walking in the direction of the back

door. 'I like to open the gate in the mornings. That is when the hens are most excited.'

'How can you tell they're excited?' He moved to catch up with her.

'They are extra chatty.'

He pressed his lips together to stop from smiling.

They exited the house, walking in silence as the dogs bounded around them, colliding with one another in the process. Astra bent to pat them as they tumbled past her.

'You're quite the farm girl now, aren't you?' he said.

'Companions have the ability to adapt to any setting.' She glanced playfully in his direction.

'That's *one* positive thing to come from the role.'

'That is all?'

'And the music.'

'What about all the other things I teach?'

'Fine. But that's it.' He watched her smile at the ground, the morning sun casting angelic light around her.

They reached the chicken palace, and Astra fiddled with the gate before pulling it wide open. The waiting hens trotted out while she looked to the house at the back. 'I suspect some are having a lazy start.'

'How could you possibly know that?'

'Because we are missing some.'

He turned to her, waiting for more of an explanation. She did not offer one.

'Primrose,' she called out. 'Oh, here she comes.'

Primrose? She had named one of the chickens. Dion watched as a freckled hen shot through the gate and came to stop by her feet. Astra bent, chatting incoherently while stroking its back.

'Such a pretty girl,' she cooed, pulling a bread crust from her pocket and offering it to the hen.

Dion linked his hands on top his head. 'Is it sensible to name the food?'

'She's a laying hen.'

'Until she stops laying. Then she's soup.'

Astra rose, a look of disapproval on her face.

'I'm just saying a hen is not the greatest choice of pet given their short lifespan.'

Astra looked down at the chicken. 'She started following me shortly after I arrived. What was I supposed to do?'

'Not name her.' He released his hands. 'Why Primrose?'

'It is my favourite flower.'

Of course. That was the scent of the perfume she wore. Primrose. 'They grow like weeds in Galen, you know.'

She met his gaze. 'I know more about your landscape than you, remember?'

'I remember.' A piece of hair had come loose from her bun, and he fought the urge to tuck it behind her ear.

Astra's expression turned serious. 'I wanted to explain my behaviour last night.'

He nodded. 'I imagine the night was very stressful.'

'Stress is not an excuse to fall apart in front of you.'

His eyebrows came together. 'It's not?'

'No. Instead of just me being uncomfortable, I made you uncomfortable also.'

'I wasn't uncomfortable.'

She looked at him like she did not believe him. 'You say that, yet I find you fleeing at first light?'

She was not the reason he was leaving. Well, not the only reason. 'I'm not fleeing, just busy, and you should go easier on yourself. No one can be strong all the time.'

'A Companion must.'

That only made him feel sorrier for her. 'Then I guess you're slipping.' He was surprised when she bit back a smile.

'As I was saying,' she went on, serious once more, 'I wanted to explain.'

He crossed his arms, waiting. Primrose remained at her feet.

'There was a Companion at Archdale,' she began. 'A friend, actually.'

'You expect me to believe you had a friend?'

'She died.'

He winced. 'I'm sorry.' There she was opening up, and he was making thoughtless jokes. 'What happened?'

Astra shook her head. 'I do not wish to burden you with all the details, only to explain that last night brought up memories I had long suppressed. I felt like I was living it all over again.'

His expression softened. 'Did your friend die during childbirth?'

Astra took a step back as though repelled by the question. 'Of sorts. It was more of a… termination.' She paused, and he waited for her to continue. 'She was supposed to be fine at the end of it, like the time before.'

He realised at that moment that there was a much darker side to the Companion life he had not considered. 'There were complications?'

All the light was gone from her eyes. 'I should have told Fedora. I thought I was being a good friend by keeping her secret.'

He stepped closer, not touching her for fear she would stop talking. 'You can't blame yourself for things that happened in that place.'

'Of course I can. There are rules, rules I broke.' She was looking down again. 'Idalia was so ill afterwards, and still I did not tell anyone. She begged me not to say anything, did not want the king finding out.'

'Sounds like you were protecting her.'

'Hardly. The secret *killed* her.' The confession seemed to wind her for a moment. She pressed a hand to her stomach, then returned it to her side. 'They laid her on the bed, and she started bleeding. Fedora knew straight away; I could tell by her expression. So I told her everything she needed to know.' She paused. 'But it was too late.'

He wished he could take away her guilt in that moment, but he knew from experience that grief did not work that way. 'I'm sorry you lost her.'

She bent and picked up Primrose. Surprisingly, the hen sat still in her arms. Astra cleared her throat. 'So that is the ugly truth about why I embarrassed myself last night.'

'By showing human emotion?' He really wanted to hold her again. Because he could not touch her, he reached up to pet the hen instead, his wrist brushing hers. 'She's surprisingly calm. Is that the Companion touch?'

Astra looked up at him, all the emotion now in check. 'Actually, I suspect it might be you. The captain effect. It seems to work for me.'

He withdrew his hand. 'Are you saying you find my presence calming?'

'Well, you got me through a storm at sea when I was certain our ship would sink.'

'You hid your fear well, by the way.'

The corners of her mouth lifted. 'Are you really surprised that a Companion can hide fear?'

'Naive of me, I know.'

She placed Primrose carefully down on the ground before straightening again. 'You were doing so well that night, all that chivalry on display, right up until the moment you left me in a cabin filled with rats.'

'I'm surprised you didn't give them names.'

She clamped her top lip between her teeth to stop from smiling.

Dion watched her mouth for a moment. 'Would you prefer me to stay at Goldmont House?'

'What for?'

'Why, my calming abilities, of course.'

She rolled her eyes, forgetting herself. He liked those moments.

'I think we will all manage in your absence.'

He tore his gaze from those cherry lips. If he did not put some serious distance between them, he was going to do something he would most definitely regret. 'Good.' He took a large step back from her, eyes going to Primrose. 'Then I'll leave you to play with my dinner.'

'Unkind,' Astra said as he turned away from her. 'I will have you know she is a fantastic layer.'

He grinned as he headed back up the lawn.

CHAPTER 20

A strange restlessness possessed Astra after Dion's departure. Despite being busy, she found her mind always drifting to him. Not in a casual sort of way either, but watching the road whenever she was out front, holding her breath when she heard a horse coming, waking and wondering if that day would be the day he returned.

It was a problem.

It had been eight days since Prince Malin had come into the world. Eight days since she had found comfort in Dion's arms. Eight days since he had held her in that way. Only eight days? Every day felt like a week.

Astra was in the drawing room when she heard a horse arrive out front. She went to the window, standing to the side so she would not be seen. It was not the captain but a woman. There was something familiar about her, but Astra could not place where she had seen her before.

Helena went to answer the door, and Astra heard her name mentioned. Stepping away from the window, she snatched up a book, opening it at a random page.

'My lady,' Helena called from the doorway.

Astra looked up. 'Yes?'

'Isolda's here to see you.'

Astra closed the book and put it down. Of course. The seamstress from Talsworth—and Dion and Helena's cousin. She followed the girl out into the hall.

A big smile spread across Isolda's face when she saw Astra. 'I'm sorry it's taken me so long to get out here. Busy, busy, and all that.' She looked past Astra to the stairs. 'Should we go to your bedchamber?'

Astra frowned. 'For?'

Isolda shook her head. 'He didn't tell you I was coming, did he? He's hopeless.'

'Dion?'

'Yes, Dion.' She walked past her towards the staircase, clearly familiar with the house. 'He called into the shop on his way to Swanton, asked me to come and measure you up for those dresses.' She spoke over her shoulder, gesturing for her to follow.

Astra looked at Helena, who just smiled back at her as though this was all very normal. Gathering the skirt of her dress, Astra followed.

'Right,' Isolda said when she reached the top. 'Which room is yours?'

The woman's warm persona put Astra at ease. 'This way.'

Once they were in her bedchamber with the door closed, Isolda spent a few moments sifting through her bag, taking out everything she needed. 'I've got some lovely fabric samples, plenty of blue, just as you requested before the mighty Elenor Talsworth poked her nose in. Don't take anything she says to heart, by the way; she's just jealous that you're living here and she isn't. We're all secretly relieved she called off the wedding. She might have loved him, but she was suggesting the children live elsewhere before they were even wed. Where was he supposed to send them?' Isolda scoffed. 'Of course she had an answer for that.'

'And what was her answer?'

Isolda gave her a knowing look. 'Her father's money. The answer to everything.'

Astra was trying very hard to follow the conversation.

'What do you think of these?' Isolda said, holding out the squares of fabric sewn together.

Astra took the bundle and began sifting through them. 'Dion asked you to come here and fit me?'

Isolda took out a box of pins. 'He didn't want you running into Elenor again. He was furious when he heard what happened.'

'I should not have let her get to me.'

'Not angry at you, at Elenor for treating you so poorly. He laughed when I told him of your response.'

Astra looked up from the fabric. 'Really? He was not smiling when he mentioned it to me.'

Isolda turned to face her. 'My dear cousin has paid for three dresses, including the addition of lace.'

Astra's hands stilled. 'Lace?'

Pins protruded from Isolda's mouth. 'Yes, he mentioned you like lace.' She ran a hand down the gown Astra was wearing. 'This is gorgeous, by the way. Who made it?'

Astra looked down at her gown. She had once had access to the best seamstresses in Syrasan. 'A seamstress at Archdale Castle.'

Isolda nodded appreciatively before crouching down to begin her measurements. 'I'm thinking practical but elegant. Simple cuts, but well fitted to this gorgeous figure of yours. We could do some lace on the collars and sleeves, perhaps over sections of the waist, a feature.'

Astra smiled. 'That all sounds wonderful.'

It was late afternoon when Isolda packed up her things

and left with everything she needed to get started on the dresses. Astra went downstairs, eating an early dinner with Sapphira. Stamitos had gone to Reave Castle for the day, promising to return that night, even if he had to ride in the dark. After their meal, Astra stood to take her usual walk to the chicken palace.

'I'll join you,' Sapphira said, taking Malin from Eda. 'I need some air.'

'That sounds awfully intimate for the two of us,' Astra replied.

Sapphira secured the prince to her front with a wrap. 'Was that a joke? I barely recognise you these days.'

'Perhaps I have been in the country too long.'

The women had just stepped out of the front door when Primrose came running up, clucking and walking in circles around them. She behaved like one of the dogs most of the time. Astra bent down to her. 'Hello, darling. What are you doing all the way up here?' The hen jumped up onto her leg. 'Don't let Eda catch you making messes on her back step.'

Sapphira shook her head. 'I'm not going to lie. This is hard to watch. What are you going to do when Hann brings her to the kitchen one day?'

'He would not dare.' Astra placed Primrose on the ground and rose. 'Even he knows she is queen of that palace.'

Sapphira drew in a big lungful of air. 'Shall we take a proper walk? I've spent too long cooped up inside. Maybe we could go down to the orchard.'

Astra leaned forwards to look at the sleeping infant, his face squashed in that adorable way. 'If you like. The prince seems happy enough. Though we probably do not have much light left.'

'You're not afraid of the dark, are you?'

'No.'

'Then let's go.'

Astra looked down at Primrose. 'Are you coming with us?'

Her head twitched, as though she were listening and thinking on the matter.

The two women strolled through the orchard, stopping to pick tart apples, which they ate while they walked. They spoke of unimportant things, enjoying the mindless conversation. Dion's name came up a few times, and Astra could feel Sapphira assessing her reaction to it.

'Have you thought any more about how you are going to return to Archdale?'

They had reached the end of the trees. The grey light would soon turn to black. They turned and walked in the other direction.

'I have been too busy to think much on it.' She did not feel the urgency to leave she had expected.

'Perhaps that has something to do with a certain captain,' Sapphira said.

'You should know I am far too practical to get distracted by handsome men.'

'Oh, you think him handsome?'

'I know he is handsome. Every woman with working sight can see that.'

Sapphira faced forwards again. 'I was worried for him when you arrived, thought you might use him in some way.'

'Thanks a lot.'

'But you've changed. Even in the short time you've been here.'

'I have conformed. That is not the same thing.'

Sapphira shook her head. 'No, you've changed.' She thought for a moment. 'Have you imagined how ridiculously good-looking your children would be?'

Astra looked at her tiredly. 'Do I seem like the type of woman who daydreams about babies?'

'No. Though to be fair, I never thought you the sort of woman who peers out of windows waiting for him to return.'

So she had noticed.

Malin began to stir in Sapphira's arms, and she patted his back. 'Do you... like him?'

'Of course I like him.'

'No, I mean *like* him, like him?'

Astra kept her gaze trained on Primrose. 'What does that even mean? He is kind, a fair employer.'

'A fair employer?' Sapphira was rocking side to side while she walked. 'You know what I mean. Romantically.'

'No' came Astra's immediate reply. 'That would not be very sensible with me leaving and all.'

'Perhaps you won't leave.'

'Of course I will leave. The plan was always to leave.'

Sapphira shrugged. 'Well, plans change.'

Astra was about to commence a sensible argument when a noise made her stop. Sapphira must have heard it too, because she turned to listen.

'What's that?' Sapphira asked. 'Is that the hens?'

Astra's blood turned cold as she registered the sound also. It was not just the sound of chickens but chickens in distress. 'The gate is still open.' Her feet began to move.

'It's probably just the dogs stirring them up,' Sapphira called out. 'Wait.'

Astra did not wait; she broke into a run towards the palace. The sound of the frantic birds grew louder. She could hear them flying about and hitting the wire. Why had she not closed the gate before the walk?

The hen house finally came into sight, and Astra stopped running. It was not dogs in the enclosure but wolves. She stood frozen in place for a moment, barely breathing. The sound of Sapphira approaching pulled her out of her useless state. She looked around for something to use as a weapon.

'Go inside,' Astra said, spotting a large stick on the ground twenty feet away. She ran to it, snatching it up.

'What are you doing?' Sapphira called after her.

The sound of snapping jaws propelled Astra forwards. 'Take the baby inside.'

'Astra, stop. They're wolves.'

But she did not stop. She could not stand back while those animals tore apart every bird in there. She was a few yards from the coop when she began shouting. 'Get out of there! Go on!' She waved her stick. Two of the wolves stopped to watch her approach. When they did not flee, she resorted to growls and hisses, but they only stared at her. She banged the stick on the wire fence, and one leapt back from it. That gave her hope.

Her gaze settled on the wolf with a limp chicken in its mouth. 'Get out of there!' It turned and fled the enclosure. That encouraged her further. She marched straight through the open gate, stick swinging at the two remaining wolves. Injured birds lay around her feet. She gripped the stick with both hands and continued swinging. 'Get. Out.'

The wolves moved back but did not leave, eyes on her the whole time. A large male emerged from the house, hen in his mouth, stopping in the doorway to look at her. Her head snapped in his direction, and she backed slowly up against the fence, her confidence faltering for a moment. He had what he came for, and she prayed he would run past her. She kept the stick raised, eyes flicking to the other two wolves that had taken a few steps in her direction. The male dropped the dead hen on the ground, large puncture wounds visible even at that distance. The surviving hens were still flapping about, too panicked to realise the gate was wide open and the wolves' attention diverted. They were all focused on her.

Astra took a menacing step in the direction of the smaller

two, swiping at them with the stick. They did not move back this time. A growl came from the large male, his head lowering a few inches, teeth bared.

Oh God.

She glanced in the direction of the gate, calculating the number of strides to reach it. Six, maybe. She tried to remember how fast wolves could run, but her mind was coming up blank. The others took another step towards her, a chorus of growls now. Slowly, she moved one foot in the direction of the gate to gauge their reaction. All three animals followed the movement with their eyes, and then the large male stepped down onto the grass. She swung the stick, putting all the force into it she could muster. That only triggered more growls. Another step towards the gate on trembling legs. This was not how she was supposed to die, mauled to death by wolves in a chicken house. The fact that it resembled a palace only increased the irony. No, that would not do.

Hurling the stick at the largest wolf, Astra sprinted towards the gate. It was not so much a conscious plan as an involuntary reaction. If she made it through before they grabbed her, she could lock them in. But would she have the strength to secure the lock? These thoughts raced through her mind as she neared the gate. She heard them behind her, in pursuit, as frightened hens dispersed in all directions. Bursting through the door, she thrust it closed behind her, then threw her body weight against it. The large male was part of the way out, yelping as the gate crashed into him. He turned his head to look at her while pawing at the ground, trying to gain traction. His shoulders slipped through, and Astra gasped as her feet slid a few inches on the ground. Damn her useless shoes. She would never be able to outrun them if they got through. Her hand fumbled with the latch. The gate was still a hand's distance from actually being able to close.

A sharp yelp rang out, and Astra looked down to see an arrow protruding from the wolf's chest. It stopped struggling, and the second she let go of the gate, it collapsed to the ground, panting a few times before going still. The wolves in the enclosure whimpered and paced. Astra stepped around the gate and pushed the dead wolf back into the enclosure with her foot before securing the lock. She stood, watching the others, her heart pounding wildly.

'Astra, move away.'

She turned to see Sapphira thirty feet from her, bow in hand. Movement in her peripheral vision made her gasp, imagining the rest of the pack coming for her, avenging the death of their alpha. But it was Hann, holding an axe and running as fast as he could.

'You all right?' he asked, out of breath.

Was she? She looked down, noticing the violent shake of her hands for the first time. Then Sapphira was there, putting an arm around her.

'Hann will take it from here. Let's go.'

Astra turned in a circle, searching, 'Where is Primrose?'

'Not now. We'll look when it's safe.'

'Primrose!' Astra looked back at the palace, where injured birds lay flapping on the ground while two wolves circled and another lay dead.

'Later,' Sapphira said. 'Let's go.'

CHAPTER 21

They met at the closest thing they had to neutral territory—the Lotheng River. Brom arrived with two men and no weapons, or at least none in plain sight. Dion went alone, not wanting to implicate anyone else without first knowing why he was there.

'You want to tell me what I'm doing here?' Dion asked. They stood beneath an oak tree, taking one another in. The rebel leader was tall, and his shoulders spanned the width of two men. He looked a lot like Jayr, minus the sharp features and patronising smirk.

'I'll get straight to the point,' Brom said. 'King Tuyon is selling children across the border.'

'To King Jayr?'

Brom nodded.

'Won't pretend I'm surprised given some of his recent comments.'

Brom ran a hand down his stubbly face, letting it rest on his inked shoulder. The markings extended up the right side of his neck. Some were likely made by his father when he had been alive and the rest by Nydoen elders. 'He's growing his army.'

Dion blinked. 'How old are the boys?'

Brom looked straight at him. 'Some as young as six.'

Dion rested his hands on his hips. 'Child soldiers with no idea what they're fighting for.' He shook his head. 'Can that man stoop any lower?'

'Jayr has always played by his own rules.'

'And you by yours?'

Brom's hand fell to his side. 'I learned the type of man I wanted to be from my grandfather. He taught me the values of our ancestors.'

Dion glanced at the slow-moving water. They were on the Zoelin side of the river. Dion had not wanted to invite trouble by bringing rebels onto Galen soil. 'What exactly do you think I can help you with?'

Brom shifted. 'Jayr sent men to Asigow to collect more boys. They passed north of the mountains two days ago. I had them followed.'

Dion waited for him to continue.

'There are thirty-two children in total. They'll be heavily guarded.'

'And you plan on intervening?'

Brom sniffed and looked behind him to where his men waited for him. 'There are families in Asigow, grieving families. They've been forced to give up these children.'

'Orphaned children under the age of fourteen belong to the empire.'

Brom regarded him. 'And you agree with that law?'

Dion was silent a moment. 'You can't just hand them back.'

'Not straight away. They will be safe with us for a while.'

Dion frowned. 'And what do you get out of it?'

The leader nodded slowly. 'Our kingdom doesn't buy

children, or people for that matter, for any reason. Children belong with their families. Failing that, they deserve a childhood free of slavery and fear. I won't stand idly by while my brother continues down this path.' He paused. 'So in answer to your question, I get to fight tyranny. Seems it's fallen to me to uphold Zoelin's values—title or no title.'

Dion felt his resolve eroding. 'You do realise this is another act of war against your own brother and king.'

Brom crossed his arms. 'The moment Jayr took the throne, I left. Knew the type of ruler he would be before his rule had even begun. He might have castles and a crown, but he's not my king.'

Dion studied him for a moment. 'What do you need from me?'

Brom glanced at his men before replying. 'Archers.'

'What's wrong with your bows?'

A smile flickered on the man's face. 'I need trained spotters to cover us from up high. Everyone knows Galen has the best archers. Your father was living proof of that.'

Dion rubbed his face. 'So he shot people?'

'Sometimes.' Brom looked down. 'I was very sorry to hear of his death.'

'It's been four years.'

Brom nodded. 'I didn't think it was smart to contact you so soon after his death.' He paused. 'It wasn't in vain, you know. He and his wife did a lot of good. There are multiple threats to Asigow children. Much of their focus was on ensuring babies born with minor defects remained alive.'

His father had kept the details from him in order to protect him, but it had all come to light when he had been sentenced. 'Where will these archers be positioned?'

'Up high, amid the trees. Jayr will have men following at a distance. If they start shooting, both the children and my men will be at risk.'

Dion shifted his weight from one foot to the other. 'I'm really surprised Jayr hasn't had you killed yet.'

One side of Brom's mouth lifted. 'Believe me, he's tried.'

Dion nodded, thinking. 'I want Zoelin weapons, so that none of the arrows can be traced back to me and my men.'

'Done.'

'When are you expecting them?'

'They're still in Asigow, probably three days away.'

Dion thought. 'And what if I say no?'

Brom's expression did not change. 'Then we go ahead without you. We're not making ultimatums here. Help if you can, keep silent if you can't.'

Dion exhaled and raked a hand through his hair. 'I'll send word when I'm on my way.'

'There you are.'

Dion looked up to see Stamitos striding along the curtain wall of Swanton Fort towards him. He pushed off the embrasure and turned to watch the prince approach. 'What are you doing here?'

'Is that any way to welcome a friend?'

Dion bowed. 'Welcome to Swanton Fort, my lord.'

'Much better.'

'Now tell me what you're doing here.'

Stamitos took a moment to admire the view of the mountains in the north. 'I never tire of that sight.'

Dion looked back also. 'Me neither.'

The prince returned his attention to Dion. 'Where were you this morning?'

'A meeting.'

Stamitos pulled a face. 'A vague response. With whom?'

Dion drew a breath, hesitating. He knew he could trust

Stamitos with his life but wondered whether he should pull him into this particular mess. 'Brom.'

'Ah.' Stamitos leaned against the embrasure. 'I recognise that look. What have you agreed to?'

'The less you know, the better.'

'Let me guess: he needs archers.' When Dion did not reply, he added, 'I would offer to help, but...' He held up his missing hand.

'I have a few men in mind.' Dion rubbed at a muscle in his neck. 'So why were you looking for me?'

Stamitos straightened as though suddenly remembering why he was there. 'Ah, yes. I have two pieces of news I thought you would want to know about.'

Dion's eyebrows came together. 'So important that you had to tell me in person?'

'One I thought you would prefer to hear in person, and the other I thought I would tell you in person since I was coming here anyway.'

Dion gave him a lazy smile. 'Start with the news you thought I would want to hear in person.'

Stamitos thought. 'Actually, I better start with the other news, as I am not entirely sure you will hear me out otherwise.'

'Go on, then.'

'King Tuyon is coming to Reave Castle.'

Dion sat with that information a moment. 'When and why?'

'A week from now. I suspect your king means to play matchmaker with one of his daughters.'

Dion winced.

'My reaction also.'

'I thought Princess Tasia of Zoelin was the front runner for that unfortunate role.'

'So did I.' Stamitos drew a breath. 'Pandarus is also

coming.'

Dion shifted. 'For moral support?'

Stamitos grinned. 'Probably. I am to board a ship and go collect him from Veanor.'

'What? He can't sail alone?'

'You know how he is.'

All too well. His mind drifted to Astra, wondering what her reaction would be to Pandarus being just a few hours' ride from Goldmont House. 'What was the other news?'

Stamitos drew a long breath. 'Now, I do not want you to worry—'

'I'm immediately on edge when you start with that.'

'There was an incident at the house last night.'

Dion stood a little straighter. 'What incident?'

'Some wolves got into the hen house.'

Dion relaxed a little. 'We can replace chickens.' Though he knew Astra would be devastated.

Stamitos cleared his throat before continuing. 'Astra was in the enclosure when it happened. She is fine—'

'What do you mean, she was in the enclosure?'

'I mean that she took on a pack of wolves armed with a… stick.'

Dion blinked, trying to decide if she was that crazy. 'Was she hurt?'

'No, but she was certainly shaky when I arrived. The animals turned on her, and Sapphira was forced to shoot one of them.'

'The wolves *turned* on her?'

'She is unharmed.'

Dion was striding away before Stamitos could finish. The prince ran to catch up.

'Where are you going?'

'Home.'

The prince exhaled. 'She did not want me to tell you because she thought you would worry.'

'She was right.' He took the steps two at a time, Stamitos on his heel.

'I only told you because she was out most of the night, searching for a hen. Are you aware that she has given them names?'

'Yes.'

Stamitos seemed surprised by his response. 'Oh, and you did not think to question her sanity? Or suggest she make a friend *without* feathers?'

'Fetch our horses,' Dion said to the young soldier waiting at the bottom. The man saluted him before hurrying off.

Stamitos grabbed Dion by the arm, stopping him. 'You don't think you might be overreacting?'

He was completely overreacting. 'Probably, but I'm going anyway.'

Stamitos released his arm, a knowing smile spreading across his face. 'All right. Well, good luck, Captain.'

CHAPTER 22

*A*t least thirty hens had been injured in addition to those taken, caught up in the chaos of swiping paws and snapping jaws. Hann had destroyed the injured hens and buried them somewhere on the property. He would not risk feeding them to the dogs for fear of rabies.

'I don't remember seeing a hen with freckles among them,' he told her, 'but I wasn't paying much attention to colour.'

Astra could not remember if Primrose had followed her into the enclosure or if she had fled the scene. She tried asking Sapphira.

'I wasn't really focused on the chickens,' Sapphira replied dryly.

Astra had snuck out that night and wandered around the property, through the orchard and paddocks, in case the hen was hiding somewhere. No luck.

The following day she continued her search, returning at dusk to ensure the gate to the palace was securely closed. They had kept the hens locked up all day as a precaution. Hugging herself, Astra leaned her forehead on the wire and closed her eyes, the lack of sleep catching up with her. Where was the rational woman she could depend on? The king's Companion? Now she was wandering through paddocks, the skirt of her dress filthy, calling out to a chicken who was likely dead. She needed to leave Goldmont House before she lost her mind entirely.

It was her fault the wolves had gotten in, her failure—and she was no good at failing.

A sound behind her made her suck in a breath and turn. She expected to see wolves, instead finding Dion. He stopped, hands raised.

'Only me,' he said.

She leaned against the gate and released her breath, watching him approach. He was wearing his uniform, looking every bit the captain of the king's army. 'When did you get back?'

He leaned on the fence beside her. 'Just now.' He glanced at the hens roaming the enclosure, yet to settle because their routine had been thrown. 'Are you all right?'

How many times had he asked her that question since leaving Galen? She was getting the impression he actually cared. 'Did Stamitos tell you what happened?'

He nodded.

'I told him not to. I hope you did not return on my account.' She said that, but she was pleased to see him. She breathed easier when he was around. He had a way of taking charge in a crisis that made her feel like she could relinquish control for a little while. 'We lost over thirty hens.' Her voice cracked a little. The man would think her a lunatic. 'Or rather, *I* lost them. I went for a walk with Sapphira. Forgot about the gate.'

He bent his head to her. 'I don't care about the hens. I came to check on you. What in God's name were you thinking taking on a pack of wolves?'

'I meant to scare them off.'

'They might not hunt you, but they will attack if threatened. They're not defenceless, especially in a pack.'

'They were killing them. I just wanted them to leave.'

He watched her for a moment. 'They would have left once they had what they came for. You should have gone inside with Sapphira.'

She was silent a moment. 'Have you seen her shoot? She was amazing.'

'Yes, I've seen her shoot.'

Astra shook her head. 'I knew there was something wrong with me when my first thought was I should learn how to use a bow for next time.'

'Come here,' Dion said, gesturing for her.

She did not move. 'Why?'

'Because you look like you need a friend.'

She dismissed him with a shake of her head. 'I am just tired.'

He tugged her to him, and she did not fight it. What did that say about her? She was not the sort of woman who found comfort in a man's arms; she was someone who found comfort in not having to seek it from other people at all. Dion draped an arm around her shoulders, and she let her cheek rest on his chest, listening to the hens.

They remained there, bathed in grey light, no one speaking. She sensed he was just as comfortable as she was.

'Thank you for sending Isolda,' she said, finally breaking the silence. She felt him nod.

'I hope she's making something appropriate for your new lifestyle. Can't have you fending off wolves wearing evening gowns.'

She looked up at him, her palm flat against his chest. 'Should I have requested fur in place of lace?'

'A warrior gown.'

She could not stop the smile, though it wavered when she became aware of how close his face was to hers. 'I think I am going to stay out here for a little longer. There is no need for you to wait around.'

'The wolves are not likely to return, if that's what you're worried about.'

'I know.' She pulled away, his arm sliding off her. 'You go ahead.'

'If you think I'm going to leave you out here in the dark, you're insane.'

She rested her head on the fence. 'I thought you said the wolves would not come back.'

'I said *not likely* to come back.' He crossed his legs, the toe of one boot balancing on the ground. 'Do I seem like the type of man who takes risks?'

She shook her head, studying his even expression. 'How long are you here for?'

'I'll leave the moment you're safely in bed.'

She sighed. 'Were you so concerned that you came all the way here just to ensure I went to bed?'

'It appears that way.'

She watched him for a moment. 'I cannot tell if you are running to or from me.' She wanted to touch the stubble on his face. In the morning it would be gone.

'Both.' He did not look away when he answered.

'Any other woman might misread such a gesture.'

He leaned closer, invading her personal space once again. 'I want you safe. You must know that by now.'

'I know that. I am just trying to figure if it is because you are a good man or whether you want something from me.'

'I do want something. I want you inside. Then I'll leave.'

She continued to watch him. 'I am very good at reading people, especially men, but you have me second-guessing my abilities.'

His grey eyes never left her. 'Perhaps you're waiting for me to overstep so that everything you think you know about men can be validated.'

The vibration of his voice had her insides twisting in knots. 'I suspect you are too proud to give in to your impulses.'

'My impulses?'

'I think you want to kiss me, but you have a point to make.'

'What point is that?'

'That you are better than most men, smarter. Too smart to fall for the charms of a Companion. Is that it?'

'That's a part of it.' He angled his head as though trying to figure her out. 'Do you want to be kissed? Is this the Companion way of asking?'

She pulled away slightly. 'If you are trying to fluster me, it is a fool's mission.'

'Because of your background or because we're too comfortable around each other now?'

'Both, I suppose. It helps that I have the option of walking away from you if I want to.'

He turned to look in the direction of the house. 'I imagine there was no walking away from Pandarus.'

'No.'

They were silent a moment.

'What was it like with him?' Dion asked. 'Before it went bad.'

Normally she would have shut the conversation down. No lady spoke of such things. But she knew he was trying to understand her better. 'In the beginning, it was all about being desired. There is excitement in walking into a room and having the king's eyes follow your every move.' She threaded her fingers through the gaps in the wire. 'But the novelty could not last. Things deteriorated. He changed, or maybe I did. He began drinking more, acting differently, until one day everything about him repulsed me. I hid it for some time. Then one night when we were leaving a celebration, he pinned me against a wall in the south corridor. Servants were passing us. His family could have walked by at any moment. I remember turning my head away from him, and he did not like that.'

'What did he do?'

She looked at him. 'He took a new Companion shortly after.'

'But kept you?'

She smiled at that. 'Pandarus is a smart man, even if his actions do not always reflect it. He likes the best, always has. Even if only for display purposes.'

'He kept you for display?'

'Yes.'

'And you played along?'

'I can put on quite a show. So can he, for that matter. He enjoyed the envy of other men, the way they looked at me.'

'Until he didn't?'

She did not reply.

'Do you want to know why I don't act on my impulses?' Dion asked.

She looked at him and nodded.

'Because I've no interest in those types of facades.'

She understood. He valued honesty. 'Are you at least tempted?'

His eyes moved down her so slowly she could feel her skin heating where they travelled. She tried not to wilt, swallowing.

'Of course I'm tempted. Look at you.' He shook his head as though shaking away the image of her. 'You swan about the place in your half dresses—'

'Half dresses?'

'Yes, half dresses.'

'Is that why you sent Isolda? To cover me up?'

'I did that for your own comfort.' He drew a breath. 'And partly to cover you up to stop other men looking at you. I'm no saint.'

'Will *you* continue to look?'

He pretended to think on the matter. 'That depends. How much lace have you requested for these new dresses?'

'Quite a bit.'

'Then yes.' A smile played on his lips. 'I'll continue to look —but always from a safe distance.'

She gestured between them. 'Do you consider this a safe distance?'

'Not at all.' He drew a breath, releasing it slowly. 'Are you ready to go inside now?'

She nodded, her body warm from his admission. 'Yes. Let us go inside.' She increased the distance between them as she stepped away from the fence.

CHAPTER 23

*T*here were two enclosed carts, sixteen children packed into each like livestock. Two drivers, plus six mounted guards to each cart. Dion was positioned on a hill with the two men he had brought with him, trying to calculate the distance.

'Can you cover that distance?' Brom asked as he mounted his horse. His men were ready to go. They would be waiting at the mouth of the gully.

Dion turned to one of his men. 'How many yards do you think that is? Two-thirty?'

'Maybe two-forty.'

Dion nodded and looked up at Brom. 'We'll make it.'

'We can move you closer, but there's risk in that.'

'We'll make it,' Dion repeated.

Brom nodded. 'Take out the drivers. Then cover us best you can. Keep one set of eyes behind you, and watch the hills. I know my brother. There'll be more.'

Dion nodded, and Brom swung his horse, gesturing for his men to move out. They disappeared silently into the trees. Dion turned back to the two men he had brought with him. Cedric and Josef had been in these mountains before. They were loyal to the cause, friends of his father once upon a time. 'You heard him. I need eyes behind.'

Cedric nodded, rose, and hurried off. Josef readied his bow.

'We'll give them some time to reach the bottom. The rest of Brom's men are in place.' Dion watched the carts, the guards surveying their surroundings. They may have been on Zoelin soil, but they knew they were on enemy territory. The mountains belonged to Brom and the Nydoen tribes.

The men positioned themselves on either side of a tree, and Dion reached for his bow. He adjusted the quiver on his back and anchored his feet. When the carts were within shooting range, he reached for an arrow. 'On my command, you take out the first driver.'

Josef nodded.

The string went taut beneath Dion's fingers. 'Hold.' He released his breath slowly, staring down his arrow at the marked driver. 'Loose.'

The moment the word passed his lips, two arrows shot through the air, striking both drivers a few moments later. One through the neck, the other through the chest. They had seconds at best before the others registered what was happening. The Zoelin soldiers would likely be expecting spears, not arrows.

'Loose,' Dion said, and the men released another round of arrows, this time hitting two guards.

Everyone was moving then, swords drawn. One of the guards looked in their direction, waving an arm.

'Loose,' Dion said, striking the man who had given the signal in the shoulder. 'You see that?'

Another nod from Josef. 'They've got men on this side.'

Dion reloaded his bow and swung it left, eyes trained on the trees while Josef focused on the men below.

'Brom's men are on the move,' Josef said, reloading his bow and watching down his arrow as Brom rode out. Nydoen men appeared from all directions, swords ready.

Dion kept his gaze fixed on the hill. 'Shoot if you have a clear shot.' As he spoke, he saw an arrow fly through the air, and adjusted his aim, spotting a Zoelin archer a hundred feet away. He released his arrow, piercing the man's neck. He exhaled, reloaded, and searched the trees once more.

'I can't shoot any more without risking the lives of Brom's men,' Josef said. 'There's too much going on.'

Dion was watching for movement in the trees, because there was no such thing as a lone archer. 'Check the hill on the other side.'

Josef reloaded his bow and let it drift back and forth along the hill for a few moments.

'Anything?' Dion asked.

'Not yet.'

Dion spotted a man twenty feet from the one he had shot. 'Got you,' he whispered.

Hiss.

He struck the man's arm, reloaded his bow, and shot again, this time getting him through the stomach. The sound of children crying drifted up to them. As if they had not been through enough already, now they were trapped in the middle of a bloodbath. Dion watched the fight below them for a moment. Brom's men seemed to have the situation under control.

Before he had a chance to comment, Cedric burst through the trees. 'Incoming, five men on horseback.' He raised his bow and swung around.

Josef and Dion turned in that direction, bows poised, waiting for whatever came through those pines. Their horses, tethered nearby, stirred.

'You're certain they're King Jayr's men?' Dion whispered.

'Yes.'

They listened. Nothing.

'Maybe they didn't see him,' Josef whispered.

The crunch of pine needles underfoot made Dion turn. A Zoelin soldier ran at him, a dagger in hand. The man screamed out when Dion released an arrow into his face, giving away their location. Dropping his bow, Dion drew his sword and slashed his neck to silence him.

Four more Zoelin soldiers appeared from the other direction. Cedric and Josef barely had enough time to draw their swords before the men were on them. Blades flew in all directions as they fought it out on the side of a mountain. One of the larger men came at Dion, ink on both arms, his neck, and surrounding one ear. Dion felt the blow of the soldier's sword in his bones when it struck his weapon. When the man swung again, Dion slipped beneath the blade, driving his weapon through the soldier's stomach and thrusting it up before withdrawing it. He turned back as another came for him, the other two occupied.

Steel screeched as their blades met. Dion heard Cedric cry out behind him and fought the urge to look. He tried not to think about what would happen if the man died. Did his family even know where he was? What he was doing?

Focus.

Stay alive.

Helena would not forgive him if he died. Everyone at Goldmont House would be forced to mourn again. Astra was still mourning the loss of her friend, her old life, and a hen. He wondered how long it would take her to erase the memory of him.

His opponent's sword locked with his, and he was shoved back into a tree. All air left his lungs, but he managed to push himself off the tree as the blade came at him again, this time lodging itself in the trunk. Dion had just enough time to drag his weapon along the man's neck. The guard's hands went to his throat as he collapsed to his knees. Dion did not stand around to watch him die; he pulled the man's sword from the trunk and returned to his men with a weapon in each hand.

Cedric was on the ground now, a hand over his side and blood seeping through his fingers. A Zoelin soldier loomed over him, weapon raised. Dion threw one of the swords with as much force as he could muster. The hilt hit the soldier's face, sending a spray of blood over Cedric. Cedric took advantage of the situation and drove a dagger into the man's leg. The soldier roared, but before he had a chance to retaliate, Dion was in front of him. He watched the man collapse before turning his attention to Josef, who was still battling with the remaining soldier. They could end this, put Cedric on a horse, and get out of there.

No such luck.

Four horses burst from the trees, riders in blue vests and their saddle blankets marked with a Z.

Dion glanced at Josef, whose face was dripping sweat. Not great odds. He positioned himself in front of Cedric. 'Keep hold of that dagger.'

Cedric nodded, ready as he would ever be. He could hear Josef still fighting as more men rode towards him with their swords raised. But before they reached his comrade, a dagger struck the chest of the first rider. Brom stepped into sight, drawing his sword and joining the fight. Two more of Brom's men appeared behind him, evening up the numbers.

He might get home after all.

A weapon came at Dion as a horse cantered past. He ducked, but the hind leg of the horse clipped his head, spinning him. The rider dismounted and came at him before his vision had time to clear. Dion raised his sword just in time to keep his head, but his attacker kept at him, forcing him back over a broken branch that almost tripped him. Dion felt the sting of a blade on his arm but continued blocking the blows to prevent a more fatal injury. Once free of the branch, he raised a foot and shoved the man with as much force as he could manage, sending him crashing backwards. Brom approached from behind, driving his weapon through the man's back. They looked at each other as the soldier collapsed on the ground between them. Dion nodded his thanks before looking around. Brom's men stood panting, their swords bloodied. Josef was crouched beside Cedric, who appeared to be alive.

'The children are secure?' Dion asked.

'They're on their way to the safe house,' Brom replied, glancing over at Cedric. 'Ensure your man can stay on a horse. We'll patch him up and have you escorted to the river.'

'Can you spare the men?'

'Yes.' He wiped his sword on the tree. 'I won't forget your help today.'

Dion nodded. 'I can see why my father liked you.'

Brom stepped up, clapping him on the shoulder. 'You remind me of him. Might even be a better shooter.' He sheathed his weapon and walked off.

Dion drew a breath and looked over at his men. Josef rose. 'Get him up. We're going home.'

'And what year was the revolt?' Astra asked, looking between the children as she waited for an answer. They were upstairs, the younger ones growing restless as they neared the end of their history lesson. Hamo raised his hand, and Astra nodded in his direction. 'Yes?'

The hand went down. '1246?'

'Are you asking me or telling me? That sounded a lot like a question.'

He looked to Meggy, who shrugged. 'I'm not sure.'

Astra suppressed a smile. 'You are correct. Try to have a little more faith in yourself.' She glanced down at her lesson plan. 'Right. Now let's talk about the invasion that followed in the year 1262.'

Before she had a chance to say another word, the door swung open and Sapphira appeared, looking as though she had come at a run.

'What is it?' Astra asked.

Sapphira looked to the children. 'Lesson's over. I need Astra for a little while. You can all go out back. Eda will collect you when it's time to eat.'

The children filed out of the room, talking in excited whispers. Astra walked over to Sapphira, waiting until they were out of earshot before speaking.

'What on earth is going on?'

'I need you to promise me you will remain calm.'

Astra's mouth flattened into a thin line. 'I am always calm.'

'I also need you to promise that you'll tell no one what you see and hear.'

Astra was wary suddenly. 'What exactly am I about to see and hear?'

Sapphira took her hand and led her out of the room, along the landing, and down the stairs. 'I can't tell you anything until I know I can trust you.'

'Then why involve me?'

'Because Stamitos is on a ship, and we need your help.'

'We?'

They reached the bottom of the stairs and paused as Eda rushed past them, clutching a bedsheet to her chest. She did not even look in their direction.

'What in heaven's name is going on?' Astra asked.

Sapphira continued to drag Astra towards the front door. 'They're bringing the horses around front.'

Astra's eyebrows rose. 'Who? What horses?'

'Promise me,' Sapphira said, 'or I'll have to send you out back with the children.'

Astra rolled her eyes. 'You have my word.'

The sun hit sharply as they stepped outside, and Astra used a hand to shield her eyes as they descended the steps. She looked towards the sound of approaching horses, spotting Dion among the men. Her stomach fell at the sight of him. He was bloodied and dishevelled, holding the reins of a horse whose rider looked ready to fall off. They stopped in front of the house, Dion dismounting and rushing to the side of the injured man. Eda flung open the sheet, and everyone moved to grab an edge so they could carry him inside.

Astra's eyes met Dion's for a moment.

'You shouldn't be here,' he said.

'She won't say anything,' Sapphira assured him.

Astra moved forwards and grabbed a corner of the sheet, wrapping it around her hand. 'I want to help.' She tried not to stare at the injured man as he was laid down on the sheet. His clothes were blood-soaked, his skin grey and eyes closed. She had no idea how he was alive. 'You can take him to my room,' she offered.

Another man dismounted and came to take the other corner. Eda headed back inside, and the four of them carried the injured man upstairs to Astra's bedchamber, placing him gently on the bed.

'Has Hann gone for the physician?' Sapphira asked.

Dion nodded.

Astra went to fetch the scissors from the drawer, returning bedside and handing them to Dion. He took them without a word, bending to cut through the clothing so they could access the wound. Astra helped him peel the clothing back, trying not to look at the blood. A deep gash ran from the man's armpit to the bottom of his ribcage.

'I'll fetch some water,' Sapphira said, rushing from the room.

Eda entered a moment later carrying clean towels. Astra took one from her and pressed it to the wound. The soldier did not react.

'He doesn't look good,' Eda said.

Astra had to agree. 'How far did he have to ride in this condition?'

'Overnight,' Dion said quietly.

'Overnight? From where?' Astra waited for him to look at her, but he did not. She reached for his arm, and he finally met her eyes. 'From where?' she asked again, watching the conflict play out on his face.

'The Nydoen mountains.'

She let go of him, then looked down at her hand. *Blood.* She sucked in a breath. 'You are injured.'

'I'm fine.'

Sapphira returned with a basin of water, placing it on the dresser. 'Physician's just arrived.'

'Let's give him some space to work,' Eda said, looking at Dion. 'And get your wound tended to.'

The other man put a hand on Dion's shoulder. 'I'll stay with him.'

'I will take a look at it,' Astra said.

'I told you all, I'm fine.'

Sapphira exhaled noisily. 'Dion, for the love of all that is holy—'

He put his hands up defensively. 'All right.'

Astra stepped out of the room and walked along the landing, listening for Dion's boots behind her. The sound both reassured her and made her nervous. She descended the stairs and headed to the kitchen so they were out of sight of the children. Dion followed her inside, stopping beside the bench and running a filthy hand down his face. He had a small cut above his eyebrow. When she reached for it, he caught her hand.

'Don't fuss,' he said.

She tilted her head. 'Who is fussing?'

He let go of her arm, allowing her fingers to explore his face for a moment. 'Head wounds always look worse than they are.'

'I know.' She picked up the pail and poured some water into a bowl, then grabbed a clean cloth and wet it. Returning to him, she said, 'Shirt off, please.'

He hesitated. 'You're not going to faint, are you?'

'No.' She hoped not.

He tugged his shirt over his head and looked down at his arm, which was wrapped with blood-soaked fabric torn off Josef's shirt.

Astra was not looking at his arm.

Good God.

His body was like the carved marble figure displayed in the throne room at Archdale. She wanted to run her fingers over his chest and stomach. Swallowing, she forced herself to focus on his arm. Even his biceps were beautiful. Removing the bloodied linen, she investigated the finger-length gash, which was still weeping. 'The physician is going to need to stitch this.'

'He's a little busy,' he said, leaning against the benchtop.

'After, then.' She wiped carefully around the wound so she could see it better. 'Are you going to tell me what happened?'

'The less you know, the better.'

She rinsed the cloth and placed two fingers beneath his chin, turning his face so she could clean the wound above his eye. 'Are you working with Brom?'

'I'm already half naked at your request. Must I face an inquisition too?'

'Yes.'

He let his head hang. 'He's not the evil man he's painted to be.'

Astra nodded. 'I figured as much.'

'Why's that?'

'Because King Jayr is the one painting the pictures, and he is the least trustworthy man I know.' She dumped the cloth in the bowl. 'I am a part of this now, so you might as well tell me everything.'

He drew a breath, hands holding the bench on either side of him, and began talking. She listened without interrupting, saving her questions for the end. When he was done, he waited and watched for her reaction.

'It is oddly heart-warming to think there is a chain of people spanning three kingdoms prepared to die for the same cause.'

'Well, we all die eventually. Might as well be for something we care about.'

Astra leaned on the bench beside him, her hand landing beside his. 'I think I may have underestimated the size of your heart.'

His eyes moved over her face. 'I can't tell if that's criticism or a compliment.'

The corners of her mouth lifted. 'Both.' She exhaled. 'So you are carrying on your father's legacy after all.'

Dion looked down at his feet. 'I never planned to, but what sort of man sees children in need and does nothing?'

'Sensible men.' Her little finger brushed his. 'What if you had died?'

'Then I'd be dead.'

'What about Helena?'

'She would have understood when she was older. But to be clear, the plan was always to return alive.'

Their arms touched.

'What you are doing is treason,' Astra said. 'Your king is aligned with King Jayr, and you are liaising with rebels without his knowledge and consent. If he finds out—'

'You don't think I know what happens next? I was there, at the execution, remember?'

She tipped her head forwards, resting it on his arm. His bare skin felt so good against hers. Her eyes closed as she struggled with the thoughts in her head and the feelings welling in her chest. 'I would prefer you to remain alive.'

He reached up, rubbing a piece of her hair between his

fingers. 'How am I to admire you from afar when you're this close?'

Her skin reacted to the vibration of his voice. She pulled back, tracing his wound with one finger, noticing a change in his breath. 'Is this still too close?'

'Much too close.'

She pressed her lips to his shoulder, his skin warm and salty.

'What are you doing?' He whispered the words into her hair.

She breathed against his skin, savouring the warmth of him. 'Forgetting myself.'

He straightened and pulled her to stand in front of him. A bloodstained hand cradled her jaw. 'Once I start kissing you, I know I won't be able to stop.'

She could not imagine asking him to stop, not with all the heat pooling inside her at the mere mention of his lips on hers. 'All right.'

He pulled back a little, studying her face. 'Then what?'

'What do you mean?'

'What happens after?'

She shook her head. 'After?'

'Then you leave Goldmont House? That's the plan, isn't it?'

She pulled away. 'We made that plan together. Now you are angry at me for it?'

He reached past her, snatching his shirt off the bench and slipping it over his head. 'I can't do this.'

'We have not done anything yet.'

'I'm not conditioned like you. I can't just switch it on and off. That's why you survived ten years in that place, isn't it?'

She hoped the shock of his words was not visible on her face. 'Yes, that is how I survived.'

He pulled the shirt down over his body. 'I can't just kiss you, then not kiss you. Feel things, then watch you leave.'

'Watch me leave? I have nowhere else to go yet.'

He exhaled, nodded. 'Did you hear what you said then? You said *yet*.'

She let out an exasperated noise. 'This is not something I am secretly plotting. We agreed I would stay here for a few months, but I have a life to get back to.'

'Oh, that's right. You want to be a mentor, to teach women to be like *you*.'

'I do not teach women to be like *me*. I teach them to be the best versions of themselves.'

He rubbed his face. 'What does that even mean?'

She was done being insulted. Looking away, she went to step past him, but he caught her arm. She pulled free of him. 'Do not grab me.'

He immediately let go of her. 'Where are you going? We're still talking.'

'*Talking*? Is that what this is?'

'Fighting, then.'

She stared at him. 'You are attacking me, and I am under no obligation to take it from *you*.'

Dion went to speak but took hold of the edge of the bench instead. All of her anger evaporated as he paled. 'What's the matter?'

He shook his head. 'Nothing.'

She watched as he collapsed to the floor.

CHAPTER 25

'Should he have woken by now?' Astra asked.

The physician snipped the final stitch on his arm and dropped the scissors onto a cloth on the bed. He bundled his instruments up and tucked them into his bag. 'Blood loss, dehydration, fatigue, and a knock to the head to finish. His body is tired.'

The fight between them would not have helped either. Why had she not sat him down to tend him? At least then if he fainted he would not have hit his head. 'But he will wake?'

'He'll be fine after some rest,' replied the old man.

Astra had more questions, but before she could ask them, Sapphira burst into Dion's bedchamber. She held onto the door handle as she caught her breath.

'The king's guards are coming down the road.'

'What?' Astra's heart stopped beating. They had to be looking for Dion. A hand went to her stomach. They knew. He would be sentenced and—

'They can't see him like this,' Sapphira said. 'We need to hide him.'

'What about Cedric?' Astra asked. 'The half-dead soldier a few doors down might clue them in.'

The physician cleared his throat. 'It's too soon to move Cedric. He's not stable enough.'

Astra's mind raced. 'There's bloodied linen in the laundry. We can't let them inside.'

Sapphira tilted her head. 'And who here's going to stop a group of armed guards? Do you expect Hann to go fetch his sword?'

Eda's footsteps sounded on the landing, and a moment later she appeared in the doorway. 'I told them the captain's at Swanton Fort, but they're not here for him.'

'Then what do they want?' Sapphira asked.

Eda's gaze settled on Astra. 'They're here for you.'

'Me?' Astra frowned. 'What do they want to see me for?'

Eda's face creased with worry. 'They're taking you to Reave Castle.'

Sapphira crossed her arms. 'Whatever for?'

'They won't tell me anything.'

Sapphira went to move for the door. 'We'll see about that.'

'Wait,' Astra said. 'I will go. If we make a fuss, they might want to speak with Dion.' Outwardly, she was composed. Inside, her heart was beating at twice its normal speed. She glanced once at a still-sleeping Dion before leaving the room.

Astra took a few deep breaths as she descended the stairs to the front entrance, smoothing down her dress as she walked. She stretched out her fingers, a technique she had used many times over the years to help her appear more relaxed. Finding a smile, she stepped through the door, counting six guards and one empty wagon. One of the men stood waiting at the bottom of the steps.

'Good afternoon,' she called out, stepping down to join him.

His eyes moved over her before replying. 'Pardon the intrusion, miss, but King Linus sent me to collect you.'

She glanced again at the enclosed wagon with its Galen flag floating gently in the breeze. 'For what purpose?'

'Not privy to that information. I'm just here to collect you.'

She looked around at the other guards, then behind her to where Sapphira stood in the doorway with her arms crossed, watching them. 'Surely His Majesty cannot expect me to leave Goldmont with strangers and no explanation.'

The man scowled at her. 'We don't wear these uniforms for fun.'

Astra grew a little taller. 'Perhaps he sent a letter?'

The man shook his head. 'Just us. The maid's fetching your things.'

Sapphira descended the steps on that point, thankfully wearing shoes. 'And exactly how long will she be at Reave Castle?'

'Couldn't tell you, my lady.'

Sapphira came to a stop beside Astra. 'She's needed here at the house.'

The guard did not appear deterred. 'Sorry, Princess, but my orders come from the king. The lady is coming with us one way or another.'

Sapphira drew a breath, preparing to continue the argument.

'It is quite all right,' Astra said, placing a calming hand on Sapphira's arm. 'Let us see what His Majesty wants.'

The guard gestured to the waiting wagon. 'This way.'

'If you put one hand on her, I'll come find you,' Sapphira said.

Astra blinked, grateful for her fierce little friend despite the hopeless situation. She knew no good would come of resisting.

'I'll send word to the captain,' Sapphira called as Astra was helped into the wagon. It was for the benefit of the guards, of course.

Astra sat, then leaned forwards so she could see the princess. 'No need to bother him at Swanton.' Also for the benefit of the guards.

'He'll want to know,' Sapphira insisted.

Eda exited the house with Helena at her side and Astra's bag in hand.

'Where are they taking you?' Helena called out, her tone laced with panic.

Astra knew what was going through her mind. 'It is just a meeting with the king. No cause for worry.' She hoped.

The three women approached the wagon together while Eda placed the bag at her feet.

'But you'll come back?' Helena asked, hands pressed to her stomach.

Astra gave her a reassuring smile. 'Please do not worry.' She had no idea if she would be back and did not want to lie to the girl. 'Make sure you help Eda while I am gone.'

Helena nodded, and Sapphira pulled her back from the wagon as the guard closed the door. A moment later, the wagon pulled away.

~

Dion's eyelids felt impossibly heavy. He struggled to hold them open as he turned his head and looked around the room, recognising his bedchamber. He had no recollection as to how he got there. Zoelin, Brom. The fight. Cedric had been injured. He was alive though. At least, he had been before…

He had been in the kitchen with Astra, her lips on his skin. Or perhaps he had dreamt that. They had argued.

Sitting up, he winced when he used his injured arm. His eyes went to the neat row of stitches. He remembered then, his hands tingling and his head dizzy. Astra had moved closer to him, asked him something. Had he answered her?

The door to his bedchamber creaked open, and Helena peered around it. She let out a breath when she saw him sitting up. 'Thank God,' she said, entering the room and walking to his bedside. 'How are you feeling?'

'Fine,' he lied. 'A bit thirsty, maybe.'

Helena poured him some water from the jug and brought it to him. She waited for him to empty it before going to refill it again. 'You collapsed in the kitchen. I heard Astra calling for help.'

He took the cup from her. 'I'm sorry to give you all a fright.'

She watched him drink. 'Did you cross the border?'

He lowered the cup. 'Why do you ask that?'

She sat on the bed, untrusting eyes never leaving him. 'Because that's a sword wound, and I heard the others talking.'

He nodded. 'I was helping out a friend.'

'The same friend our father helped before they beheaded him?'

He could barely meet her gaze. He certainly did not have it in him to lie to her.

'It's all right,' she said, sparing him the explanation. 'Father once told me it's what good men do.'

Dion exhaled and lifted his eyes to her. 'You're not a child anymore, are you?'

She shook her head. 'You can't keep things from me. I'm on your side. I'll always be on your side. If something happens to you, I don't want to guess at the reasons. I don't want to find out after the fact, not again.'

He gestured for her to come closer. She shuffled along the

bed, and he pulled her to him, kissing her forehead. 'He wanted to keep us safe. That's why he kept things from us, and that's the only reason I kept this from you.'

'What about what I want?' She pulled back to meet his gaze once more. 'I don't like secrets. No more. Promise me.'

He exhaled. 'I promise to share what I can.'

Her shoulders relaxed a little. 'Does Astra know everything?'

He blinked. 'Yes. Why do you ask?'

'Because the guards came and took her away.'

Dion's eyebrows pinched together. 'What are you talking about?'

'An hour or so ago, King Linus sent men to collect her. She won't say anything, will she?'

Dion shot up off the bed, his foggy mind racing with possibilities. If King Linus suspected anything of his recent activities, he would come for Dion directly. He pressed his knee to the bed to steady himself. 'Did the guards know I was here?'

Helena shook her head. 'Eda told them you were at Swanton.'

He nodded. 'Good.'

'Are you going after her?'

'Yes.' He ignored the pounding in his head and went to dress.

Helena watched him from the bed. 'Can you even ride in your condition?'

'Sure.' At least he hoped so. He needed to go and find out what his king was up to. If it was not about him, then perhaps it had something to do with King Tuyon's impending visit. Or Pandarus. He did not know which was worse. 'Do me a favour, would you? Tell Hann to saddle my horse.'

Helena rose and hurried from the room.

Guilt pounded Dion's gut as the pieces of his earlier conversation with Astra came back to him. He realised at that moment that he had wanted her to choose him over the life she was still chasing. But instead of making himself the more appealing option, he had made her feel small and shallow—and she was neither of those things. If he did not fix things with her quickly, he would lose her to that other life forever.

CHAPTER 26

$\mathcal{R}$eave Castle was larger than Astra had imagined, its walls standing more than fifty feet high and stretching farther than she could see. Guards paced on top of it, armed and watchful. The wall was surrounded by a moat, the only point of entry being a heavily guarded drawbridge. It lowered in front of them, and Astra flinched when it hit the ground with a mighty thud. The horses trotted over it, their hooves creating a rumble of thunder that sent ripples across the water.

Astra had seen drawings, but they had not prepared her for the reality of the castle. As the wagon passed through the wall, she was immersed into the bustling life of the outer bailey. To her right were neat rows of houses with a small church sitting behind them. To her left was a barn with grassy enclosures where livestock grazed. The stables sat at the far end, with the gallows and scaffold tucked against the inside wall. The wagon did not stop, following the dirt road right up to the inner wall.

No one paid them much attention as they passed, the wagon not slowing or stopping until they reached the inner wall. The portcullis lifted in front of them, and the guards' eyes followed the wagon as it passed through the arch. Astra was met with a small lake surrounded by green lawn scattered with ducks. Manicured shrubs lined the road all the way to the front entrance of the castle. Astra smoothed back her hair and straightened her dress as a young man rushed forwards to open the door of the wagon. She took the offer of a hand, stepping gracefully down onto the paved road and looking around.

The guard from earlier appeared. 'This way,' he said, gesturing to the entrance.

Astra followed him up the stone steps that seemed to go on forever. When she stepped inside, she stopped, taking a moment to absorb the beautifully decorated entranceway with its framed paintings and brass candelabras nestled into the walls. She hurried after the guard, the eyes of previous Galen kings following her. 'Where are you taking me?'

'King Linus is waiting in the throne room.'

She was not even going to be permitted time to freshen up before being presented.

They passed the Great Hall, where ceiling-high green banners hung from each wall and a beautifully decorated high table sat along the back. The guard led her up some stairs. Two maids came from the opposite direction, stepping aside when they caught sight of them. They eyed Astra curiously as she passed. At the top, two guards stood to attention outside of the throne room, their eyes ahead.

'Tell His Majesty King Linus that I have the lady,' her escort said when they reached the door.

One of the men disappeared inside while the other snuck glances at her. The guard reappeared a moment later and opened the double doors. She had no idea what she would find on the other side. An entire room full of men? Just one king? She glided in, head high and hands loosely clasped in front of her. Looking around, she saw only King Linus and his advisor, Philo, seated alone at the large table. Two men she could handle.

Philo stood as she approached the table, always the gentleman. Astra lowered into a curtsy. 'Your Majesty. Philo.'

Philo nodded. 'Astra.'

'Please, take a seat,' King Linus said, gesturing to the chair opposite him. Then he turned to the guards. 'Tell my daughters I wish to see them.'

'Yes, Your Majesty.' He turned and marched out of the room.

She had no clue what was going on. Walking around the other side, she lowered herself into a chair. As soon as she was seated, Philo sat also.

'I apologise for bringing you here with no explanation,' the king began, 'but I thought it best we discuss the matter in person and privately, of course.' His eyes moved over her. 'It seems country life agrees with you. You look as radiant as ever.'

She responded with a warm smile. 'Time in the sun. The children seem to prefer the open air, and I prefer happy children.'

'You are settled at Goldmont, then?'

'For the time being.' What was he fishing for?

He leaned back in his chair, regarding her. 'I understand Captain Dion was not at Goldmont House when you departed. Would you like me to send word to him at Swanton of your whereabouts?'

'That will not be necessary, thank you.' Hopefully she could get back there before he learned of her departure. 'What is it I can help you with, Your Majesty?'

'I shall get straight to the point.'

Astra waited.

'We have some very important guests arriving at the castle tomorrow.'

Story of her life. They were always important. 'I see.'

'King Tuyon of Asigow will be among them. If my memory serves me correctly, he was quite fond of you.'

Dread pooled inside her. 'Will this be his first visit to Reave Castle?'

'Yes.'

'A first for our kingdom,' Philo said.

Astra glanced at him. 'May I ask what has enticed him this far south?'

King Linus leaned forwards, resting his elbows on the table. 'We are considering a match.'

'A match between whom?'

Philo spoke up. 'Princess Joneta and King Tuyon.'

She sat with that information for a moment. He was going to marry off one of his daughters to a man who sold Asigow children. 'Are you sure that is wise?'

King Linus appeared to be struggling with that exact question.

'I thought you might be able to guide me on that. You have spent some time with him.'

Slept with him, he meant. 'What exactly do you wish to know?'

Sensing the king's discomfort, Philo spoke up once more. 'Perhaps you could tell us if he was respectful during your… interactions.'

Astra looked between the men. 'Yes, mostly, but I know how to earn that respect. I have ten years of training with an excellent mentor. A woman without that experience might struggle.'

'My daughter has no experience with men,' Linus said.

'A man like King Tuyon is a brave starting point. Once your daughter crosses that border, she will be on her own.

There will be little you can do to protect her from here. It will come down to her.'

King Linus stared at his hands. 'I am aware you heard the rumours of a union with King Jayr's sister, Princess Tasia.'

'Yes.'

He hesitated. 'And you understand that such an alliance would not be good for my kingdom?'

They needed some sway north of the border. 'Yes.'

He looked up. 'Your king was smart in handing his sister over to King Jayr. She rules at his side. Syrasan is somewhat protected through their union.'

'At present, Galen has no such protection,' Philo added.

Astra looked between them. 'Queen Cora suffers at the hands of her husband, as I am sure you have heard. She is strong, so she stands a chance at surviving the match. Can you say the same for Princess Joneta?'

King Linus cleared his throat. 'Let me assure you she has been raised with such a role in mind.'

Before Astra could respond, the doors opened, and the two princesses entered. Astra watched them walk to their father, curtsying before him. Astra and Philo rose.

'Allow me to present my daughters,' Linus said. 'My eldest, Joneta, and my youngest, Beatrix. This is Astra, former Companion to King Pandarus of Syrasan.'

Astra curtsied, and the women nodded a greeting. 'My ladies.' She rose, focusing on Joneta, who stood back from her sister, hands clasped so firmly in front of her that her fingers were white. One look at the nervous blonde and Astra knew she would not survive five seconds with King Tuyon. Her gaze travelled to the younger brunette, who was studying her with unblinking green eyes. There was a woman who might stand a chance against such a man. 'May I speak freely in front of the princesses, Your Majesty, or would you prefer to talk in private?'

Linus waved a hand. 'You can speak freely.' He gestured to the chair. 'Please, sit.'

As she took her seat, the doors to the throne room opened again, and everyone turned to watch the guard enter.

'Forgive the interruption, Your Majesty, but Captain Dion is here.'

Astra looked to the door, her heart speeding up.

King Linus scratched tiredly at his grey beard. 'Send him in.'

Astra watched as a uniformed Dion strode into the room as if he had not collapsed on the kitchen floor earlier that day. He glanced in her direction, and she saw immediately that he was angry.

'Your Majesty,' he said, stopping in front of the king. 'I received word that one of my employees was taken from my house without explanation.'

'She's not in any trouble,' Linus replied. 'Rest easy, Captain.'

Dion's gaze flicked to the princesses. 'Then I trust you won't mind me sitting in on this… meeting?'

'Fine with me,' Linus said, growing impatient. He turned his attention back to Astra. 'You were saying?'

Dion walked around the other side of the table and pulled out the chair beside Astra, letting the legs screech across the floor before sitting. His eyes met hers for a moment. 'Forget I'm here.'

She wanted to ask how he was, then reprimand him for coming, but instead she returned her attention to the king. 'As I was saying, Your Majesty, if you do not mind me speaking freely in front of your daughters…'

'Please.'

'If you insist on going ahead with your plan, then might I suggest Princess Beatrix as a match for King Tuyon.'

Everyone turned to look at Beatrix. The princess did not wilt but straightened.

'Me?' she asked. 'Why me?'

'Because you are stronger than your sister,' Astra said plainly.

King Linus stared at his youngest daughter like he was trying to see something. 'How can you possibly tell that?'

'Body language does not lie, Your Majesty. Princess Joneta, while very beautiful, would be better suited to a gentler man.'

Dion shifted beside Astra as he realised what was happening, and King Linus and Philo exchanged a look.

'You're quite sure?' Philo asked.

Astra looked at Beatrix once more. 'That she is up to being the Queen of Asigow? No. That she is the best chance of the two? Yes.'

Linus seemed unsure. 'I hate to put so much on such young shoulders.'

'I can do this,' Beatrix replied.

Joneta placed a hand on her father's shoulder. 'Even a stranger can see she will make a better queen than me.' There was no disappointment in her tone, only relief.

Linus nodded and patted her hand. 'That will be all, girls, thank you.'

The princesses gave a small curtsy before leaving the room.

Astra waited until the door closed before asking, 'Is that all you needed from me, Your Majesty?'

The king cleared his throat. 'Actually, there is one more thing.'

Dion leaned forwards in his chair. 'What's that?'

The king looked at Dion. 'I would like Astra to prepare my daughter for the introduction.' His gaze shifted to Astra. 'And I think your attendance at the feast would be helpful. You could speak with King Tuyon, see where his mind is at.'

'Play spy, you mean?' Dion asked.

Philo spoke up at that. 'To find out simple things, like why the marriage with Princess Tasia is yet to go ahead, for example.'

Astra blinked. 'Simple things.'

'You are a Companion,' King Linus said. 'You can talk a man into or out of anything, can you not?'

Perhaps he meant it as a compliment.

'Actually,' Dion said, 'Astra is a governess in my household. Perhaps you could find someone else for the task.'

Philo was still looking at Astra. 'Before you shut down the idea—'

'Astra's too polite to shut it down,' Dion interrupted, 'so I'm shutting it down on her behalf.'

King Linus linked his hands in front of him. 'The arrangement would be mutually beneficial, of course.'

Dion went to speak, but Astra raised a hand to silence him. 'I thank you for your concern, Captain, but I am quite capable of speaking for myself.'

Linus looked between them before continuing. 'King Pandarus will also be attending. Not only will this give you an audience with him, but I will make sure he knows that you mentored my daughter.'

Astra stared at him, her fingers pressing into her legs. 'King Pandarus will be attending?' She heard Dion's chair creak.

Philo nodded. 'We thought it might be a good opportunity for you to... recapture his attention, remind him of your abilities, if that is your wish.'

'Sell herself also?' Dion said. Astra's gaze snapped to him, but he simply stared back at her. 'You can tell them no.'

He was right, of course, but so were they. It would be the

perfect opportunity, perhaps her *only* opportunity. Dion's eyes seemed to be pleading with her, making it impossible to think clearly. She turned her attention back to King Linus. 'King Tuyon might have certain expectations if I attend. Have you considered that?'

'The king has difficulty keeping his hands to himself,' Dion said, translating.

Astra drew a calming breath.

Philo spoke up again. 'If you are concerned about your safety, we could have a guard follow you.'

Astra shook her head. 'A bodyguard will only make the king suspicious.'

'He's a predator,' Dion said. 'You will need someone.'

She looked at him. 'I will need privacy to gain his trust. The man is not going to open up to me in a room full of people.'

'Then I'll do it,' Dion said. 'I'll be your guard. I can be discreet.'

Astra was about to object when she realised there was no one she trusted more. Though she would have to lay down some rules.

'Very well,' King Linus said. 'It seems the captain of my army is intent on keeping you safe. Anything else?'

Astra thought. 'I will need as much time with Princess Beatrix between now and the feast as possible.'

'I understand.'

'As well as access to your best seamstress.'

Linus's brow creased. 'My daughter has plenty of dresses.'

Astra smiled politely. 'You will need to trust me on this, Your Majesty.'

The king gave a reluctant nod. 'Very well.'

'And one more thing.'

Linus waited.

'I am going to need a harp.'

CHAPTER 27

When they exited the throne room, Dion did not wait for Astra. He marched ahead, the western sun pouring through the windows, hitting him every few strides. He felt the heat of it.

'Captain,' Astra called out.

He did not stop. In fact, his pace quickened. He needed some air and some space from her.

'Captain, stop.'

She was already out of breath trying to catch up to him. That was his weakness. He could not listen to her struggle. Stopping, he waited for her to reach him. 'What?'

His tone made her pull up. 'Where are you going?'

'To get some air.'

'I will come with you.'

'No.'

She was silent a moment, her fingers twitching at her sides. 'Did you ride here?'

'You know I did.'

She lowered her voice. 'You should be in bed, resting.'

'Probably, but instead I'm forced to come here and deal with this shit.'

She was quiet a moment. 'What are you so angry about?'

He closed the distance between them, a little too fast judging by the way she stepped back. 'What am I angry about? How about you volunteering yourself as a pawn.'

She searched his face. 'They presented a mutually beneficial opportunity.'

'You think that is an opportunity?' He tried to remain calm. 'Please, explain the opportunity part to me.'

'To get my life back.'

'Your *life*?' He wanted to shake her. 'You call what you had at Archdale a *life*?'

She opened her hands. 'It has been my only life for the past ten years.'

He raised a finger at her. 'You have a life at Goldmont that doesn't require you to sell yourself.' He pointed the finger down the corridor. 'Those men in there don't care about you. They're using you.'

'I know that. I am using them right back.'

'You're whoring yourself out to them, but you seem to think if you don't lift your skirts this time, you can call it something else.'

She flinched. He had never seen her flinch. He immediately lowered his hand. 'You're better than the life you're planning for yourself.' He shook his head, his frustration spilling over.

'I thought you understood.'

'And I thought you'd grown up.' He drew a calming breath. 'What is your big plan, by the way? To parade yourself in front of Pandarus and hope he gets an urge?'

'What? No.'

'Then what?'

'To demonstrate my skills as a mentor.'

He shook his head, anger colliding with pity. 'You spent ten years proving that.'

'He just needs reminding.'

Dion brought his face closer to hers. 'He wagered you in a game of cards. Where's your self-respect?'

She looked off down the corridor. He could see her heart thudding through her dress.

'This is the life I chose a long time ago.' She drew a breath before continuing. 'Where I come from, a daughter is an enormous burden. My parents planned to marry me off the moment I came of age. I was fifteen when the first offer came along. Father said no. Not because I was too young but because they knew a better offer would follow. I was never going to get a say. Can you imagine me in that life, birthing baby after baby, wondering how on earth I am going to feed them in the cold season?' She paused. 'I saw an opportunity, and I went after it. If that makes me a bad person, then that should make it easier for you to hate me.'

He was standing too close, getting high off her scent. He took a step back, trying to clear his head. Whatever he was feeling, she must have felt it also, because there was confusion on her face as she also moved back. He tried again. 'I can appreciate a self-sufficient woman, one with drive and ambition, but I don't believe for one second that you really want that life. You must know you deserve better.' He paused, giving her time to absorb his words. 'I think you're just afraid.'

She shook her head, rejecting the suggestion. 'No. For once, the decision is mine.'

'You're letting fear drive your decisions.'

She was still shaking her head. 'The only thing I have agreed to is helping your king.'

'Who's made his own daughter part of this.'

'That is what kings do.' She was whispering but animated.

'Open your eyes. That is the world we live in. We cannot all run around saving lives and fighting for our beliefs. Some of us just want to survive.'

He stared hard at her. 'You don't get to turn this around on me to make yourself feel better.'

She pressed a hand to her brow. 'You know what? Perhaps you should just leave. Go back to Goldmont House, or run away to Swanton Fort, like usual. Normally you just avoid me, so I have no idea why you are suddenly injecting yourself in my business.'

His eyes burned through her. 'Really? You have no idea?'

Her breaths were coming faster now. 'I did not ask for your help. In fact, I told them not to tell you.'

'Too bad. I'm here, and I'm not leaving.'

She swallowed and looked away.

'I wish you had said no,' he continued, 'but you didn't. I'm angry, but I'll get over it. I'm not abandoning you.' He let out a breath and backed away. 'I just hope you know what you're doing.'

CHAPTER 28

*A*stra had two days to prepare Princess Beatrix. That was not a lot of time. The princess's Zoelin was adequate at best, and since it was the only language they shared, Astra spent most of their time on that. She also taught body language tricks, best practices for conversation, and acceptable limits for physical contact. They had dress fittings, played with colours on her face, and selected jewels, shoes, and perfume for the feast. They treated her hair with oils to add shine, plucked unwanted hair, scrubbed her teeth with charcoal until they gleamed, and polished her skin until they could see their reflections in it. They practiced smiling, flirting, disinterest. Astra even organised for some men to attend whose sole purpose was to fight for the princess's attention. King Tuyon would soon pay attention if it became a competition. They found a partner so the princess could practice dancing, Astra ruthlessly critiquing and dissecting every move.

'Eyes up. Looser. Where is that curve in your back? Again.'

Dion managed to avoid her for the entire two days. He

always managed to eat at different times, and on the few occasions that she saw him from afar, he barely looked in the other direction. But true to his word, he did not leave the castle.

'I'm not going to abandon you.'

She played his words over and over in her mind, recalling his expression. All that disappointment. It had been difficult to digest.

It was not until the afternoon of the feast that he finally came knocking at her door. She had thought it was the seamstress and called out, 'Come in.'

The door swung open, and Dion leaned casually on the door frame, choosing not to enter. He always had a way of looking at her that made her stand a little straighter.

'So, you are alive,' she said.

'Thought it best to stay out of your way.' He looked around the room. 'What time should I collect you for the feast?'

She regarded him. 'You want to escort me there?'

His expression did not change. 'I'm your bodyguard for the evening. I'll be close by all night.'

'What happened to discreet?'

'Have a little faith. You do your job, and I'll do mine.'

She looked down. 'Still angry at me, then?'

'No.' His tone was softer this time. 'Just want this night to be over.'

Her eyes returned to him. 'Well, thank you for staying.'

He watched her for a moment, as though trying to read her. 'Do you need anything?'

She shook her head. 'The seamstress will be delivering my dress shortly. All I have to do is get myself ready and pray that Beatrix is up to the task.'

'How has it gone with her?'

'Fairly well. Though her Zoelin is not strong, which may work against her. Good communication is key.'

Dion nodded. 'I agree.'

She felt like that was aimed at her. 'Well, just come by when you are ready.'

He glanced down at his uniform. 'I am ready.'

She could not stop the smile. He was not one for dressing up. 'Then come back when *I* am ready.'

His mouth tilted up. 'Don't worry. You'll be great.'

She felt some relief knowing she had him back onside—sort of. 'Thank you.'

He reached for the door, pulling it closed as he stepped back. 'See you tonight.'

Dion had wanted to leave, many times, but he could not bring himself to do it. The next best thing was to stay far away from her. He had seen her a few times with the princess, had even stood at the entrance of the great hall when she had been teaching Beatrix how to dance. Her face had been so serious, her arms folded in front of her as she circled the pair like prey, calling out instructions that seemed overly critical. But what did he know? He had not been watching the princess, his eyes on Astra.

He had run into King Pandarus out front when he arrived. Dion had bowed, the appropriate greeting for a king. The man had nodded once in his direction as he passed.

'Captain.'

Then he had stared at Pandarus's back, imagining the king's hands on Astra while she faked pleasure—until she could not. Then he imagined his own hands on her, her body responding as it had that day in the kitchen. He recalled the change in her breath when he touched her, the heat that had pulsed through him when she pressed her lips to his arm. *His arm*. He could only imagine the effect of her mouth on his. He had imagined it every day since, been driven mad by the thought.

His head had gone in a strange direction over the previous week, occasionally visualising a life with her. He would return to Goldmont House, filled with that familiar anticipation, and find her chatting away with Eda in the kitchen. Her polished hands would be covered in a dusting of flour, the same hands she had once pressed to his thudding heart.

He was going to be in a lot of trouble when she left.

When he had eventually gone to see her, she had called out for him to come in, but he did not dare set one foot inside her bedchamber, remaining safely at the door. A few seconds into their conversation, he had realised he could not stay mad at her. Instead, he found himself reassuring her.

That evening, he had a quick wash, gave his boots a polish, and strapped on his sword. He wandered down the corridor to Astra's bedchamber, knocked on the door, and then walked over to the opposite wall, preparing to wait. He knew how long it took ladies to prepare themselves for an evening, so he was surprised when her door opened and she stepped out into the corridor, dressed up and ready to depart.

He froze in place when he saw her. His lungs seemed to stop working for a moment.

She wore a silk gown in the palest of pinks. The sleeves were gathered atop her shoulders, held in place with a cluster of embroidered leaves in various colours. His gaze travelled down her lean body, pausing at her breasts, which, to her credit, were fully covered, giving the illusion of modesty. A sliver of bare skin trailed down to the plaited belt wrapping her waist. He should have stopped there, but his eyes moved over her round hips and all the way down the skirt of the dress, which fanned out at the bottom. The hem was finished with feathers and a scattering of pearls.

Astra adjusted the gold cuff on her arm, the rings on her fingers catching the light. 'I know you are not big on compliments, but you could say *something?*'

Dion dragged his gaze up one bare arm and along her slender shoulder, neck, until he met her eyes. What to say? Nodding to the hem of her dress, he said, 'I guess we know what happened to Primrose.'

Her mouth fell open, and she looked down at the feathers. Why in God's name had he said that? He should have told her she looked beautiful. Breathtaking, even. Perhaps recited a sonnet—but he did not know any sonnets.

She looked up at him. 'You… you cannot say things like that.'

To his relief, he realised she was holding in laughter.

'That is truly horrible. I am still grieving.'

'Your dress suggests otherwise.'

She breathed out a laugh, then covered her mouth, looking off down the corridor. Heaven forbid someone see her having an honest moment. Regaining control of herself, she smoothed down her long hair, which was out and swept to one side, reaching all the way to the top of her breast. He really needed to stop looking at her.

'Are you ready?' she asked.

No, he was not ready. 'Before we go, I just want to say that there's not a king in the history of kings worthy of you right now.' The air returned to his lungs. He could breathe again. 'Now we can go.'

Astra stared at him for a moment, lost for words for once in her life, then walked off ahead of him.

It was not the best idea to walk behind, as he was yet to explore the back of her. The dress was open, and he could not tear his gaze from her. It roamed the bare flesh between her shoulder blades, sinking down the visible line of her spine. She walked with her hips gently swaying and head straight, as though she were balancing a crown. A disobedient lock of hair floated around her right ear, and he wanted to put it back in its place. He shifted his gaze as they rounded the corner. Soon they would arrive, and the moment she stepped inside, every pair of eyes would be upon her. Every man, woman, guard, servant—and most certainly every king. There was not a chance in hell that Pandarus would not sit up and take notice, not with those lips painted the colour of peaches, those arms bronzed from long walks with chickens.

They paused at the entrance, Astra readying herself for show and Dion readying himself for vultures. She fixed her hair, catching that one stray piece, now part of a unified cascade of deadly fire.

Dion stepped closer, his knee brushing her skirt. 'Don't leave this room without me. Understand?'

She turned to look at him, eyes moving over his face. 'Do not worry yourself, Captain. I have done this dance many times.'

He needed to stop looking at her lips whenever she spoke. 'I mean it. Don't leave this room without me.'

She faced forwards again, and he stepped back and watched her enter the hall.

CHAPTER 29

$\mathscr{A}$stra had never seen so many women at a royal feast. Galen was not a kingdom that hid away its wives. Though she suspected their presence did not stop the men behaving badly, judging by the way their gazes followed her. She spotted Princess Beatrix speaking with Queen Catrain. Beatrix whispered something to her mother, who looked in Astra's direction, giving a small nod of acknowledgement. Astra lowered into a curtsy, then watched the princess approach. She gestured for her to slow down, give the men time to enjoy her on the move.

While she waited, she had a look around. To her right stood a group of women who lingered by their husbands. One glance in their direction told Astra that they did not approve of her—or at least her gown. They were the type who wore theirs buttoned up to their necks with sleeves to the elbow. The husbands, on the other hand, seemed to very much approve of Astra.

To her left were the ladies of court. Their dresses did not button up to their neck, and their expressions were more curious than disapproving. The single men were close by, easy to spot with their predatory glances and inability to be subtle. Astra paid them no attention, her eyes going to the group of men gathered in front of the high table. King Linus, Prince Stamitos, King Pandarus, King Tuyon, and now Dion, who had wandered up to join them. Their eyes met briefly. At least he was not loitering behind her. It seemed he could be discreet after all.

'I met him,' Beatrix said, joining her. 'Did everything exactly as you instructed.'

'Good.'

Beatrix leaned in. 'He did not seem very interested.'

'Of course not. He is a guest in your father's home. Perhaps you could present me to your father. Then I will be able to gauge for myself.'

'Good idea.' Beatrix turned, adjusting the skirt of her crimson silk gown. She looked every bit the lethal queen Astra had hoped she would.

The moment the women stepped up to the group, the men stopped talking and turned in their direction. Astra allowed herself one glance at King Tuyon to see who he was looking at. Straight at her. Not ideal, but the night was young. Her eyes flicked to Pandarus, who struggled to hide his surprise at seeing her there. His gaze travelled down her body, predictable as ever. If other men were looking, then so was he.

'Excuse me, Father. I wanted to present Astra. She joins us from Goldmont House this evening. I believe you are all acquainted.'

'Your Majesties,' Astra said, curtsying. Then she looked to Stamitos and Dion. 'My lord. Captain.'

Stamitos gave her a wry smile, and Dion barely looked at her.

'I was hoping to run into you,' King Tuyon said.

She smiled warmly. 'I was going to ask you to save me a dance, but I do not imagine you know any Galen dances.'

His eyes shone at her. 'A walk instead, perhaps.'

Dion would not like that. 'Sounds lovely.' She turned her attention to King Linus. 'So kind of you to invite me. The scenery on the journey here was simply breathtaking.'

'I understand the captain keeps you quite busy. I figured you deserved an evening of fun. I do hope you will honour us with a performance tonight.' He looked at Pandarus. 'A marvellous talent. I imagine she is greatly missed at Archdale.'

'Greatly,' Pandarus said, speaking for the first time.

Her eyes drifted to him, her face a blank canvas. The best approach if she wanted him to take notice was to pay him as little attention as possible while remaining respectful. 'How is your family, Your Majesty?'

'Well, thank you.' His tone had lost the sharp edge present last time they had spoken.

'I am pleased to hear it.' She looked back at King Linus. 'You best keep a close eye on Princess Beatrix tonight, Your Majesty. I have never seen so many men light up at the sight of a woman.'

'You are far too kind,' the princess replied, touching a hand to her collarbone exactly as they had practiced.

Tuyon finally looked at Beatrix.

'She is quite the prize, is she not?' Astra asked, directing the question at Tuyon.

His eyes moved over the princess. 'Yes.'

They had some work ahead of them, but it was a start.

Music struck up behind them, and Astra considered her next move. Turning to Dion, she asked, 'Would you care to dance, Captain?'

All eyes went to Dion, who had not been expecting that question. Out of the corner of her eye, she could see

Pandarus looking between them. She did not dare look in his direction.

'All right,' Dion said. He gave a small bow to the group. 'Please excuse us.'

Astra curtsied and took the arm Dion offered her, fingers resting lightly on it. She glanced sideways at him as they walked away. 'I should have probably checked that you could dance before asking.'

'I've been told I'm rather good.'

His voice washed over her like warm water. 'By whom?'

'By the women I dance with.'

She took in his playful expression. 'I am counting on it. One wrong step and I will abandon you on the dance floor.'

'I'm surprised you asked. I assume this is one of your ploys to get your king's attention.'

She wished that had only been her only motive, but she was curious to see if he was any good. The fact that Pandarus was looking in their direction was a nice bonus. 'You know me so well' came her reply.

They joined the line of dancers, men on one side and women on the other.

Dion looked down at her dress. 'Will your gown stay in place if I spin you?'

'Exactly how fast do you intend to spin me?'

'That depends on your answer.'

She pressed her lips together. They were flirting, and it needed to stop.

Dion glanced down the line of men when the next song began, and when they all stepped forwards, so did he. Astra held her breath as he came towards her, circling before stepping back into line with the other men. Now it was her turn. She held his gaze as she stepped up to him, the smile gone from her face. The intensity of his stare made it impossible to look away. She turned around him and stepped back into line with the other women, feeling oddly nervous. Next time, they both stepped in, palms joining. She was worried that her clammy hands would give away what she was feeling inside. When they stepped apart, she made a point of opening her fingers to let her skin breathe, looking away from him to ease the intensity.

Spinning around, she braced for his touch again. His right palm caught her hip, and she could not look up, knowing what was next. He moved behind her, his large hand sliding to the small of her back. The warmth of it made bumps appear on her arms. She swallowed thickly, hoping he would not notice. Then he was in front of her, his face inches from hers, his other hand swallowing hers whole.

'Look at me,' he said.

She lifted her eyes to him, trying very hard to relax her brow.

'Better.'

They began turning, their hips a careful distance apart. Her gaze fell again, focusing on the top button of his tunic.

'Why can't you look at me?'

A valid question. She forced her eyes up. The effort was enormous. 'I am looking at you.'

He searched her eyes. 'I'm not that bad, am I?'

His technique was flawless, every move graceful. 'Actually, you are very good, and you know I do not hand out compliments easily.'

The music stopped, and the other couples stepped apart. Applause ensued. Neither of them moved. His hand still held hers, his fingers pressing into her back.

'The dance has finished,' she said, not moving. She needed him to let go first.

His hands were unrelenting. 'You don't have to do this, you know. You don't have to leave.'

She took a small step back, and he released his grip on her. 'Thank you for the dance, Captain.'

A stranger approached her. 'May I have the next dance?'

Astra turned to give him her full attention. 'I would love to.' She permitted herself a quick glance in the direction of the kings, finding Beatrix speaking with King Tuyon and Pandarus looking straight at her with an expression she had come to recognise over the years. Possessiveness. Jealousy. He would lose his mind to it eventually and realise his mistake.

The man led her away from Dion, despite the fact that they were already standing on the dance floor. He needed to claim his own space, unwilling to share her for the few moments he had. Astra glanced back at Dion, who stood with a disapproving expression. In another life, she would have told the stranger no and danced every dance with the only man to ever make her look down at her feet.

But that was not the life she had chosen.

The evening progressed like a form of slow torture for Dion. Not only was he forced to watch Astra dance with more men than his stomach could handle, but he was also forced to watch King Pandarus and King Tuyon undress her with their eyes. King Tuyon might have been talking to Princess Beatrix, but he was watching Astra like an eagle ready to swoop down at any moment. Pandarus mingled with other guests, but he appeared to be in a permanent state of agitation that could only be attributed to one thing.

He was no better than them, his own body twitching and tightening each time a hand moved on Astra's back or someone leaned in to whisper in her ear. Her smile never faltered.

'I was not expecting to see you here' came the familiar voice of Elenor Talsworth.

He turned his head as she stopped beside him, and then they both looked out at the dance floor. He had been so focused on Astra all evening he had not even seen her. 'You're looking well.'

'I always thought you hated these types of events. Perhaps you just hated attending with me.' Her tone was teasing. 'Are you here for work or pleasure?'

Torture, apparently. 'Work.' He watched as Astra changed dance partners again. When would she tire?

'Interesting work you are doing nowadays.'

'Don't know what you mean.'

Elenor laughed. 'You know exactly what I mean. She is very beautiful, but she is also a *Companion*. I thought you were smarter than that.'

He had thought so once. 'She's not a Companion. She's a governess.'

Elenor gave a small laugh. 'Well, your governess has captured the attention of the entire room. She must be *very* good.'

He drew a breath, not wanting to talk about Astra with her. They both watched as Pandarus walked onto the dance floor, touching a hand to Astra's back as he asked her a question. The gesture was familiar, the exact gesture one would expect from a couple who had spent ten years together. She nodded, excused herself, and then turned to face Pandarus.

'If you are waiting for a second dance with her, it might be a bit of a wait,' Elenor said, trying to sound amused but coming across jealous.

'I'm not here to dance.' The music started, and he watched as Pandarus broke all the rules of etiquette; his fingers splayed on the exposed part of her back, elbow bent so her hips were pressed to his. She just went along with it. No discomfort, no reason for Dion to go out there and interrupt the moment.

'We danced rather well together at one time,' Elenor said. 'We used to have fun.'

He glanced briefly in her direction. 'We did.' Then his father had been sentenced, and Elenor's biggest worry had been how it would reflect on her.

'How about a dance? For old times' sake.'

Dion's eyes narrowed on Pandarus's hand, which had slipped beneath the fabric of Astra's dress. 'I'm working. Sorry.'

'You danced with *her*.'

'That was work.' Pleasure. Torture.

King Linus, who was now seated at the high table with his wife, tapped his cup with a fork. The room fell silent. 'I would like to invite Lady Astra up to play something.' He gestured to the far end of the raised floor, where a harp and stool sat.

Tentative applause broke out.

When Dion looked in Astra's direction, he found her looking back at him—or rather, straight at Elenor. It was the first time her smile had faltered all evening, but it was so fast he doubted anyone else would have noticed. Turning her back to him, she excused herself from Pandarus, gathered the skirt of her gown, and glided towards the harp. When she reached the platform, half a dozen men rushed forwards to take her hand as she stepped up. She thanked the man who reached her first and went to settle herself on the stool. When she released the skirt of her dress, it fanned around her like an upside-down flower. She pulled the harp closer so the shoulder of it rested on her breastbone.

Dion glanced about the room. All eyes were on her. King Tuyon had moved closer to watch, Princess Beatrix following like a shadow. His shoulder rested on the wall, arms crossed, the hint of a smile on his lips. Astra did not even glance in his direction. It was her moment—her escape. Soon, she would leave them all behind.

Astra ran her fingers along the strings, then fiddled with the pins on the neck of the instrument. She closed her eyes, running her fingers along them one more time. Dion waited for her eyes to open again, but they did not.

There was a long silence before she began. Then her delicate fingers moved across the strings, producing a melody. He did not recognise the song, but he appreciated the beauty nonetheless. She was gone, lost to the music. It built then, faster and faster, her fingers moving at an impossible speed. He wondered where she was in that moment, wished he could follow her. There was a hole in him suddenly. The entire room was still. The women who had looked on with disapproval moments earlier now sat in awe, exchanging bewildered looks with those around them. She could win over anyone eventually. Her eyes did not open once. She was one with the instrument, feeling her way through the entire piece note by note. His heart expanded at the sight of her free. Free from every man there—even him.

As the song neared its end, her hands slowed, her fingers plucking at individual strings in a way that evoked emotions he seemed to have lost control of. He heard a few sniffs around him, though not from Elenor, who stood with a pinched expression.

Then silence.

The silence seemed to stretch on forever while everyone waited for her to come back to the room. Slowly, her eyes opened, returning to them. She looked around as if she had forgotten she had an audience. Applause began, a scattering at first, then growing louder as more people joined in. Those seated stood. Those who were standing stood taller, edging forwards as the hands came together, faster and faster.

'Oh, she is good,' Elenor said, joining in the applause.

Dion knew it was not meant as a compliment. He joined the applause, his eyes never leaving Astra as she pushed the instrument away and stood to curtsy. That had been her life at Archdale. She had spent years perfecting her craft and performing in front of distinguished guests. Her life there had been bigger than Pandarus. It had barely been about him at all but an act that benefited both of them.

And what had Dion done?

He had stripped her of her music and offered her chickens. He had deprived her of the one thing she actually enjoyed, the thing she needed more than anything else. The honest part of her. He understood that now. It was not only her talent but her gift, her love. It was payment for her hellish existence.

Elenor's applause stopped. 'Is that blood on your tunic?'

Dion stopped applauding and looked down at his sleeve before meeting her gaze. 'Sparring injury.' He covered his sleeve with his hand and looked around the room to ensure no one else had noticed. 'Excuse me,' he said, already backing away. 'I need to go clean up.'

He glanced once in Astra's direction. If he was quick, he would be back before she even noticed he was missing.

CHAPTER 30

King Tuyon was waiting to help her down from the platform. She glanced past him to where Pandarus stood, visibly annoyed. He had been too slow. Everyone was playing their roles perfectly, and she was on a high after her performance. She searched for Dion again, catching sight of him just as he left the room—with Elenor Talsworth in tow. Her belly tightened at the sight of her following after Dion. She recognised jealousy when she felt it, though this felt different to what she had experienced in the past. With Pandarus, it had been about being his first choice. With Dion, it was about every other woman staying the hell away from him. She watched the door for a moment, the one he had disappeared through when he abandoned her. So much for "don't leave this room without me".

'Take a walk with me,' King Tuyon said.

She dragged her gaze back to him and nodded. 'All right.' Princess Beatrix had retreated to the high table, looking disappointed. But the evening was not over yet. 'I need a break from all the dancing.'

He offered his arm, and she took it. They made their way

towards the exit. Perhaps she would run into Dion outside while having some alone time with the king. Maybe he thought his presence would be less suspicious with another woman at his side, just a couple of lovers strolling in the dark.

The pair stepped out into the corridor, following it all the way to the entrance. Astra resisted the urge to look around for him. If she expected Tuyon to open up, she needed to relax so he felt at ease with her. She slid her shoulder blades down her back, a contented sigh passing her lips as they exited the castle. Descending the steps, they made their way towards the garden.

'Such a beautiful castle,' she said, looking around at the budding trees. 'What is your palace like in Asigow? Paint me a picture.'

He guided them onto the path that weaved between the flowerbeds. 'You want to know if we have pretty gardens like these?'

'I am picturing trees and swans paddling in icy ponds.'

He glanced down at her, a smile on his lips. 'I've a number of palaces. I move around a lot.'

Seemed like a good enough opening. 'Is that why you have not taken a wife? I imagine it would be a lonely exis- tence for a queen with her husband away all the time.'

They reached the roses that ran either side of the path. The smell overtook the air, and Astra breathed in deeply. King Tuyon slowed to watch her.

'It's not a position you just give out to anyone. She will be queen of an empire, mother to the future king. She needs to be up to the role.'

Astra pretended to think on that for a moment. 'Princess Tasia of Zoelin was rumoured to be a suitable match, was she not?'

'Yes.'

She looked up at him. 'But you hesitate.'

'Call it a gut feeling.'

She took careful mental notes. 'You have hesitations about the princess?'

'Not her specifically but her kingdom. Change is coming, so I'd prefer to wait.'

'What a tease you are.' She smiled up at him. 'What secrets is King Jayr keeping this time?'

He glanced down at her. 'This time?'

'I have known him since he took the throne. He is always up to something.' She made sure she kept her tone light.

'Right now, he's just trying to keep a hold of his crown because the kingdom's divided.'

'Divided, yes, but Jayr is the rightful heir.'

Tuyon nodded. 'If only his people liked him.'

She kept her pace even. This was not where she had expected the conversation to go. 'You think Brom will make a move for the throne?'

'Maybe. If he doesn't, the Zoelin people may act on his behalf.'

She looked around. 'Then I suppose it is a good thing King Jayr has the support of Syrasan.'

'But not Galen.'

She looked up at him again. 'Why do you say that?'

'Another gut feeling.'

She needed to be careful now. She pulled herself closer to him. 'I was under the impression King Jayr and King Linus were allies of sorts.'

They turned a corner.

'I suspect King Linus has multiple Zoelin alliances,' Tuyon said.

She felt her stomach knot. 'Why do you say that? Another gut feeling?'

'Something like that.'

He could only be referring to Brom, but Astra did not want to push him for fear of making him suspicious. 'Well, then I think you are smart to wait.'

A smile played on his lips. 'I'm glad you approve.'

Astra looked up at him. 'May I speak freely?'

'Don't you always?'

She gave him her sweetest smile. 'Perhaps you should align yourself with Galen instead. You could marry one of the princesses. Princess Beatrix seems more than interested.'

He laughed once. 'What makes you say that?'

'A gut feeling.' She watched his eyes for a moment. 'Galen has been at peace for years, has a strong army of highly skilled soldiers prepared to lay down their lives for their king without question, as well as the full support of Syrasan.' She paused. 'And Beatrix is a born queen.'

He laughed again, reaching up and touching her hair. 'You know, if you had an ounce of royal blood, I'd marry you.'

'And I would drive you mad.'

'Perhaps I should hire you as my advisor instead.'

She laughed this time. 'You joke, but we both know I would be very good.'

'Because you know the minds of men?'

'Because I know the minds of men better than they do.'

He regarded her. 'I think I believe you. You were at Pandarus's side for so long.' He brushed his fingers down her cheek. 'He's been watching you all night, no doubt regretting his wager.' His eyes moved over her face. 'Might you share my bed this evening?'

Her face gave nothing away. 'You have already had me in your bed. Where is the fun in that?'

He emitted a noise that was half growl, half laugh.

Footsteps sounded on the path behind them, and they both turned to look. Astra expected Dion to appear through the darkness, but it was not him. It was Pandarus—a visibly drunk Pandarus. He stopped a few paces from them, his jaw tense as he looked between them.

'I wonder if I might have a private word with Astra.'

She felt as though she were being saved by the devil.

King Tuyon leaned his weight on one foot, a smirk on his face as he regarded the jealous king. 'By all means.' He looked back at Astra. 'Perhaps I'll see if Princess Beatrix wants to teach me to dance.'

She lowered into a curtsy, a knowing smile on her face. 'I hear she is very good. Thank you for the walk, Your Majesty.'

Tuyon winked at her. 'Come find me if you change your mind.'

She kept her expression playful as he turned away and walked slowly past Pandarus. The two kings eyed each other as their paths crossed; then Pandarus focused on Astra, not speaking until Tuyon was out of earshot.

'Change your mind about what?' he asked as soon as they were alone.

Astra lifted her chin. 'Teaching him to dance.' A lie, but she was a lady.

He closed the distance between them and took her hand. '*My* turn for a walk.'

His words were slurred, and she could smell the wine on his breath. 'All right.' Dread coiled inside her. It was time to play the Companion again—and play her well. She tried to keep up with him, but he was walking too fast, and her foot rolled on the uneven surface. When she stumbled, he did not slow his pace. That was not a good indication of his mood.

'Please slow down, Your Majesty.' When he did not listen, she pulled her hand from his and waited for him to turn around. 'I am happy to walk with you, but you will need to *slow down*.'

He stepped up to her, using his height to intimidate.

'Who do you think you are speaking to? Have you forgotten how things work? I set the speed, and you keep up.'

She stared up at him, unblinking. 'Perhaps you have forgotten that I am no longer yours to command.'

The corner of his mouth tugged. 'What I had forgotten is how good you are at these games. Fire and ice. You mean to make me jealous and then feign innocence.'

She had wanted him to take notice—and she had succeeded. 'That is a rather colourful interpretation. King Tuyon asked me to go for a walk, and I agreed.'

'I am not talking about Tuyon.'

She blinked, confused.

'I am talking about Captain Dion.' He watched her reaction to his words. 'You are sleeping with him.'

She made herself as tall as possible. 'You are overstepping, Your Majesty. My personal affairs are no longer your business.'

'But what is interesting is that you are not required to. He wanted you freed, do-gooder that he is. Does not believe in people as property. He is proving himself quite the humanitarian of late. He is your employer, is he not?'

She tried to decipher his cryptic words. 'Yes, he is my employer.'

He shook his head, like a disappointed parent. 'Oh, Astra. Please tell me you were not stupid enough to fall in love with that man. I mean orphans and chores? Is that what you are settling for nowadays?'

She felt her cheeks heat with… anger? Embarrassment? 'It is a big step up from being a wager in a game of cards.'

'Ah, that.'

'Yes, that.'

'You know I was drunk.'

It was definitely anger she was feeling, a decade's worth

bubbling to the surface. 'You were *drunk*? That is your explanation for so easily discarding me?'

He brought his face closer to hers. 'I made a mistake. Is that what you want to hear?'

The whispering of words was no doubt meant to be seductive, but she felt only repulsion. Then his lips came crashing down on hers, the action too hard, his mouth too cold. Everything inside her screamed. Her hands went to his chest, shoving him away. He took a small step back, his eyes widening in surprise. Panic filled her. She had never said no to the man in her life, and she had certainly never been unable to control her reaction like that. 'Forgive me,' she said immediately, her mind grabbing for an explanation. 'You caught me off guard.'

He was slightly breathless, his eyes smouldering now. 'You want me to work for it, is that the game? You want to hear that I am sorry?' He closed the distance between them, taking hold of her face at an awkward angle. She swallowed against his fingers. 'Perhaps you want me to fall to my knees in front of you, bury my face between your thighs until you scream out your forgiveness?'

He was insane if he thought she wanted that.

His mouth found hers again, opening this time. The action made Astra's stomach twist with repulsion. Had she really thought she could just go back to pretending after weeks of reprieve? Dion had been right. She was not the same person. She could not stay still while Pandarus touched her.

Stepping back from him, she drew a breath. 'I think I should return inside.'

'What?'

'I am sorry.' Sorry that she could no longer tolerate the scent of him, feel of him, or even the sight of him in that moment.

When she turned to leave, Pandarus grabbed her by the wrist and tugged her roughly back to him. 'You dare turn your back on your king.'

Astra tried to pull her hand free, and when he did not let go, she pushed at his arm. 'Let go.'

'This is how you respond to my apology.'

There was no blood getting to her hand, no air to her lungs. '*Apology*? You are hurting me.'

'Shut up and listen for a moment.'

Shut up? She was two breaths away from screaming, from clawing his face.

'The lady has asked you to *let go*.' Dion's voice sliced through the dark like a blade.

Astra's head snapped in his direction. He stood six feet from them on the path, his black eyes fixed on the hand holding Astra's wrist.

'So let her go,' Dion finished.

It took drunk Pandarus a moment to register who was speaking. 'Ah, Captain Dion. We were just talking about you.' He looked between the two of them. 'It seems even you are not immune to the talents of my Companion, you on your high horse with your superior morals.'

Astra realised at that moment that Pandarus's anger stemmed not from the fact that she had, presumably, fallen for another man but a *better* man. People like Dion, good people who stood for things outside of their own self-interest, were a threat to men like Pandarus. He was forced to confront his own shortfalls when measured against them.

'I warned you she was good. Did I not? The morning you came to me and requested she be freed, I told you she would get what she wanted and leave you a shell of your former self.'

Astra stared at him. He had painted her as a monster. That explained where Dion's distrust of her stemmed from.

'I'll continue to look—but always from a safe distance.'

'Though I am still trying to figure out what my lovely Astra is getting out of this little arrangement,' Pandarus continued. He pretended to think for a moment. 'Did you pay for the dress? The jewels? She does love pretty things. Sold her soul for them once.'

Astra tried to pull her hand free again, but Pandarus held tight.

Dion took a few more steps towards them, remaining calm. 'Astra is under my protection this evening, Your Majesty. If your hand does not let go of her, I'll be forced to cut it off.'

Pandarus only grinned. 'You are speaking to a *king*. You dare draw your sword and I'll have your head.' He released Astra with a shove.

Dion caught her with his good arm and pulled her behind him. Astra brought her hand to her chest, her other one going protectively over it. Pandarus's eyes followed her every move.

'Wait until your king hears of you threatening his guests,' Pandarus said.

Dion's eyes remained on him, his body rigid. 'Just doing my job.'

Pandarus laughed at that. 'I bet you are. Your father would be so proud of your latest efforts—if he were alive.' He turned away, unsteady on his feet as he prepared to leave.

He knew something.

Dion went to follow after him, but Astra touched a hand to his elbow. He stilled, glanced at her, then looked back at Pandarus. They watched as he made his way back up the path, his pride in tatters. Dion waited before turning to face her. For a moment, they just stared at one another.

'I'm guessing that was not the first time he's grabbed you like that,' Dion began.

'He is just drunk.'

'Don't make excuses for him.'

'I can handle him.'

'Like you handled him then? Looked very much like he was handling you.'

She could see he was trying to contain his temper.

'I told you not to leave that room,' he continued, his hands balled into fists at his sides.

'And I told you that I needed time alone with King Tuyon in order to gain his trust.'

'And Pandarus?'

'He just showed up. What would you have me do?'

'Return to *me*.' He was getting angrier. 'I'm trying *very* hard right now to understand why you want to go back to *that*.' He pointed after Pandarus.

She looked back down the path where he had disappeared. 'It would not be like this if I were a mentor. Mentors are respected.'

Dion's hands went into his hair. 'How can such a smart woman have such stupid thoughts? If that man doesn't respect you now, he's not going to suddenly respect you with a different title.'

'Do you think you are being respectful right now, calling me stupid?'

His eyes narrowed. 'I called you smart.'

'Oh, yes. Smart with stupid thoughts.'

He dragged his hands down his face. 'He doesn't respect you.'

Astra blinked. 'He would if I were in that role. You do not understand how things work there.'

'I understand better than you think. I understand that you were one exchange from being struck or having that pitiful excuse for a gown torn off you. If you had just stayed at the feast—'

'You were not even at the feast! I saw you leave with Elenor Talsworth.'

He closed his eyes in exasperation. 'My wound was bleeding. Elenor spotted blood on my sleeve, so I went to clean myself up. She followed because she was worried.'

'That is so considerate of her.' She detested sarcasm, yet it poured freely from her. 'Did she help you undress too?'

Dion regarded her for a moment. 'Careful, you sound like a jealous wife.'

'I am not sure what is more offensive, the jealous accusation or the image of being your wife.' She paused. 'I have shared Pandarus with more women than I care to count. Jealousy is a waste of my energy.'

He brought his face to hers. 'Perhaps it's different with me. Have you ever considered that?'

Her breathing was laboured, her heart racing. 'You have made it perfectly clear from the very beginning that you are *far* too superior to lower yourself to a *Companion*. I get it, of course. You were heeding Pandarus's warning.'

'Stop.'

'He is such a reliable source.'

He took a firm hold of her arms. 'Stop.'

'Perhaps it is me. Better go admire me from afar, Captain.' Her voice cracked during that last part, exposing her for the big fraud she was.

He stared down at her, his eyes moving over her face. 'I've been admiring you from afar all evening.' His voice was a deep whisper. 'And it's killing me.' He let go of her. 'I'm done playing bodyguard.'

Astra took a greedy breath of air, hands going to her hips for balance. 'Done?' The word was like a small death.

His shoulders dropped a few inches. 'I'm done pretending, done torturing myself.' He pressed a closed fist to his brow, then looked at her with a broken expression. 'The hair, the laugh, the smile, the lips, the dress—'

'You mean the *half* dress?'

An exasperated noise escaped him. 'You're killing me.'

'I am killing *you*?' She struggled to get the next words out. 'Do you have any idea how terrifying it is to feel emotions you have suppressed for a decade?'

'You mean human emotions?'

She stared boldly back at him. 'It is all a big joke to you.'

He shook his head. 'I shouldn't have said that. I'm sorry.'

'Imagine being told you are a goddess, then discovering you are mortal, ordinary.'

He reached one hand up, smoothing back the locks of hair that were now spilling in all directions. 'There's nothing ordinary about you.' He brought his forehead to hers, his fingers resting along her jaw where Pandarus's had sat moments earlier. 'And I like that you were jealous,' he whispered.

Astra was sure he could see her heart pounding through her gown. There was so much happening in her body. Her cheeks were hot, her limbs trembling. There was a relentless pull at the base of her stomach, a heavy sensation between her thighs. She knew what it was, what it meant—and it terrified her. Where was the control? The carefully planned reaction? The rehearsed seduction? She was trapped in a body she did not recognise, her face moving closer until her nose brushed his.

Dion pulled back a few inches, looking at her with the same tortured expression he had worn that day in the kitchen. His breaths were coming as fast as her own. He brought his lips to her forehead, and she pushed up into the sensation. He smelled so familiar now, so safe. She tipped her face up so his lips brushed her cheek until his warm breath mixed with her own. His other hand came up to her face, and he finally pressed his mouth to hers. Heat tore through her until her entire body hummed with the sensation of him. Her hands slid up his neck and into his hair. Every touch and movement was bliss. Her hips instinctively moved forwards in search of his. The moment they touched, Dion released an unsteady breath, which she inhaled, not wanting to waste any part of him. He traced his fingers up her bare arm, her shoulder, down her back until he found the opening of her dress. Her breath hitched at the feel of his rough fingers, and her body melted against him. A small whimper passed her lips.

A whimper.

She had never whimpered in her life.

The realisation made her pull away, a hand going over her burning lips. She was not in control—and she needed to be.

'Sorry,' she said.

He kept a hold of her arms. 'Don't say that.'

She was trembling, and the more she became aware of it, the worse it got. 'I just need a moment.' She pulled out of his grip, skin still warm where his hands had been, breathing deeply. *Better.* The Companion was returning.

Dion linked his hands on top of his head, watching her. 'You all right?'

That question. 'Yes.' She had some control back in her voice. 'We should go inside.'

He was silent a moment. 'Is that really what you want, to go back in there and continue the charade?'

No. She wanted to stay outside with him, kiss him, encourage his hands beneath her dress again. 'Yes, of course. I have a job to do. A kiss does not change that.'

'A kiss.' Dion held his knees for a moment. 'Well, I can't watch you with those men. Not after that.'

She forced her hand away from her mouth, trying to think through the fog of him. 'All right. I need to bid good evening to some people, speak with the king, and then I am done. I can return to my bedchamber and forget this entire evening ever happened.' She barely knew what she was saying.

He straightened, his intense gaze on her again. 'Fine, but no more disappearing acts—unless you want a scene.'

Astra nodded and stepped back from him. 'I understand.' With her eyes down and plenty of distance between them, she walked back up the path.

CHAPTER 31

*R*eturning to the feast was too much for Dion. His body felt heavy, his mind too busy. People approached, spoke to him. He nodded, said things he was barely aware of, eyes following Astra like one possessed. She was calm, collected, every hair back in place. Looking at her, you would think the kiss never happened. Though "kiss" was an inadequate description of what it was. He had sacrificed a part of himself in a ritual he had not realised he was participating in. How was he supposed to go about his evening after finally *tasting* her?

'Every man who meets her feels exactly as you do right now,' Pandarus said, coming up beside him.

Dion shifted his body away. Judging by the smell of drink on the king's breath, he had made no effort to sober up. If he had been any other man, Dion would have broken his face for the way he treated Astra earlier, but his title made him untouchable. Dion continued watching her, saying nothing.

'A lord once told me he would cut off his own arm if it meant he could sink into her for just a few seconds.'

Dion blinked. 'He sounds like a real catch.'

Pandarus laughed through his nose. 'Every man here is imagining what lies beneath that skirt.'

Dion refused to be baited. Astra was talking with King Linus, no gestures or facial expressions of any kind, just quiet conversation. They could have been talking about anything. As soon as she was done, they could go. Dion's gaze drifted to where King Tuyon was dancing with Princess Beatrix, all of Astra's hard work playing out in front of everyone.

'We're all animals,' Pandarus continued, as if they were having a conversation. 'Men love the chase. I do. Even now, having had her more times than I can remember.'

Dion forced his hands to relax, afraid of what two readied fists might lead to.

'And we all have a price.' Pandarus wore a cocky smile. 'I know Astra's, but tell me, Captain, what was your price for betraying your king?'

Dion looked around before meeting his gaze. 'I think you should lay off the wine, Your Majesty.'

Light danced in Pandarus's eyes. 'I hear you are an excellent archer.'

If he was fishing for confirmation, he would not get it from Dion. 'Good fighting skills are a basic requirement of any soldier—and man, for that matter,' he added, knowing he was playing with fire but unable to help himself.

Before Pandarus could reply, Elenor appeared in front of them, lowering into a curtsy before the king.

'Your Majesty,' she said as she rose. 'Forgive the interruption. I wanted to check on Captain Dion here. He has a rather nasty sparring injury.' She turned her attention to Dion. 'Has it stopped bleeding?'

Talk about bad timing. Dion was careful not to react in a way that would make the king more suspicious than he already was. 'I'm fine. It's just a scratch.'

Pandarus looked between them, and Dion could practically hear the wheels turning in his head.

'You cut yourself with a wooden sword, Captain?'

'No, Your Majesty. We were foolish enough to use sharp weapons.'

Elenor tutted. 'I saw the stitches. You could have lost your arm.'

Dion really wished she would stop talking.

'Sounds like a rather serious sparring match,' Pandarus said, his eyes never leaving Dion.

Dion looked in Astra's direction and found her making her way towards them. He was hoping to avoid letting her anywhere near Pandarus, but he knew rushing off in the middle of that particular conversation would do him no favours. He watched her approach, her expression pleasant and seemingly unfazed by the company he was keeping.

'Your Majesty,' Astra said when she reached them. She curtsied before Pandarus, then threaded her arm through Dion's. 'I am ready to leave.' She glanced at Elenor. 'Only if you are finished here, of course.'

'I'm done.' He placed a hand over hers and gave a small bow to the king. 'Please excuse us, Your Majesty.' He looked to Elenor as he rose. 'Have a pleasant evening.'

A bitter smile was frozen on Elenor's face. 'Of course.'

They left the hall with everyone watching them until they were out of sight. Neither of them spoke during the walk. When they reached the steps, Dion gestured for Astra to go ahead of him. She gathered the skirt of her dress and began climbing. He watched her back, the way her shoulder blades shifted with each stride, the way her spine moved. He could not look away, and that was how he knew he was in trouble. He was no better than all the other men leering at her that evening. Once she was safely in her bedchamber, he would return to his own room and shout into a pillow until he felt some relief.

'Wait here,' he said when they reached her door. He stepped inside, walking a lap of the room, checking under furniture and behind drapes.

She laughed from the doorway. 'Who exactly are you expecting to find hiding under my bed?'

He tried not to look at her tempting smile. 'One of your many admirers. Seems they all remained at the feast this time.'

'Good to know.'

All that was left to do was walk past her and leave. 'Do not open your door to anyone,' he said when he reached her. 'Your king is drunk enough to show up in the middle of the night.'

'I am not allowed to open my door to my own king?'

His eyes grazed over her. 'You can let him in when he's sober.' The words tasted bitter in his mouth. 'I'd prefer not to sleep at your door like a dog.'

'I can handle Pandarus,' she assured him. 'I am a highly trained Companion, remember?'

Dion rested a hand on the hilt of his sword. 'I too am highly trained. I'd prefer not to have to use that training, if it's all the same to you.'

Astra made no move to go inside.

That was his cue to leave. Any further delays and he would be tempted to take hold of her face again, push her up against the door frame and consume that perfect mouth while her hands explored his chest. 'Goodnight, Astra.'

'Goodnight, Captain.'

Somehow he managed it. With his body screaming in protest, he turned away from her. He listened for the sound of her door closing behind him. It took a while, but he heard it eventually. He glanced over his shoulder to make sure she had gone inside.

When he arrived at his bedchamber, he pushed the door open with far more force than was necessary and closed it with the same level of enthusiasm. Drawing a breath, he looked around the room, which felt an awful lot like a cage in that moment. He needed some air, a walk, a run, a sparring partner willing to get hurt. He needed a way to clear her from his mind. Hard to do when his clothes smelled of her. He unbuttoned his tunic and tossed it in the corner, then brought the front of his shirt up to his nose, smelling it. He was thoroughly contaminated. Tugging his shirt over his head, he tossed that in the corner also, then paced the room for half an hour before he finally collapsed face down on the bed.

It was going to be a long night.

A soft knock made him look up. He stared at the door for a moment, knowing it was her. Yet he did not move. Why? Because he knew what would happen once he opened it. She would own him.

Another knock, louder this time.

'Dion?'

Astra's voice seeped through the gaps around the door. She had said his name. Not 'Captain,' his name.

He pushed off the bed and walked over to it. Taking hold of the handle, he drew a breath before tugging it open. He leaned on the edge of the door, hopefully looking more relaxed than he felt. Astra's face was scrubbed clean, her hair plaited to one side. She wore a dress he had never seen before; blue cotton with lace—an entire dress. She looked just as beautiful as she had an hour ago. No, more so, because all of her lovely freckles were on display. He tried to calculate how long it would take him to kiss each one, but his mind was not up to simple math. 'What's wrong?'

She looked at his bare chest, then everywhere but at him. 'Do you believe what Pandarus told you about me?'

'What?'

'The day you had me freed.'

He could see she was nervous. 'No.'

She looked up at him then. 'Why not?'

'Because he doesn't know you like I do.'

She searched his face. 'Can I come in?'

He did not step aside. 'I told you, I'm not interested in a Companion.'

'I know. I am not here as a Companion, I am here as me.'

She was completely vulnerable in that moment, exposed to rejection. He knew that was not an easy position for her. 'Are you sure about this?'

She shook her head. 'Not at all.'

The only thing left to do was step aside and let her feast on his remains. Blood pulsed in his ears as she passed, then turned and waited for him to close the door. She was not hiding behind a stoic expression or layers of carefully applied paint. Her hands hung at her sides instead of neatly folded. She had come to him raw, offering up something real.

'I don't even know where to begin with you,' he said, still drinking in the sight of her.

She stepped up to him, face turned up and eyes searching his. 'Touch me like you did before.'

He ran his fingers along the lace of her dress. Her breath changed immediately, and his eyes travelled up to watch her face.

'Keep going,' she breathed.

He removed the ribbon from the end of her hair, undoing the plait with his fingers. 'You're so beautiful.' His feet shifted closer, his hands going into her hair. He kissed her softly, not trusting himself yet. 'Beautiful inside and out.'

'How can you tell what is inside?' she whispered into his mouth. 'Maybe I am hollow.'

He pulled back, his thumbs brushing her jaw. 'You're not hollow.'

She pushed herself up onto her toes, taking his mouth again. There was that hunger, that rush, that pleasure that made him forget everything else. A shudder ran through her, or maybe through him. Hard to tell in the moment. All he knew for sure was that she needed his legs to stand, and he needed her mouth to breathe. Without her, he would slowly suffocate. Perhaps her heart would beat for both of them.

Astra's head tipped back, and his mouth found her neck, their bodies speaking another language. She sucked in a breath and he stopped, needing to see the pleasure on her face. Her head rolled forwards, her lips parted and her expression pleading.

'Don't stop again.'

He nodded, understanding, and watched her head tip back once more.

CHAPTER 32

*P*anic hit Astra like a charging ox when she woke beneath the weight of an arm. She looked down at it, following it all the way up to its owner, then relaxed. Not Pandarus. Not King Tuyon.

Dion.

Her mouth stretched into a smile as she took in his squashed face, his soft snores filling the room. She rolled onto her side to face him. The snores stopped, he drew her closer, and then the snores resumed. Her body was loose, numb. She flexed her toes, feeling smug and utterly satisfied. The night replayed in her mind, and her ears burned at the memories.

She had thought herself a long way from *firsts*—but she had been wrong.

It was not that lying with Pandarus had never felt good. At the start it had, but never *that* good. She had never built, exploded, and melted in that way. No man had ever pushed her beyond a pleasant sensation. Dion had made it his priority, proving she was not broken as she had once thought. She was not naive. She had always known there was more; she had just never known there was more for *her*.

Lucky, lucky her.

Dion's arm twitched, making her smile again. She committed his face to memory. Every hard line of his jaw, his straight nose, his messy eyebrows pointing in all directions, his hair that stuck up on one side. She resisted the urge to smooth it down, not giving in to perfection. She preferred him dishevelled, because it was further proof that last night had indeed happened. Her gaze travelled down to his parted lips, his stubble that had appeared overnight, down the curve of his thick neck—the one she had held on to. She peered into the dark shadows of his chest and torso, remembering the feel of his body. She was used to Pandarus's physique, which had always been lean but not *strong*.

Footsteps passed the door, making her hold her breath. Real life awaited them on the other side. They could only hide away in his bedchamber for so long. She shut her eyes tightly, not wanting to think beyond that moment. She had no idea what she was supposed to do. What would Dion expect her to do? When she opened her eyes again, she found him watching her. She felt nervous, terrified, happy, like she was seeing in colour after years of black and white.

'How do you look this good first thing in the morning?' he asked, his voice thick with sleep.

'I was just thinking the same thing about you.'

A playful smile came and went on his face. 'What a glorious mess we've gotten ourselves into.'

She wriggled closer, dragging the sheet with her, not ready to surrender to reality.

'Don't do that.' He tugged the sheet down. 'Let me enjoy you a while longer.'

She pressed her lips together to stop from smiling. 'You don't think we have enjoyed ourselves enough?'

'No.' He reached up, taking a gentle hold of her chin. 'I'm done for, aren't I?'

'Yes, your soul is mine.'

He laughed, his hand going to rest on her hip. 'A strangely erotic thought.'

'We need to talk about something serious.'

He propped himself up on one elbow. 'I'm listening.'

She drew a breath before beginning. 'I think Pandarus knows about your excursion north.'

'Oh, that.'

'And King Tuyon knows that Galen men were involved in the rescue of those children.'

'So?'

She took hold of his face. 'So that means two kings have theories.'

Dion placed a hand over hers. 'What they don't have is proof. Pandarus was just mouthing off.'

He bent and kissed her, and she savoured the feel of his warm lips.

'Please don't worry,' he said. 'King Linus isn't going to act without proof.'

She released his face. 'They will not find any proof, will they?'

He shook his head. 'No.'

She stared up at him. 'Tuyon seems to think Brom may one day be king. Is that what you think?'

Dion lay beside her again, drawing her close. 'I think eventually he'll have no choice because Jayr will self-destruct.' He kissed her forehead. 'Stop worrying about things that haven't happened yet.'

'I have been trained to think many steps ahead.'

'Well, un-train yourself. We have more important things to talk about.'

She searched his face. 'Such as?'

'Such as what we're going to do now that our souls are bound together for life.'

She suppressed a smile, ignoring the flutter of excitement inside her. For the first time in her life, she was an equal participant in bed—and it felt good. 'I made no such commitment.'

'Not verbally.'

'I told you last night I do not have all the answers.'

'And I told you a few days ago that once I started kissing you, I wouldn't stop.' His lust-filled gaze fell to her lips.

She sighed. 'I can barely think past last night.'

'I have an idea how to bring your focus to the present.' His hand travelled along her thigh.

Astra could not stop the smile. 'Aren't you… tired?'

'No.' He kissed her.

She was surprised at how familiar his mouth felt already. She closed her eyes, telling herself not to think.

'I can't watch you with that man,' Dion murmured into her mouth. 'Just the thought of his hands on you makes me crazy.'

The thought of Pandarus's hands made her feel sick. 'I believe that ship has sailed. I am not expecting an invitation to Archdale any time soon. Last night did not exactly go to plan.'

He pulled back, looking at her. 'Your plan to dress up, play your harp, and flirt with every man but him until he was driven mad by the sight of you?'

She gave him a disapproving look. 'That is a rather simplistic view. The aim was to remind him of why I am the best choice for mentor.'

'He doesn't want you as a mentor. He wants you in his bed.'

She regarded him for a moment. 'Right now he does not

want me at all. I believe my plan turned to dust the moment I left that room on your arm.'

Footsteps made them both look in the direction of the door, but they continued past. Dion turned to look at her.

'Let's go home.' His tone was gentle.

'Home.' She repeated the word, testing it out. Goldmont House was the closest thing she had to a home. 'I worry you are expecting too much from me. I did not change overnight, Captain.'

'We're back to "Captain" now?'

She exhaled. 'If I stay, I will be relying on your fleeting generosity and affection.'

'Why do you assume they're fleeting?'

She gave a knowing look. 'Experience.'

'I'm not Pandarus.'

'I know that.' She pressed a palm to his chest. 'I was only supposed to stay at Goldmont until I found my feet, remember?'

'Last time I checked, there was only one mentor role available. You need a new plan.'

She covered herself with the sheet. 'I am not going to fight with you naked.'

He tugged the sheet down again. 'This is the only way I'm prepared to fight with you.' He grinned at her. 'Sorry, but there's no running from me now. I did warn you.'

'Well, you are in luck, because I have nowhere to run *to*.'

He squeezed her leg. 'It's settled, then. We return to Goldmont, go straight to my bedchamber, and remain there naked for the rest of our lives.'

She laughed and rolled to the edge of the bed, snatching up her underthings. 'That is your big plan?'

'If I had said get married and have eight children, I fear you would've fled.'

She glanced over her shoulder at him while she dressed. 'I

will come to Goldmont for now, because Sapphira needs me, and the children need me—'

'Are we going to pretend last night and this morning never happened?'

'Nothing did happen this morning.'

'Stop putting clothes on, then.'

She smiled to herself. 'I acknowledge last night happened because I suggested it, remember?'

He fell back on the bed, watching her. 'I feel a "but" coming.'

'But there are lots of things to consider. If we continue like this, that will make me what? Your mistress? Do you see the irony?'

'So marry me, then.'

She rolled her eyes. 'Charming offer, but we both know I am not housewife material.'

'Says the woman with twenty-two children.'

She could not stop the laughter that time.

'You need time to come around to the idea,' he said seriously. 'I understand that.'

She turned to face him. 'And you do not? Captain "I would never be so foolish as to fall for a Companion" is suddenly all-in?'

He shrugged. 'I knew what I was in for when you pushed your way through that door.'

'Pushed?'

He winked at her. 'I'm a patient man. I can wait.'

'Mmm.' She stood, her dress in hand. 'All right. Let us go to Goldmont before Pandarus comes looking for me.'

His expression was serious again. 'I meant what I said. I don't want his hands on you.'

'And I told you that ship has sailed.'

He did not look convinced. 'What if he did show up? Asked you to return to Archdale as his Companion?'

She drew a breath. 'I would tell him no. I am not interested in being his Companion.'

Again, he appeared sceptical. 'You'd really tell him no?'

She got back onto the bed and crawled to him. 'Do you really think I could bear to share his bed after *last night*?'

His warm arms went around her. 'Are you saying I've ruined other men for you?' He looked pleased by the thought.

'No, I am saying you have woken my appetite for better lovers.'

He dug his fingers into her ribs, tickling her. 'Take that back and I'll stop.'

She jumped in surprise. She had not been tickled since she was a child. 'No.'

He pinned her to his chest and tickled her harder. Her head tipped back, and a squeal of laughter came out.

'Say it.' He was grinning. 'I've ruined other men for you.'

She squirmed against his chest. 'All right.'

'All right, what?'

'You have ruined other men for me.'

He stopped tickling and brought his mouth to hers, capturing her dying laughter.

CHAPTER 33

*D*ion had lost the fight, and he had never been happier about anything in his life. It was not like she broke through his walls but that he had picked up the largest hammer he could find and smashed through them of his own accord. There was no turning back as far as he was concerned. He did not need any time to think about what was next. She was next, in whatever way she would have him. He was offering up all the tiny pieces of himself she had been chipping away at since their first meeting at Archdale. Perhaps that was when he lost the fight.

Now he stood outside of her bedchamber at Reave Castle, waiting for her to gather her things. He watched the corridor, one foot tapping madly, expecting Pandarus to show up and ruin everything. The door swung open, and Astra stepped outside carrying her bag. She was wearing one of the dresses Isolda had made for her, hair piled on top of her head and lips unpainted. He was looking forward to a time when he would not come apart every time he caught sight of her.

She offered a smile. 'Ready.'

He took her bag and gestured for her to go ahead, eyes

moving both ways down the corridor as they headed for the stairs. At one point the toe of his boot clipped the back of hers. She glanced over her shoulder at him.

'Why do I feel as though I have another shadow? I am not going to run off, you know.'

He increased the distance between them, not wanting to scare her away before they had even reached Goldmont House.

'Pandarus has not even emerged from his chambers yet, if that is what you are worried about,' she said.

'How do you know that?'

She slowed to walk beside him. 'I asked the maid.'

He kept a lookout anyway, ready in case the king lurched from a dark nook and tried to drag her back to Syrasan.

On their way out, they ran into Stamitos on the front steps. He informed them that Pandarus had gone a little hard on the wine the night before, then took a letter from his pocket and asked if they could pass it on to Sapphira. Stamitos was expected to remain at the castle with Pandarus and sail with him to Veanor at the end of the week.

'Of course,' Dion said, tucking it into his pocket.

Stamitos looked between the two of them for a moment.

'Did something happen last night?'

Astra feigned surprise at the question. 'Why do you ask?'

'Because you are both acting weird. Very... civil.'

Dion spoke up. 'You've spent too much time with your brother. Your sense of normal is warped.'

A smile spread across Stamitos's face. 'Oh, I see now. All good. Off you go. As you were. Pretend I know nothing.'

Astra walked off, head shaking.

Dion clipped the prince's shoulder as he passed. 'Very smooth,' he whispered before following after her. He heard Stamitos laugh behind them.

~

They were welcomed at Goldmont by a visibly relieved Sapphira and Helena.

'Thank God,' Sapphira said, walking down the steps towards them. 'When I received your letter, I almost fell over. Please tell me Pandarus is on his way back to Syrasan.' She looked past them. 'No Stamitos?'

Astra hugged the princess while Dion retrieved the letter for her. 'Pandarus leaves at the end of the week. I am afraid Stamitos will be accompanying him.'

Sapphira took the letter and ran her finger over her name written in his hand. 'Of course.' Her eyes retuned to Astra, taking in her appearance. 'Did you leave the castle wearing that?'

Astra looked down. 'Yes.'

Sapphira pulled a face at Dion that apparently he understood, because he smiled. 'You just look so...'

'So what?'

'Relaxed. No. Too much. Less uptight?'

Astra frowned. 'What a terrible compliment.'

'It wasn't a compliment. It was a comment.'

Astra glanced at a grinning Dion. 'Well, you look exactly the same.' She gestured at Sapphira's bare feet.

'I like to be consistent.'

Dion cleared his throat and turned his attention to Helena.

'How did it all go?' Sapphira whispered to Astra while he was distracted.

'Fine.'

Sapphira's eyebrows rose. 'Fine? You were taken by the king's guards, brought before the Galen king, asked to play matchmaker with his daughter, get information out of King Tuyon, whom most sensible people steer well clear of, all while trying to sell your skills as a mentor to King Pandarus, and all I get is *fine?*'

Astra lifted her shoulders. 'Well, I am here, so it seems my mentor skills were not too impressive.'

Dion must have been listening after all, because he spoke up at that. 'Pandarus was too drunk to notice much outside Astra's more *tangible* attributes.'

Sapphira pressed her lips together to stop from smiling. 'I see. I must say, I'm surprised he just let you leave.'

'It's not his decision,' Dion replied. 'She doesn't belong to him.'

Sapphira breathed out a laugh. 'Since when has that stopped him from getting what he wants?'

'I'm going to get cleaned up,' Dion said, throwing an arm around his sister.

Astra exhaled. 'Dion—'

'I'll see you at dinner,' he said before walking off.

Helena gave Astra a warm smile as she passed, which she returned. Sapphira waited for Astra to look back at her.

'What?' Astra asked upon seeing her expression.

'Did something happen between you and the captain?'

'Why do you ask that?' Her gaze drifted to him.

'Because you called him *Dion.*'

Astra knew there was no point in lying. 'Yes, actually.'

Sapphira leaned in conspiratorially. 'Do tell.'

'You are not mad at me?'

'You left Pandarus at Reave Castle and returned to Goldmont with our favourite Galen captain. How can I be mad at you?'

Astra watched him disappear through the door. 'I think Pandarus knows about Dion's trip to Zoelin.'

Sapphira's happy expression collapsed. 'Normally I would chastise you for changing the subject, but I'll allow it in this instance. What did Pandarus say exactly?'

'You know him, it was all very cryptic.'

Sapphira nodded. 'He likes to play games.'

Astra looked around before continuing. 'The thing is, it is not just Pandarus. King Tuyon said some things as well about Galen's involvement with the rebels.'

'It's recent news. Everyone's talking. Everyone's got a theory. What they don't have is proof. King Linus is not going to act on rumour, not after what happened to Dion's father.'

'That is what Dion said.' Astra thought for a moment. 'You make it sound like his father was executed on a whim.'

'Might as well have been. King Jayr wanted him dealt with, and the old king eventually obliged. The backlash was enormous. I've no doubt that is what finally killed him in the end.' She paused. 'So how did you leave things with Pandarus?'

Astra shook her head, wishing she could erase that part of the evening from her mind. 'It was a disaster. He was drunk—'

'There's something new.'

'We got into a fight. Then Dion showed up—'

'Always the hero.'

Astra let out a breath. 'The thing is, it was the only plan I had.'

'Well, I'm glad it didn't work out. It was a foolish plan.'

Astra pressed her lips together. 'I would have made a good mentor.'

'I know that, but it wasn't to be.'

'I lost control.' She hesitated before adding, 'I pushed Pandarus.'

Sapphira looked almost proud. 'About time.'

'I pushed a *king*.'

'A king who's had it coming for years.'

Astra released a breath. 'I failed, and I never fail at anything.'

'Returning here isn't failure, it's fate. Enjoy your freedom from Pandarus. Though it sounds like you have enjoyed it already.'

Astra felt her cheeks heat.

'Are you blushing? Companions don't blush. It's Fedora law.'

Astra waved her off and turned for the house. 'Walking away now.'

Sapphira's laughter followed her. 'Did you ever think that one day we would live under the same roof and not hate each other?'

'It is temporary,' Astra called over her shoulder.

'Admit it,' Sapphira shouted. 'You *like* me now.'

Astra shook her head, biting back a smile. 'Go put some shoes on.'

CHAPTER 34

*D*ion might have agreed to give her time, but what he did not give her was space. For the next four days, he travelled to Swanton Fort at first light. He took care of business as usual, and then he would return home to her every night. While he usually missed dinner, he always tried to make it home for her nightly walk down to the chicken palace. They would stroll side by side, sharing stories from their day. She would tell him funny things the children had said and done, and he would laugh. She got a strange thrill from making him laugh. It was a sound she had grown to love, a noise so contagious that she could not help but join in.

On day five of their new routine, Astra wandered to the front window to see if Dion had arrived home yet. He was not there, but she knew that even if he missed the walk, he would be home in time for the knock on his door later in the evening. Astra wandered down to the chickens on her own, checking that the hens had settled for the night before securing the gate. After an exhausting day, including caring for five sick children, she did not feel ready to return indoors. The still air and quiet anchored her. She stood hugging herself, watching the sun sink behind the Bolltree Hills. She felt a rare moment of contentment that almost fooled her into thinking it could last. Perhaps she was just a deluded peasant who had aimed too high. Perhaps Dion was telling the truth. Maybe he would not tire of her, and their life together would be enough for both of them.

The sound of a chicken pulled her from her thoughts. She looked around, because it had not come from the palace ten feet behind her but close by. It was not uncommon for a stray to be discovered after lock-up.

Another cluck.

Astra turned in circles, searching. 'Where are you?'

The hen spoke, as though answering the question. Perhaps she was going mad, but she could have sworn it sounded like Primrose.

'Primrose?'

And there it was again, her pretty little cluck, coming from… where? Astra ran to the maple tree, looking up at the branches. 'Primrose?'

Another cluck.

Astra gasped when she spotted the hen at the top of the maple tree. It was unmistakably her with her trademark freckles and black-and-white tail feathers. A smile spread across Astra's face. 'There you are, my clever girl. Where on earth have you been hiding? I thought you dead.' She reached her hands up, gesturing towards herself. 'Come on. If you got up there, you can get down.'

The hen watched Astra from her perch.

'Please tell me you can get down.' Astra looked around, sighing. She could get Hann, but he was too old to be climbing trees. She stepped up to the trunk, touching the lowest branch, which sat at chest height. Her eyes travelled up the long trunk. She had climbed trees as a child. Letting out an exasperated sigh, she kicked off her shoes, fearing she would tear the silk covering on the bark. 'All right, I am coming up, but I want it known that I am not happy about the fact.'

Gripping the branch, she began walking her feet up the trunk, but the skirt of her dress restricted her legs. She stopped and hitched it up, tucking the hem into her undergarments, and tried again. When she finally sat crouched atop the branch, she peered in the direction of the house to ensure no one was looking. She would be absolutely mortified if Sapphira saw her in such a compromising position. The teasing would be relentless.

Satisfied she did not have an audience, she continued up, surprised at her agility given she was by no means athletic. She went higher and higher, until she was just a few branches below Primrose. 'All right. That is absolutely as far as I am coming. I am not falling to my death for you.'

The chicken's head twitched from side to side, watching her with interest.

Astra reached up, rubbing her fingers together, encouraging the hen closer. Thankfully, Primrose obliged, walking along the thin branch until she was within reach. Astra rested her hip against the trunk of the tree and took a firm grip of the bird, pulling Primrose to her chest. Breathing a sigh of relief and very determined not to cry, she buried her face in the hen's back.

'This does not mean you are forgiven,' she whispered into the feathers. Primrose nuzzled her hair, clucking so softly it sounded like a purr. 'All right, let us not make a fuss. You are all right now, and I have you.' Holding the hen tightly, Astra looked warily down at the ground.

And there stood Dion.

~

What in God's name is she doing? She was at least forty feet up, her dress bunched at her hips and feet bare.

'Ah... I found Primrose,' she called down to him.

He tried really hard not to smile. 'I see that.'

She cleared her throat. 'She was stuck.'

'Was she?' He could not stop the smile this time.

Astra glared at him. 'I needed to get her before the wolves did.'

She looked absolutely adorable in the fading light with a twig poking from her hair. 'And what's your plan now?'

She held Primrose a little tighter. 'To descend in a calm and logical manner?'

He nodded. 'Is this a skill Fedora taught you?' He really needed to stop smiling.

'I am about to start throwing things at you.'

'Start with the hen. She can fly, you know.'

Astra drew Primrose even closer.

Shaking his head, Dion began to climb the tree. 'Stay where you are.' He could feel her eyes on him as he climbed. She did not object, saying nothing until he reached her, one hand resting lazily on the branch above them.

'I will admit,' she said, 'you did that far more gracefully than I did.'

He chuckled and brushed his thumb over her cheek. 'Next time wait for me. You don't have to fight off wolves and rescue chickens alone anymore.' He leaned forwards and kissed her. 'Give her to me.' He took the hen from her, ensuring her wings were trapped. 'I'll help you down.'

'I got up without your supervision.'

He kissed that smart mouth of hers again. 'Well, I feel better helping you on the way down.'

Instead of climbing, she rested her head against the trunk,

watching him. 'I watched the sun set before. It never fails to impress.'

Dion kept a hold of the branch above. 'You should see the view from Swanton Fort. It's something else. I'll take you there one day.'

Her expression did not change. 'You are impairing my ability to form a sensible plan, Captain. You, this house, those children and their infectious laughter.' She looked west. 'These Galen sunsets.'

He shrugged. 'Your plan may be disrupted, but mine is going perfectly.' He grinned at her. 'All ploys to keep you here.'

'Do you consider yourself a large part of that ploy?'

'Why do you ask?'

'Because you did some rather unspeakable things to me last night, which has me very suspicious.'

'I wouldn't dare presume.'

Primrose struggled against his grip for a moment, then went still again.

Astra watched the hen. 'I fail to see how it would all work.'

'It's working well as it is.'

'As a scandalous affair?' She looked up at him again. 'I am certain Eda has said something to Hann, because he can barely raise his eyes to me.'

'Perhaps he heard you last night.' He saw colour rise in her cheeks, enjoying that he could make her blush after years of being conditioned against it. He bent to kiss her again, the action gentle. Neither of them moved, breathing against each other. 'I want you to stay, not just for me but for yourself.'

She brought a hand to his cheek. 'I keep trying to be logical, but I cannot think past you. I am going in circles.'

'I can live with circles if they come back to me.' He brushed his nose along hers.

She let go of his face, leaning her head against the trunk again. 'Do you really think you could be happy with me?'

'You already make me happy. I run my horse into the ground every night just to get a few extra minutes with you, even if it's to stand across from you in the kitchen while you help Eda.'

Her lips twitched. 'You mean when you loiter in the kitchen undressing me with your eyes?'

'It's that obvious?'

She nodded.

Of course he had to kiss her again. What other option was there? 'There's something erotic about watching you do chores badly.'

'Badly?'

He leaned away. 'Haven't you noticed that Eda rewashes some things?'

'Oh.' Astra thought for a moment. 'Well, there you go. More evidence that I am no good at playing wife.'

'You don't have to play anything anymore. Just stay and be happy.'

'As your mistress?'

'Mistress, wife, lover, distant cousin I took in. I don't care, just stay.'

She exhaled, her face serious again.

'What are you overthinking now?' he asked.

She hesitated before answering. 'Do you know what people would say behind your back? What they probably already say?'

'You should know me well enough by now to realise I don't care.' He leaned forwards to kiss her a final time. 'And please don't run away because I said *wife*.'

She exhaled. 'I have nowhere to run to, remember?'

'Then the odds are in my favour.' He was silent a moment, the only sound the incessant chirping of insects. 'I'm going to get you out of this tree, and I'm going to take you inside and give you another reason not to leave.'

'That is the extent of your plan?'

He thought for a moment. 'And get some more chickens, perhaps.'

'Masterful.' She smiled. 'After you, Captain.'

CHAPTER 35

During breakfast the next day, the children asked if they could take their lessons outside. Astra agreed, inviting Sapphira to join them for the company and fresh air. The women split the children into two groups, setting a task for the older ones before sitting with the younger children. Prince Malin lay on a blanket beside his mother, little arms flailing. Everyone had removed their shoes, and for once, Astra did not object. When the prince began to grizzle, Astra picked him up to give Sapphira a break, pacing the length of the blankets where the children were sprawled. Sapphira let her daughters climb on her lap so they could enjoy the novelty of their mother's undivided attention.

Astra kept an eye on the sun, partly to ensure the children finished at an appropriate time but also as a means of counting down the hours until she would see Dion again. She was just about to end the lesson when she heard the dogs bark out front. Moments later, Stamitos strode across the lawn towards them. Sapphira jumped up and ran to him. The second the young princesses spotted their father, they squealed and ran after their mother. Astra stopped to watch the reunion.

'Look at your crazy little family,' she whispered to the baby in her arms. 'Syrasan is counting on you to be the one who wears shoes.' He was sound asleep with no idea what she was saying.

When Astra looked back in their direction, she found Stamitos and Sapphira staring at her with matching worried expressions. *Now what?* 'All right. Time for lunch,' she said to the children. 'I want everything packed up. Helena, could you supervise the younger ones, please?'

'Yes, my lady.'

Astra smiled at her as she stepped past to help the others, then made her way up the lawn, a bad feeling enveloping her. *Please do not let it be Dion.*

When she reached them, she handed the baby to Sapphira. 'My lord.'

Stamitos nodded a greeting. 'King Pandarus is here. He wants to speak with you.'

'I can tell him you're ill,' Sapphira said immediately. 'Contagious.'

Astra drew a long breath, knowing there was no point in delaying the inevitable. 'It is all right. Where is he? Inside?'

Stamitos shook his head. 'He is waiting out front.'

She looked down at her dress, wondering if she should change.

'Don't you dare,' Sapphira said, reading her mind. She handed the baby to Stamitos. 'Want me to come with you?'

Astra shook her head. 'It is all right. Excuse me.'

'There's a reason I had my children here in Galen,' Sapphira called to her back. 'That place is toxic.'

Astra would hear Pandarus out, tell him she had no interest in being his Companion, and then he would be on his way before Dion arrived home and all hell broke loose. She did not change her dress, walking straight through the house, ignoring Eda's pity-filled face as she passed her in the entranceway.

Out front, Astra looked around for Pandarus, spotting him over at the small training yard the children used for archery practise. He was standing by the target holding an arrow. She walked over to him. Before her departure from Archdale, he had barely raised his eyes when she entered the room; now he was watching her carefully. She held his gaze, lowering into a curtsy when she reached him. 'Your Majesty.'

He looked around. 'So this is Goldmont House. Not much to look at.'

She looked around also. 'I think it is charming.'

He scrunched up his nose before looking at her again. 'Good to see you well. You fled Reave Castle so fast after the feast I feared something was wrong.'

She forced a smile. 'I was ready to go home.'

'Home? That is an interesting word choice.'

'Well, I live here.'

He looked down at her dress. 'I feel I am partly to blame for all this.'

Her eyebrows rose. 'Only partly?'

He laughed off the comment and took a step towards her. 'I am returning to Syrasan tomorrow. Ship sails late afternoon.'

She nodded. 'I pray you have better weather than we did on our journey here.'

'Stamitos told me about that. I am glad he was there to take care of you.'

'Actually, Captain Dion took care of me.'

He regarded her for a moment. 'He paints himself as quite the hero, does he not?'

She watched him coolly. 'I know him to be a rather modest man.'

'Of course you do.' His tone was patronising.

She drew a breath before speaking again. 'What is it you wanted to see me about, Your Majesty?'

He sniffed and considered his words. 'I wanted to apologise. My behaviour the other night was… well, I must blame the wine.'

There was the Pandarus she recognised, the one who was never responsible for anything. It was the wine's fault. 'You travelled a long way to apologise.'

His eyes never left her. 'I also wanted to invite you to return to Archdale Castle with me. Let me make amends.'

She could have predicted the script. 'I am so sorry that you travelled all this way—'

'As mentor,' he finished.

She had not predicted that part. She waited for her body to respond to his words. *Mentor.* Where was that fire that usually ignited in her belly when she pictured herself in the role? Nothing.

'What about Fedora?'

His liquid eyes remained on her. He was a handsome man, but she felt nothing when he looked at her that way. 'There can only be one mentor. I have already sent word to Archdale that you will be replacing her.'

How long had she waited to hear those words? 'And where will Fedora go?'

He was taken aback by her response. He did not have an answer, had clearly not given any thought to the woman who had served so loyally in his household for years. 'She will not just be thrown through the gate if that is what you are worried about.'

She continued to watch him. 'I am sure you can understand my concern, as if I were to accept, I would one day find myself in the same position.'

He gave her a patronising smile. 'Ah, already thinking to the future like a mentor.'

'I am wondering how far into the future that will be. Ten years from now? Ten days?'

His smile faltered. 'Ten days? Really, Astra.'

She was oddly angry given what he was offering. 'You will have to forgive my scepticism, but history has shown me that your wishes can change rather suddenly.'

He wet his lips and looked in the direction of the stables. 'I was expecting you to show a little more gratitude. This is what you want, after all.'

Was it? The fact that she was attacking him instead of falling at his feet suggested otherwise. 'I do not trust you.' The words just spilled out of her, and she could not take them back.

He stared at her with genuine surprise, then down at the arrow in his hand. 'Do you know what distinguishes these arrows from other weapons?'

She was thrown by the sudden change in topic. Perhaps that was his intention. She glanced down at the arrow Dion had brought from Swanton Fort, knowing the children would enjoy using weapons made exclusively for the king's army. 'No.'

He turned it in his hand. 'It has a three-inch steel head, goose feather fletching, and an extra inch of cedar wood. Most arrows are made from pine, but King Linus wants the best for his army.' He lowered the weapon. 'You have changed.'

'I have grown up.'

He nodded, slowly. 'You want more. You have always wanted more. I used to admire that about you.'

She swallowed. 'It is not about more. It is about protecting myself.'

He looked around again. 'What would you say to a legally binding agreement?'

She blinked, careful to keep her face neutral. 'What sort of agreement?'

'One that protected you, that ensured you remained at Archdale for an agreed period of time.'

Such a thing had never existed before. The king was under no obligation to keep women in any position. 'And what would happen at the end of my service?'

His eyes returned to her. He seemed to be enjoying the power play. So predictable.

'And still you want more. What will be enough?'

Astra's heart was racing. 'I want a house.'

His head tipped back with laughter. 'A house, she says.'

She was not laughing. 'Not just for me, for retired mentors and Companions should they need it.'

He looked at her like she was crazy. 'They are called brothels.'

She looked away at that. Better not to let him see the disgust in her eyes. She spotted Primrose coming towards them and willed the hen to stay back.

'Oh, do not be like that. It was just a joke.' He took both her hands in his. When he did, Primrose came right up to him, wings flapping wildly. He shoved her away with his boot. 'You cannot be serious about the house.' Primrose came at him again, and he laid the toe of his boot into her this time. 'What is wrong with this chicken?'

Astra pulled her hands free and went to stand in front of the hen. 'I thank you for bringing me your offer, Your Majesty, and wish you a safe journey back to Syrasan.'

He frowned at her. 'You were serious about the house?' He took in her unflinching expression. 'And if I agree to this *house*, you will return to Archdale with me?'

Her hands were sweating, her mouth dry. 'I would need to see the agreement first.'

Primrose made a move to go around her, and she blocked the hen with her foot. Pandarus continued to look at her while he thought. Stepping forwards, he brushed his lips over her cheek. The scented oil he had used that morning burned the small hairs inside her nose. She fought the urge to cough while imagining Dion arriving home to see Pandarus's lips on her. Guilt pounded her chest.

'I will have the agreement written up this afternoon.' He spoke the words into her ear before straightening.

She panicked then. What had she done? Had she agreed to leave? No, she had agreed to view his written offer, an offer that might never eventuate once he came to his senses. But if he did send it, she would be forced to make a decision. And tell Dion. And he would... what? Shout? Break things? Fall on his knees and beg her not to leave? Shrug and tell her to pack her things? Tell her he was right about her all along?

'Let Stamitos know I am ready to leave,' Pandarus said, stepping back.

Astra nodded, curtsied, and left with her heart pounding in her ears. 'Good day, Your Majesty.' Primrose ran alongside her, loyal to the end. When she reached the front door, she bent, picked up the hen, and carried her inside the house.

CHAPTER 36

*D*ion knew something was wrong the moment he entered the house. It was in the eerie silence and Eda's inability to meet his gaze when she came out to greet him.

'Everything all right here?'

Eda nodded, still not looking at him. 'Astra's out back.'

Her tone had his feet moving. He exited the house and strode across the lawn in the direction of the chicken palace, spotting Astra in her usual place, facing west, lit up by the orange glow of the setting sun. At least she was on the ground, with no sign of wolves. He could see Primrose walking the boundary of the enclosure.

His eyes returned to Astra. She was hugging herself far too tightly given how warm the evening was. A bad feeling settled in his gut.

'I've never returned to such a morbid house,' he called, making her jump. 'Sorry. Thought you heard me coming.'

She smiled weakly. 'These Galen sunsets.'

He walked right up to her, slinging an arm over her shoulders and pulling her in for a kiss. She was stiff against him, and he drew back to look at her properly. 'All right. What's the matter?'

She considered her words. 'Pandarus came by today.'

He tried very hard not to react in the way his body wanted to. 'Oh?' He removed his arm, hands going to his hips to give them something to do. 'What did he want?' She was looking at the buttons of his tunic, which told him he was not going to like her answer.

'He wants me to return to Syrasan with him.'

He took a step back. 'And what did you tell him?'

She swallowed. 'I told him I needed to think about it. I wanted to talk to you before—'

'Leaving? You want my blessing, is that it?' His restraint had not stretched as far as he had hoped. 'You're not actually considering going back to that place, are you?'

She finally raised her eyes to him. 'When you hear what he is offering, you will understand why.'

Dion took another step back. 'Whatever he's offering you, let me tell you right now, it's not enough.'

'He is making me mentor.'

Dion rubbed his face with both hands. 'Please tell me you're not that gullible. He's just telling you what you want to hear.'

She appeared wounded by his words. Her chin lifted slightly. 'He has put everything into a legally binding agreement.'

'Astra—'

'I negotiated a house, a place for women with nowhere else to go afterwards. He has agreed to a future in which I am not left relying on charity.'

He drew a breath, but the pain in his chest prevented him from getting enough air. 'Is that what you think this is?' He gestured between them. 'Charity?'

'It was in the beginning. You were being kind. It is not a smart way for me to live.'

He shook his head. 'I can't believe you. You're being manipulated, and you're blind to it.'

She swallowed a few times. 'I was just as sceptical as you, believe me. I thought I might never hear from him again, that he was testing me in some way.' She breathed. 'But he sent the agreement this afternoon, agreeing to everything I asked for.'

He closed the distance between them. 'Oh, what an honourable man your king is.'

'Do not do that.'

'Do what?' He began to pace, that energy building in him again.

'Make *me* feel stupid because your ego has taken a hit.'

He stopped walking. 'My ego?' He stepped up to her so fast that she actually stumbled backwards. He caught her in a firm grip, bringing his face to hers. 'My ego? You think I'm angry because of my *ego*?' When she looked down, he shook her, and her eyes snapped up to meet his again. 'This isn't a game to me. I love you. It's really that simple. I love you, and I want you to choose this life. I want you to choose *me*.'

Her eyes welled up. 'It is not that simple.'

'It *is* that simple.' He eased his grip, scared he might hurt her. 'Stop being so weak. It doesn't suit you.' When her gaze dropped again, he said, 'Lift your eyes to me this second and tell me what you want.'

She raised her eyes to him. 'You know I do not make choices with my heart. You said it yourself, I can just switch it on and off.'

He let go of her arms and stepped back. 'So this is you switching it off?'

Her eyes moved rapidly. 'No.'

'So stay.'

'Until you are sick of me?'

He took a calming breath. 'Don't you dare confuse me with him.'

'I have to be practical. Pandarus is offering me a life after men, when all the beauty has faded, when I have nothing left to offer. I will have a house, somewhere to go. We all will.'

'Is this really about a house?' His voice was raised now. 'I will build you a goddamn house.' He knew he had gone too far by the way she flinched at his words. She looked away, fighting back tears. Would it have killed her to cry, show some remorse?

He tried again. 'Tell me what I can say to make you stay. You are loved and wanted, not just by me but by those children in there, by Sapphira, Eda, Hann. You will be free to come and go as you please, in charge of every aspect of your life. You can be whoever you want to be, wear whatever you want to wear, teach whatever you like.'

She bit down on her lip so hard he was expecting blood to pour down her chin at any moment.

'Tell me what you're thinking, because I can't read your mind. Five minutes alone with Pandarus and the Companion mask is back on.'

She let out a pained noise. 'We are having the same fight, over and over. You say I can be whoever I like, except the person I am, is that it?'

'No—'

'I have been consistent all along.' She thrust a finger at her chest hard enough to leave a mark. 'The problem is you do not like me for who I am. You are so intent on changing me.'

He linked his hands atop his head. 'Don't turn this around. I love you. All I'm asking is that you don't walk away.'

She stared at him, hands pressed to her stomach as

266

though holding all the pieces of herself in. 'Look at us. What chance did we ever stand?'

He took an unsteady step back, his chest tearing with the movement. 'You're speaking like you've already made up your mind.'

She blinked back tears. 'I wanted to talk to you.'

'You wanted me to ease your guilt, and I won't do it.'

Her eyes pleaded with him. 'You are not even trying to understand. You could throw me out any time you like. You hold all the power here.'

He groaned. 'No, I'm powerless against you. I tried to stay away. I too tried to be sensible and practical, remember?'

'Perhaps we should talk later when we have both calmed down, had time to think.'

'I don't need time to think.' He watched her face contort as she struggled with her emotions.

'I am in love with you too,' she said. 'Dangerously so.'

The confession winded him for a moment. He did not dare speak.

'I have loved you for some time.' She swallowed as though it pained her to say it. 'That is why I cannot trust my heart right now. I must use my head. Despite what you believe, there is no switching you off.'

His hands were curled into tight fists. 'So choose me, and I promise to never give you a reason to doubt your decision.'

More tears spilled down her beautiful face. She brushed them away like they were acid on her skin. 'This is not a choice between you and him. You know that, right?'

'I can't.' He raised a hand to silence her. He had reached his pain threshold. 'I can't listen to your excuses anymore. You want to go live in a castle with your abusive lover? Go.' What on earth was he doing? 'I'll have Hann take you right this second if you want.'

Her hands went over her face, and he watched her body

shudder with the arrival of tears. He should have gone to her, but his feet did not move. A part of him needed to witness her pain. 'I'm offering love, protection from men like Pandarus, a home for as long as you want it. That's what I'm offering. That's it. You will never be a mentor here. Your expensive dresses will fade and eventually fall apart, as will your shoes.'

She was crying quietly into her hands, saying nothing.

'I'm not selling you a dream here, just an ordinary life I think you'd grow to appreciate. If that's really not enough, then leave. Get out of here.'

Suddenly exhausted and unable to contain his own emotions any longer, Dion turned and walked back in the direction of the house, shutting out the sound of crying that followed him.

CHAPTER 37

*H*ann drove Astra to Reave Castle. The journey was a solemn affair, neither really speaking outside of a few comments about the weather. Astra sat with the agreement on her lap. She had made some last-minute amendments that Pandarus would want to review before signing.

When she arrived at the castle, she found the royal wagon waiting out front, loaded and ready to depart. Pandarus was making his way down the steps. A smug grin spread across his face when he spotted her. She continued towards him, and he greeted her with a kiss to the cheek instead of the usual way one would greet a mentor.

'I made a few amendments,' she said, handing him the parchment. He did not even glance at it.

'I shall review them on the way.' His eyes narrowed on her. 'What is the matter with you? You look positively dreary.'

She had forgotten to smile, to make him feel like the luckiest man alive. No, she had not forgotten, just could not manage it. Dion had not come to her bedchamber. She had not gone to his. Instead, she had sat on her bed staring at her packed bag, reading and rereading the agreement. Then at first light she had left, skipping the goodbyes. They would have only weakened her resolve. 'Just a little weary from the early start.'

He looked down at her dress. 'Thankfully, you have enough time to change before we depart. You are not at Goldmont House anymore.'

Astra had not given any thought to what she put on that morning. She looked down at her dress. Pandarus was right, it was not fit for her new role. 'Of course, Your Majesty.'

Inside the castle, a maid showed Astra to a room. She changed into a blue silk dress, painted her face, braided her hair to one side, and replaced her sturdy boots with elegant slippers that were far from comfortable. She covered every freckle with a thick coat of powder and painted her lips a blood red. Better if she did not recognise herself when she looked in the mirror. Dion would have shaken his head if he saw her.

When Astra returned to the wagon, she found the king already inside and Stamitos on horseback. He glanced in her direction, nodding a greeting before facing forwards again. All that disappointment in just one glance. He was Dion's friend; of course he would disapprove.

A servant stepped forwards to help her into the wagon. She took the hand offered and stepped up. Pandarus nodded to the seat beside him. She sat down, eyeing the agreement tossed carelessly on the seat opposite.

'Alone at last,' he said, planting a hand on her thigh.

'Have you had a chance to look over the amendments?'

'I just sat down, but there is plenty of time. Right now I would rather look at you.'

She cleared her throat. 'Your Majesty, I will not be boarding that ship without a signed agreement. I trust you understand.'

Pandarus exhaled and leaned forwards to pick up the agreement. 'We have plenty of time to get reacquainted onboard.'

Astra knew she was going to have to give Pandarus a refresher on how the king-mentor relationship worked. There was no getting reacquainted, no hands on thighs, no long suggestive stares. But she would let him read the agreement first, make sure he was on board with the big things before she began nitpicking.

'I shall take in the scenery,' she said, moving closer to the window and looking out. 'I do not imagine I will be returning to Galen anytime soon.'

He laughed at that. 'My dear, you will not be leaving the walls of Archdale for some time.'

She blinked as they passed through the outer wall, her eyes already growing heavy with the motion of the wagon. She really should have slept instead of sitting up all night waiting for Dion to… what? Burst through the door and try to talk her out of it? He had already done that—and she had left anyway.

Astra tried to focus on the green hills, the grazing horses, sheep gathered in the shade, anything but herself. She thought about Primrose. She had gone to visit the hen before she left. The only person she had been able to face was not even a person but a chicken. What a coward she was.

Leaning her head against the wall of the carriage, she closed her eyes.

Astra woke to a warm hand roaming beneath her skirt. For a moment, in her dreamy state, she thought it belonged to Dion. She had woken that way before, with a smile already on her lips as fingers traced the length of her thigh. But as she became more aware of her surroundings, the gentle rock of the wagon, she bolted upright in a panic.

'I had forgotten how beautiful you are when you are asleep. A true rose,' Pandarus said.

His voice was too close, his hand too high. Her insides screamed as she caught hold of his hand through the fabric of her dress. 'Your Majesty, you need to save your appetite for Mira. This is not appropriate.' She turned to look at him, taking in his hungry expression.

'You always were a tease, but I played along then, so I can play along now.'

'This isn't a game to me.' Dion's words came back to her. He was not one for games. He was nothing like Pandarus.

As Astra took in the king's devilish smile, the one she had seen a thousand times before, aimed at various women who passed in and out of his life, she felt nothing. It was the same nothing she had felt the entire time as his Companion—only then she had thought it was her. Dion was not a big smiler, but when he did, it was so warm she felt the heat of it in her bones. His eyes would turn a shade lighter, as though his joy was pouring through them. He had smiled more in the previous week than in the months she had known him. *She* had done that.

Then she had left.

'What is the matter with you?' Pandarus asked. 'You look sickly.'

She shook her head, trying to shake away thoughts of Dion. 'Did you sign the agreement?'

He studied her for a moment. 'I have a question about one of your changes.'

She nodded. 'All right. Perhaps you could remove your hand from beneath my skirt so we can discuss it.'

He slowly withdrew his hand, dragging his fingernails along her skin as he did so. 'I was offering you a minimum of five years in the role. You changed it to two.'

She straightened the skirt of her dress. 'In case the arrangement does not work out.'

'You mean in case you miss your lover and wish to flee back to Galen.'

Here we go. 'Your Majesty, what I do once our agreement comes to an end will be my business alone.'

'What is the point of giving you a house if you will not be living in it?'

'Who says I will not be living in it?'

His hand returned to her thigh, causing her to jump slightly. 'I watched the two of you very closely. A Companion will always do what she has to in order to survive, but it did not look like an act to me.'

He was fishing for some sort of confession, but she would give him no part of that life. The fleeting time spent with Dion was theirs alone. 'I am coming to Archdale to mentor, not play the virgin maiden.' She was getting too bold.

'Be that as it may, we cannot have loose women teaching good morals, can we?' He watched her face as his hand climbed higher, the tips of his fingers brushing where they should not.

Astra realised at that moment that she had lost her ability to shut him out. She could not decide if that meant she was broken or fixed. A mentor would say broken; Dion would say fixed. 'Stop.' She grabbed hold of his hand, this time pulling it off her and releasing it some distance from her leg. The damage was done then. She had rejected him, embarrassed him. There was no coming back from it.

Pandarus's eyebrows rose, slowly. 'You want *me* to stop?'

He pulled back a little to see her properly. 'You did not tell the captain to stop, did you?'

She thought about trying to save the situation, but resentment simmered away in the pit of her belly until it spilled from her mouth. 'No. I did not tell him to stop.' She got a strange thrill from saying those words aloud. The pain in her stomach eased for a moment. The power of speaking her truth. There was no stopping her then. 'I do not want you to touch me ever again. There is no *need* for you to touch me ever again.'

He looked genuinely confused for a moment, but then all the muscles in his face began to tighten. 'You dare speak to me in that way. I should tear your dress off and colour you with my belt.'

For some strange reason, she tried to imagine those words coming from Dion's mouth. It would never happen. 'Stop the wagon.'

'What is the matter with you?' He snatched up the agreement, thrusting it in her face. 'You have everything you wanted.'

No, she had nothing she wanted. She had left it all at Goldmont like a fool.

'You do not get to deny me.' Spit flew from his mouth when he spoke. 'You should be falling at my feet, praying I can look past your filthy actions.'

She felt her face twitch with anger, anger so violent she was afraid she was going to physically harm the king of Syrasan. Her eyes went to the agreement in his hand. Snatching it from him, she tore it in half and tossed it out the open window. 'Please stop the wagon.' Her hands were trembling, but not from fear.

His eyes were ablaze then. 'You have not thought this through. What is your big plan exactly? To run back to your lover and pray he will take you back after seeing firsthand how shallow you really are?'

She held his gaze. 'I said stop the wagon.'

He leaned close, bringing his lips to her ear. 'Do you really think I am going to let you embarrass me? The only way you are leaving this wagon is if I throw you out. Agreement or no agreement, you belong to me now.'

Astra pushed herself back on the seat, trying to get away from him. Short, blunt fingernails sank into the soft flesh of her arm, holding her in place. 'You have nowhere to run to. No one else will want you now, not even *him*.'

'Stop the wagon!' she shouted.

'Are you planning on walking?' He released his grip on her and moved away with a warning on his face. 'I suggest you behave.'

She looked to the window to gauge the speed they were travelling, her breaths coming faster and faster. Then, shooting up, she grabbed hold of the wagon door, shoved it open, and jumped. She landed on her feet, then fell forwards onto her knees, one elbow scraping the road. Wincing, she pushed herself up, eyes going to the torn fabric and her stinging knees. A few scrapes, nothing broken.

'Halt!' Pandarus shouted.

Astra glanced back at the wagon. Stamitos, who was riding up front, turned to see what the delay was. A look of confusion passed over his face when he saw Astra standing there. She heard Pandarus curse under his breath as he stepped down and stormed towards her. She planted her feet.

'Get back in the wagon,' he hissed, clearly not wanting anyone else to hear their exchange.

Stamitos was now trotting towards them.

She shook her head. 'No. I chose to come, and now I am choosing to leave.'

He stepped up to her, his shoulders squaring as he brought his face to hers. 'Get back in the wagon!'

Astra's breathing was erratic, her pulse racing. 'No.'

He raised a hand to hit her, but before he had a chance, Stamitos drove his horse between them.

'What in heaven's name is going on?' he asked, looking between them. His gaze fell to Astra's bleeding elbow. 'Good God. What happened to your arm?' He looked accusingly at his brother for an answer.

Pandarus stepped around the horse to get to her.

'Easy, brother,' Stamitos warned.

'Astra was just getting some air,' Pandarus said, his voice calm. 'Now she is getting back in the wagon.'

She shook her head, mustering whatever bravery she had left. 'No I am not.'

For a moment, no one said anything. Then Stamitos, realising what was happening, said quietly, 'Brother, you cannot make her go with you.'

'Stay out of it,' Pandarus snapped, not looking at him. He brought his lips to Astra's ear. 'You could barely raise your eyes to him when the two of you were dancing, and yet you have no problem raising your eyes to me.'

She swallowed. 'I am sorry.'

'You are a disgrace.'

She stepped back from him. 'I am walking away.'

'You are too late,' Pandarus said. 'He will not be there.'

Astra's eyebrows came together. 'What are you talking about?'

'Your lover. Captain of the Galen army.' The corners of his mouth lifted in a half smirk. 'And traitor—just like his father.'

A cold feeling enveloped Astra. 'Dion is no traitor.'

'You sure about that?'

Stamitos moved his horse closer. 'If you have something to say, spit it out.'

Pandarus crossed his arms and looked between them. 'I am talking about the beloved captain crossing the northern border and joining forces with rebels, killing Zoelin allies.'

'Are you drunk?' Stamitos asked, holding the reins a little tighter.

Pandarus shook his head. 'It seems Captain Dion was a little sloppy with his deceit.'

Astra's heart stopped beating.

'King Jayr's men found a Galen weapon onsite,' Pandarus said.

Astra's eyes narrowed on him. She remembered Dion telling her there was nothing left behind to find. He would never be that reckless. 'You are lying.'

Pandarus's nostrils flared. 'An arrow. Three-inch steel head, goose feather fletching, with that trademark extra inch of cedar wood.'

She sucked in a breath. 'What have you done?'

Pandarus's anger was replaced with a smug expression. 'The guards would have been and gone by now.'

Stamitos's horse stirred. 'What guards? What are you talking about?'

'The ones King Linus sent to Goldmont House this morning to search the premises and arrest Captain Dion.'

Stamitos's eyes widened. 'My wife and children are there. You did not think to tell me?'

'I am telling you now.'

Stamitos swung his horse and offered his good hand to Astra. 'You coming?'

She stared at Pandarus, hating him more than she could have ever thought possible. What a blind fool she had been.

'Astra,' Stamitos said.

She looked up at him, then stepped forwards to take his hand. He hoisted her up behind the saddle.

'Who said you could leave?' Pandarus shouted.

'You have gone too far,' Stamitos said, shaking his head. 'You better pray no harm has come to my family.'

Pandarus's lip lifted slightly, and he threw his hand up. 'Go. Better hurry. Treason is punishable by death.'

*D*ion sat on the front steps of Goldmont House with his head in his hands. He had listened to the cart pull away from the house just before sunrise while pacing in his bedchamber. He had laid awake all night thinking about what he might say to her, but he had said it all the day prior. She knew how he felt—and now he had her reply.

He was supposed to go to Swanton Fort that morning, but he could not even bring himself to stand up. She had destroyed him, and he had no one to blame but himself. What had he expected from a Companion? It was laughable how naive he had been, how reckless.

'She's gone, then?' came Sapphira's voice behind him.

He lifted his head when she took a seat beside him, resting his elbows on his knees. 'Yes.'

Sapphira sat Malin on her lap, and he looked over at Dion with wide eyes. She sighed. 'I guess we need to make sure the children lock up the chickens moving forwards.'

Dion only nodded.

Sapphira turned Malin around so he could see the road. He flapped his arms happily. 'I really thought she might stay.'

Dion reached out and let the baby take hold of his finger. 'This wasn't enough for her.'

Sapphira glanced sideways at him. 'It was plenty for her. She was just at Archdale too long.' She breathed out, head shaking. 'She was miserable there. How could she not be? You're always measuring your self-worth by the attention paid to you, always lonely.'

'Well, she went back, so it can't have been that bad.'

Sapphira ran a hand over her son's silky head. 'Do you remember when the entire west fence came down in the back paddock, and we were all surprised to learn the oxen never crossed the boundary?'

Dion nodded. 'Astra knew the fence was gone, if that's where this is going?'

Sapphira leaned forwards. 'She has been in that same paddock for ten years. It's scary to venture out. Better to be unhappily confined than find herself lost in the unfamiliar.'

'She was not lost. She had us.'

'I'm not sure if you remember, but we were not exactly friends at Archdale. She was still learning to trust us. Then Pandarus shows up, offering her exactly what she wanted, what she *needed*. We can't judge too harshly.'

'I told her I loved her.'

Sapphira's face pinched with worry. 'That explains why she fled. Those three words are like Companion repellent.'

He rubbed his hands together. 'And she said it back.'

Sapphira sat a little straighter. 'What?'

'She told me she loved me.' He met her eyes. 'Why do you look so surprised?'

'She actually uttered the words "I love you"?'

He tried to recall her exact words. 'She said, "I am in love with you too. Dangerously so".'

Sapphira let out an enormous breath. 'Oh, Dion. And you just let her go?'

'Was I supposed to lock her in her bedchamber until she changed her mind?'

'She's a Companion.'

He pinched the bridge of his nose. 'Yes, everyone's gone out of their way to reiterate that point, thank you.'

'She's been trained *not* to fall in love.'

'I know.'

Sapphira was looking at him like he had missed something important. 'Do you understand what a big deal it is that she felt that, let alone admitted it aloud? It goes against every fibre of her being.'

'Doesn't matter now. She left.'

'She got scared.'

'She made a decision.'

'The wrong decision.'

His head went back in his hands, and he took a few breaths before speaking. 'I saw the way Pandarus treats her. Is it always that bad?'

Sapphira sighed. 'Depends on the audience. He's unpredictable. He will treat her well enough for as long as it suits him.'

Dion lifted his head and looked at her. 'I walked away first, you know. I laid out my offer and walked away, as though it were a business deal and I was calling her bluff.'

Sapphira pulled Malin closer. 'You tried to call a bluff on a Companion? Terrible idea.'

'I left her in tears, bastard that I am.'

Sapphira's legs stilled. 'Wait. Astra *cried*?'

'Yes.'

Sapphira shook her head as she processed that new piece of information. 'I've only ever seen her cry once. It was the night Idalia died. She hid her face from everyone, like she'd contracted leprosy. She wouldn't let anyone comfort her. Not that anyone knew how to. The sight of her in tears was more unsettling than the corpse on the bed.' She looked away.

'I should've gone to her last night, but I wasn't in a good way.'

'You could go after her now.'

'Too late. Too much damage done.'

'Oh, please.' She looked at him tiredly. 'Don't be such a defeatist.'

He shook his head. 'Even if I did, and she agreed to return, I'd never be able to trust her. I'd be waiting for her to get a better offer and leave.'

Sapphira looked at the road, eyes narrowing. 'Do you hear horses?'

Before he had a chance to reply, a group of horses entered the property, eight guards flying the familiar green flag.

'Now what?' Dion asked, standing and descending the steps.

Sapphira followed after him, facing Malin to her and placing a protective hand over his head. She pressed him to her chest. A minute later, the horses came to a halt in front of them and two men dismounted, making their way over to Dion.

'What's your business here?' Dion asked, glancing down at the scroll one of them was holding. That was not good.

'Captain Dion,' the man said, unrolling the parchment and holding it up for him to see. 'This is a warrant for your arrest. You are being charged with treason and will be brought before King Linus.'

Sapphira stepped forwards. 'What proof do you have of this accusation?'

Dion closed his eyes. 'It's all right. Take the prince inside.'

The other guards dismounted and marched towards the house.

'Search the entire property,' said the guard with the scroll.

'For what?' Dion asked. 'There are children inside.'

Two men approached Dion, each taking an arm. No one answered him.

Dion turned to Sapphira. 'Tell Eda to take the children out back, away from the house, until they're done. And take care of Helena.'

'What about—'

'Please.'

She stared at him for a moment, then nodded before hurrying up the steps as the guards tugged him in the other direction. He glanced once at the house as they led him away.

Dion was marched into the throne room, where King Linus and Philo stood waiting for him. Philo appeared uncomfortable, not surprising given the two men had known each other their whole lives. King Linus's icy stare bored into him. The guard stopped him about eight feet from them, remaining at his side.

'It seems your family is determined to make a fool of the crown,' Linus began.

Dion looked between the two men, saying nothing. He would let them speak first.

'I thought we had an understanding,' Linus continued. 'I put you in that role as a show of good faith. I would not punish you for your father's mistakes, and you would not punish me for his death.' He looked at Dion, his expression conflicted. 'Instead, you repeat his mistakes.'

Philo looked down. Linus did not seem to notice.

'It has been brought to our attention that you assisted Zoelin rebels in an attack against their king.'

Dion remained calm. 'Brought to your attention by whom?'

'The crown does not buy into rumours,' Philo said, raising his eyes. 'But when Galen weapons are found at the site of the attack, we cannot dismiss proof.'

Dion frowned. 'What weapons?'

Philo walked over to the table and picked up an arrow. He returned, tossing it on the ground between them. Dion stared down at it. It was one of theirs all right, but there was no way it came from Zoelin. He looked up his king.

'And who supposedly found this arrow?'

'Our ally, King Jayr of Zoelin.'

That made no sense. 'He sent it to you?'

'He sent it to King Pandarus. Asked him to find out where it came from.'

That made a lot more sense. Pandarus had taken it from the house. Of course, King Jayr would back whatever story the little mole told because he had a debt to settle also. 'I haven't taken any Galen weapons into Zoelin.'

'So you deny the charges?' Philo asked.

Dion lifted his chin. 'I would never implicate the crown by using army-issued weapons.'

'But you do not deny aiding rebels?' Linus snapped.

Dion swallowed. 'I never did so in your name, Your Majesty.'

'In your father's name, perhaps.'

Dion looked him straight in the eye. 'King Jayr is buying young boys, some as young as six. Slaves. He's building his army.'

Linus rubbed his forehead. 'All the more reason to keep them as *allies*.'

'Historically, our allies have been in line with Galen's

284

values, its morals. We are a kingdom that protects its vulnerable people, not exploits them.'

Philo cleared his throat. 'We can only take care of our own, Captain. We start poking around in other people's business and we will find ourselves at war with a very dangerous enemy.'

'The bottom line is,' Linus continued, 'you liaised with rebels without my consent.'

'I acted to protect children when their own king failed them. I gained nothing from it. There was no money exchanged, no political considerations whatsoever.'

'Clearly,' Linus said, his eyes dark. 'And once again, my family is forced to clean up the mess. King Jayr wants blood for the men he lost.'

'The blood of child soldiers isn't enough?'

'Watch yourself, Captain,' Philo warned.

Dion fell silent, and Philo turned to the king, waiting. Linus stared at the arrow lying between them for the longest time before speaking.

'Based on the evidence, and your admission, I have no choice but to charge you with treason.'

Philo looked down, eyes closing for a moment. The punishment for treason was death.

'We always have a choice,' Dion said. 'My father chose to help people, yours succumbed to political pressure, and now history repeats itself.' His legs were heavy. 'I accept the charge, but for the record, the evidence provided by your so-called ally is bogus. I recommend you be very careful who you trust moving forwards.'

The anger was gone from the king's eyes. 'I hereby sentence you to death.' There was no malice in his tone. 'Because of the unique circumstances, the fact that your motives were not malicious but well-meaning, I am going to permit an honourable death, via sword.' He paused a moment. 'I am sorry for it, because I liked you a great deal, but you have forced my hand.'

Dion's mouth was numb, and Philo still struggled to look at him.

'Put him in the tower,' King Linus said to the guard. Then he turned to Philo. 'Make the necessary arrangements.'

'*Treason is punishable by death.*' That was all Astra could think about as they rode east.

'I am going to Reave Castle,' she told Stamitos once they were some distance from Pandarus. 'They will have taken him there.'

'I have to go to the house.'

She touched his arm. 'I know. Take me as far as you can, then go to your family.'

'What will you do?'

'Walk.'

He glanced down at her shoes. 'In those?'

She should have left her boots on. 'I will be fine.'

'It will probably take you an hour from the dropping point. Follow the same road all the way to the castle.'

She nodded. 'That arrow Pandarus was referring to, he stole it from the house yesterday.'

'I figured as much.'

'They cannot sentence him with false evidence, can they?'

Stamitos's mouth flattened into a thin line as he guided his horse around the bend. 'They can do whatever they like.'

She had been afraid of that.

Twenty minutes later, they came to a fork in the road. Stamitos pulled up the horse and lowered Astra down onto the ground. 'I will join you as soon as I can.'

She nodded and watched as he swung his horse around and galloped off in the other direction. Drawing a breath, Astra headed south. It was her fault—all of it. She had placed a target on Dion's back at the feast. She had wounded Pandarus's pride to the point where he was prepared to watch a man die rather than risk coming off second best.

Astra was about halfway there when her heels began to bleed. The shoes were designed for leisurely strolls on the arms of men, not long treks on dirt roads. She pushed on, bringing a hand to her collarbone where perspiration had gathered, the high sun now beating down on her.

A small cart came towards her, travelling in the wrong direction. The driver cast a wary glance at her as he passed. She must have looked ridiculous marching along in her torn dress and silk slippers, which were now shredded and filthy. Blood trailed from one elbow to her hand. She had realised too late, and it had set on her skin.

Soon after, two horses approached, once again travelling in the wrong direction. She had hoped someone might stop, but judging by the wide berth the riders gave her, she suspected she was not going to have much luck with that. She nodded a greeting in their direction while peeling locks of hair from her face. Everything was sticking to her sweaty skin.

How much farther?

She tried to remember what Fedora had taught them about Galen law. Only that it was similar to Syrasan in that, once charged, sentencing was usually swift. Why had she thought of that? Her feet moved faster still, now rubbed raw.

It was almost half an hour later when Astra saw Reave

Castle rise from the trees. She blinked with relief, glancing down at her feet, shocked to discover red patches on the expensive fabric. She paused at a tree, removing her shoes and leaning on the trunk as she inspected the mess of blistered and bloodied skin. She wriggled her toes before shoving her feet back into them and continuing on her way.

When Astra finally approached the outer gate of the castle, she realised they might take one look at her and not let her in. She wiped her face and smoothed back her hair, thinking of a cute story she could laugh about with the guards. Maybe she was travelling by cart, lost a wheel, and was forced to walk. Maybe they would not even look that closely at her.

Finding her best smile, she continued towards the guards. The men looked in her direction and straightened. At least she had their attention. Now to deliver her adorable story in which they got to play the hero. But before she had a chance to speak, a notice plastered on the wall across the water snagged her vision. Her feet stopped. Her lungs stopped.

On this day, Captain Dion of Goldmont House has been found guilty of treason. Sentencing will be carried out this afternoon. The event will be open for public viewing.

Event.

They were calling his death an event. It was a tragedy, a mistake, surely. To take the life of a man so loyal, so caring of others. Helena would have to face yet another family member gone from her life.

'Miss?' came the voice of one of the guards.

Her gaze snapped back to him, hands shaking at her sides. 'Has the execution taken place yet?' What if they said yes?

What if she was too late? She would fall down and never get back up. She was sure of it.

'Crowd's gathered. Just waiting on the prisoner to be brought down from the tower. You here to watch?'

She was having trouble connecting the word prisoner to Dion. 'Yes.' She attempted a smile and failed. 'Could you let me through please?'

He noticed her feet then, stepping back a little to see better. 'That blood?'

She looked down, disturbed by the sight suddenly. 'Yes.'

His eyes returned to hers, suspicious now.

'Astra!'

She turned at the sound of Sapphira's voice. The princess cantered up on horseback, her son wrapped to the front of her.

'They are going to execute him.' She blurted the words the moment the princess was within hearing range.

Sapphira's expression hardened. 'They came to the house this morning, tore it apart and took him away. Helena's beside herself.'

'Get me inside,' Astra whispered. 'We do not have much time.'

Sapphira took her hand and marched past the guard towards the gate, the horse trailing behind them. 'Let us through.'

'Halt,' the guard behind called, rushing to get in front of them again.

'I am Princess Sapphira of Syrasan, and I am not asking you again.'

Astra wanted to hug her.

The guard looked Sapphira over and then turned, nodding at the other guard. The drawbridge began to lower. The moment it touched the ground, the women ran across it. Inside, the shopfronts were closed, the roads empty. Their eyes narrowed on the crowd gathered in the distance. Astra searched the scaffold tucked against the inner wall. People were packed around it.

'Tell me we are not too late,' Astra choked out.

Sapphira shook her head. 'There he is.'

Astra searched the scaffold again, spotting him at the back as he was marched up the steps by two guards. Her heart lodged in her throat at the sight of him walking to his death, hands bound behind his back, his eyes on his feet, shoulders slumped forwards. She barely recognised him.

And now she was out of time.

Astra broke into a run towards him. No, not a run, a sprint. She had never moved so fast in her life. Her feet pounded the gravel, sending one shoe flying. She did not even break stride, barely registering the sharp rocks underfoot.

'Wait,' Sapphira called, holding on to her son and trying to catch up.

'I need to get up there,' Astra shouted over her shoulder.

'What are you going to do?'

She had no idea. A chill pulsed through her as she watched the guards push Dion to his knees. Another man appeared, his broad shoulders filling her vision as he rose like a demon from hell.

The executioner.

'Stop!' Astra thought she shouted, but the breeze just carried the word away.

The women reached the edge of the crowd, and Astra began pushing through. People turned, glaring, but she did not look back at them, too afraid to take her eyes from Dion. A man stepped forwards to speak, but Astra could not hear him over the buzzing in her ears. Some final words for the condemned, perhaps. He stepped back, and the executioner took his place. A guard offered up a sword to the man, and he reached one muscled arm out to draw the weapon from its sheath.

'Move,' Astra said, throwing her body weight against spectators. Fedora would have fallen down with shame. She was less than ten feet from the platform now. 'Stop.'

A woman turned to look at her, but not the executioner, who knew better than to pay attention to the crowd. His only focus was the clean removal of the captain's head. Dion was looking straight up, focused on something in the sky. He seemed shut off to the scene around him. How else did one face death?

Five feet.

Astra turned sideways to fit between two large men.

Three feet.

Two.

One.

She reached for the scaffold, her fingers brushing the edge before she finally grabbed hold of it. She tried to pull herself up, her eyes on the executioner. He was adjusting his grip on the sword, ready.

'No.' The word slipped out of Astra like a breathy plea. Someone grabbed hold of her leg, and she was hoisted up in the air until her chest crashed against the timber floor. It was stained with blood. She got her knee up, heard her dress tear, felt the remaining shoe slip from her foot. All of these things she was aware of while transfixed on Dion. Captain of the king's army and protector of stray Companions. She pushed herself up onto her feet, saw one of the guard's heads snap in her direction. She was past him before he had time to react. The executioner raised his weapon. She opened her mouth to scream, but nothing came out. Dion's eyes pressed shut, bracing for death.

Reaching for him, Astra leapt in front of the swinging blade.

CHAPTER 40

*D*ion disappeared. He closed his eyes and went away, just like Astra did each time her hands landed on the strings of her harp. Anywhere but there, kneeling on that scaffold, facing his mortality. He had seen men die this way, watched them lose control of their bladders, occasionally their bowels. He had seen them cry and beg for their lives.

Better to not be present at all.

He had glanced once at the crowd as he climbed the steps, thankful his sister was not among them. Though as he knelt, he had imagined her reaction to the news. That was worse than death itself. He looked up instead of out, escaping to the enormous expanse of blue above. It was like staring into Astra's eyes. He could waste hours doing that—*had* wasted hours doing that.

How would she learn of his death? Pandarus would make sure she knew, would likely tell her himself. He would enjoy watching the shock play out on her face. He was that type of man.

Dion caught his thoughts, not wanting to spend his final

moments thinking about Pandarus. He let his mind drift back to Astra: her smile, her serious face as she watched the sunset, washed in the colours of the sun. Astra crouched in the middle of the lawn, stroking Primrose's back. Whenever he had glimpsed her like that, he had taken a mental picture, wishing he could have it painted and hung in the entranceway.

Astra with her big heart.

Astra who had weakened his resolve with one glance in his direction.

Astra tucked beneath him during a storm.

She was his final thought as the sword was raised, his eyes pressed shut.

How many freckles? He struggled to remember despite counting them enough times.

The weight of something slammed into him, and he sucked in a breath. Was that it? Was that death? It was not so bad. No pain, only suffocating weight and the scent of primrose.

Something shifted against him, breaths coming hard and fast on his neck.

What the hell is happening?

He opened his eyes. Not dead after all, but clearly hallucinating. Astra was wrapped around him, the blade of a sword sitting two inches from her neck. Dion looked up at the executioner, whose eyes were filled with panic. He had nearly taken her head off; it was all there in his expression. The sword shook in his hands as he lowered the weapon and took an unsteady step back. It was just a hallucination, surely, his mind's way of processing his death. But her grip on him did not ease. Her breath did not slow.

'Astra.' He spoke her name aloud to see what would happen.

Slowly, she peeled herself off him and looked around,

panting. When her eyes found his, he knew it was real. His mind struggled to catch up, to process what had happened. She had just put herself between him and the blade. Panic rose as his eyes moved over her, checking for injury.

'You all right?'

She swallowed, nodded. Her gown stuck to her body like a second skin. Paint streaked her cheeks, and a film of sweat covered her face. Wherever she had come from, she had come at a run. And there was blood on her arm.

'You're hurt.'

'I am fine.'

His eyes met hers again, his hands tied behind his back and hers holding him tightly still.

She exhaled, the breath shaky, and brought her face close to his. 'I will not let you die.'

'You need to leave.' That was his first impulse. Get her away from the danger, away from the grief of watching someone you love die. She would see it for the rest of her life, as he did. 'Leave,' he hissed. '*Now*.'

The smallest shake of her head as she let go of him and stood on trembling legs. He recognised that expression on her. She was not done.

King Linus was climbing the steps now, looking less than pleased. 'What is the meaning of this? Have you lost your mind?' He was looking at Astra, who remained between Dion and the executioner.

'No, Your Majesty. I assure you I am quite sane.'

Dion caught sight of her bloodied and bare feet. What in God's name was going on? He looked around and spotted Sapphira to his left, looking just as shocked as he was. She was supposed to be home with his sister.

'Unless you wish to be locked up for interfering,' Linus said, 'I suggest you leave this platform at once.'

'The evidence was false. That arrow did not come from Zoelin. It was taken from Goldmont House yesterday.'

Murmurs broke out in the crowd, and Dion looked down, knowing she was fighting a losing battle.

'This is not a trial,' Linus said.

'Perhaps it should be. I am sure the people standing before you would like to hear of the captain's so-called crimes before witnessing his death.'

Dion looked up. 'Astra—'

'No.' She raised a hand, not even close to done judging by her expression. 'If evidence has no part to play in your death, then they must have another solid reason for ending your life.'

Philo, who had been loitering by the stairs, spoke up at that. 'We have his confession.'

'There was no trial because he admitted to the crime,' Linus finished.

Astra did not even blink. 'You mean treason? There is not one person standing before you who would wish this man dead for what you have called treason, for lack of a better word.' She turned to the crowd, addressing them. 'Who would like to hear the details of why this man is being put to death?'

The king ran a hand down his beard. 'Guards, take her away.'

Dion tried to get to his feet but was quickly shoved back down. A man in the crowd pushed to the front.

'I want to hear what she has to say,' he shouted.

The woman beside him nodded. 'Let's hear it, then.'

Astra turned back to Linus, waiting for his response. A few carefully selected words and she had the spectators eating out of her hand.

The king looked out at the crowd, then at Philo, who responded with the slightest nod of his head. Sighing, he said, 'I will permit you to speak, but one sniff of misinformation and I will have you locked up.'

Dion sank down onto his heels.

If there was ever a time Astra needed to excel at a role, it was now. The only way Dion's life would be spared was if the people before her demanded it. So, she would give the performance of a lifetime. She could do it. For Dion, she could be anybody. It was too bad she looked like a desperate beggar instead of a woman in control.

She glanced back at Dion. He was slumped on his heels, watching her with a mix of adoration and defeat. *Not yet, my love.* She was a long way from giving up.

Turning back to the crowd, she adjusted the skirt of her gown to cover her bare feet and pushed her hair back from her face. Yes, she was outwardly a mess, but inside she was pulling it together. She would show them that.

Movement was the best way to capture their attention, so she began walking slowly along the platform. All eyes followed. Only then did she begin talking, her gaze moving from person to person, as if the story was being told just for them. First, she told the story of Goldmont House and the captain with the enormous heart who had opened his house to children with nowhere else to go—children he was not obligated to care for. She maintained eye contact for the right amount of time, long enough for them to feel the sincerity of her words, but not so long as to single them out and cause discomfort. The *Companion* length of time.

Once she had set the stage and painted a picture of the man before them, a man who gave so much and asked for nothing in return, she moved on. 'Now you are probably more curious than ever to learn of the treasonous act committed by this beloved man. So what is treason?' She stopped walking, ensuring she had everyone's attention. 'It is a crime against one's kingdom, an attempt to kill or over-throw the king or monarch. Or in this instance, the act of betraying one's king.' She turned to Dion. 'Let me tell you about Captain Dion's *terrible* crime.'

Dion's eyes were fixed on her, his expression so full of admiration that she wanted to go to him and take his beautiful face in her hands. She smiled at him before turning her attention back to the crowd.

'His crime, his only crime, is that his big heart does not care for borders. If there is a Galen child in need of help, and he is in the position to help, he will. If there is a Zoelin child in need of help, he will do what he can. If there is an Asigow child in need, and by that I mean taken from loving families who want them very much, sold across the border as slaves to be turned into soldiers, *child* soldiers as young as *six*'—she paused, looking around—'he will help.'

Astra drew a breath and continued walking. 'Now look at the child closest to you. Is it your own?' She looked between their faces. 'Imagine a world where, if you died, that child became the property of your king. Instead of grieving with their family, they are taken from the only life they know, at a vulnerable age, and sold to a foreign king who means to exploit them.' She swallowed. 'We do not have to imagine it. That world is just over the border.' She pointed north. 'Asigow orphans under the age of fourteen are property of the empire, their childhoods over the moment they lose their parents.'

Astra glanced at Sapphira, who looked like a proud mother. She gave Astra a nod of encouragement.

'Captain Dion's father was also a traitor. Or put another way, he also had a big heart that did not care for borders.' She looked back at Dion, who watched her with shining eyes. 'He died right here, for a similar cause, because people who do not share our values wanted him to mind his own business.' She stepped to the edge of the platform, raising her voice. 'But child slavery is everybody's business. Children drowned at birth due to minor defects is everybody's business. Boys handed swords at age six and trained to kill is everybody's business.'

She took the crowd's silence as a good sign.

'That is it. That was Captain Dion's crime. He was told to mind his own business, but he did not, because he was in a position to help, and that is what *good men do*. You can call it treason if you like, but that is just a dirty word for being a compassionate human being.' She pointed at Dion. 'We should be admiring these men, their bravery, and holding them up as examples to our own children. We should be celebrating them, not killing them off.'

The crowd was nodding in agreement now. She was winning them over. She glanced at King Linus, who had noticed also. Astra searched for the perfect words to finish.

'As captain of the king's army, Dion has a responsibility to his kingdom, one he takes very seriously. But as a man, he has a responsibility to those in need—regardless of what side of the border they are on.'

Astra looked at Dion again, filled with adoration for him. She had meant every word she said and prayed everyone had felt the sincerity of them.

'Untie the man,' someone called out. 'He's no traitor.'

Everyone was nodding in agreement, talking, restless, and looking to the king for a response.

Astra walked over to King Linus. 'Your Majesty, this is not just about Dion. This is much bigger than him.' She lowered her voice.

He looked around before speaking. 'Your dramatic

display might have worked on them, but I cannot afford to be swept away by feelings.'

She looked him straight in the eyes. 'You are appeasing King Jayr, and I understand why, but I strongly suggest you think carefully before you act. Have you given thought to the enemy you will be making?'

His eyes narrowed. 'Speak plainly.'

She moved closer. 'When Brom takes the throne from his brother, and he will'—she paused for emphasis—'you will have already drawn a line in the sand. Four years ago, your father made a very big mistake. This is your chance to send a different message, to demonstrate Galen's values to your neighbours. You may lose a few friends in the process, but you will gain the respect of the people who matter.' She glanced over at Dion, who was watching them. 'If you execute him, you will be severing your only tie with Brom, the man who will replace King Jayr when the time comes.' She turned back to Linus. 'This is not the opinion of a Companion but of King Tuyon himself.'

King Linus rubbed at his beard, thoughtful, conflicted. He looked again to Philo, who gave another small nod. Exhaling, Linus stepped up to the edge of the scaffold to address the people. 'If it is your collective wish, I am prepared to pardon Captain Dion.'

Cheers erupted, every person before them now onside.

'Very well,' King Linus said. 'I hear you, and I must respect the wishes of my people.' He looked over at the guards standing behind Dion. 'Release him.'

Applause broke out, people whistling and clapping at the king's decision, or perhaps Dion's bravery—Astra was not sure which. She watched as Dion was pulled to his feet, his eyes still fixed on her. She exhaled, swallowing back the tears and focusing on the relief. The joy would come later once she had calmed down.

King Linus gestured to one of the guards, and the man walked over to where he stood. 'Take the lady to the tower.'

Astra blinked, not sure if she had heard correctly. 'What?'

'Some time in prison might make you think twice about interfering next time.'

'Your Majesty—'

The guard took her arm and led her off the scaffold before anyone knew what was happening.

CHAPTER 41

D ion sat on the stone floor at the top of the tower, his back against the wall, staring ahead. Astra was seated on the floor on the other side of the bars, doing the same. King Linus had not liked being shown up in front of a crowd. He had wanted to make a point. Dion also had a point to make, but just as he was preparing to take the tower apart brick by brick, Philo had placed a calming hand on his shoulder.

'Easy, Captain. She'll be out in a few hours.'

The king had permitted him to go sit with her for the short time she would be imprisoned. He had gone straight to her, seeing the relief on her face when she saw him.

'You all right?' he had asked.

A nod. 'Yes.'

They had sat in silence then, processing the day's events.

Dion was still trying to figure out how he was alive at the end of it all. The answer was, of course, Astra. 'You saved my life.' He was ready to talk.

She turned her head to look at him. 'Given I am the reason you were arrested, it felt like the least I could do.'

'You ran in front of a weapon. What if he had not been able to stop in time?'

She shrugged. 'It would have gotten quite messy, I imagine.'

He looked at her then. 'How can you make jokes?'

She drew a slow breath. 'I am probably still in shock. I could hardly stand back and watch you die.'

'Yes you could.' He looked down at her bloodied feet. 'What happened to your feet?'

She wiggled her raw toes. 'I wore the wrong shoes, and it was a long walk.'

'How far did you walk?'

'Not far.'

He was silent a moment. 'You need to tell me what happened, or I'm going to imagine terrible things.'

She faced forwards again. 'I realised, at a very inconvenient distance from the castle, that I wished to return to Goldmont House.' She tucked some hair behind her ear. 'Pandarus was not particularly understanding of my dilemma, and things got a bit... dramatic.'

'Did he hurt you?' Dion could not keep the edge out of his voice.

'Not really.'

'Not really?'

She blinked slowly. 'He definitely shocked me. The mention of your arrest was not a particularly fun moment.'

'I'm surprised he told you before I was dead.'

She thought on that. 'He had nothing to lose at that point. Perhaps he thought I would change my mind if I had no one to go back to.' A smile played on her lips. 'I jumped out of the wagon while it was moving. It was the craziest thing I have done in years.'

'While it was moving?' He looked at her elbow. 'That how you hurt your arm?'

'My arm, my knees, my reputation as a refined woman.' She looked at him, smiling. 'But it felt so good.'

He relaxed when he saw the pride in her expression. 'What did Pandarus do then?'

'He got mad, demanded I get back in the wagon. I wish you could have seen his face when I told him no.'

'So I could smash it with my fist?'

She suppressed a smile.

'Want to tell me why you jumped from a moving wagon to begin with?'

She lifted her shoulders. 'Because he refused to stop.' She swallowed. 'And because I realised I had made a terrible mistake.'

He searched her face. 'Really?'

'Yes.'

He was quiet a moment. 'Tell me about your terrible mistake.'

Her hands twitched in her lap. 'For the first time in my life, I had the freedom to choose, and I chose wrong.'

'So you abandoned your king, walked to Reave Castle, and threw yourself in front of a sword.'

Her bottom lip disappeared between her teeth. 'I did not exactly plan that part.'

'Clearly.' He hated that she had been so reckless. 'I understand why you did it. You felt responsible somehow, didn't want my blood on your hands.' A small scowl appeared on her brow, but he ignored it. 'Now what?'

She turned her body to him. 'Like I said, I had planned to return to Goldmont.'

'For how long?' He should have been falling over himself with gratitude, but instead he was raising a wall between them.

'Must I set a departure date?' She kept her tone light.

He pulled his knees up. 'Just want to be clear on your intentions this time to prevent any confusion.'

She tilted her head. 'My intentions? Are my intentions not clear?' She waited. 'Look at me.'

He kept staring ahead. 'You're welcome there for as long as you want.'

She nodded. 'What about what you want?' When he did not reply, she reached through the bars and took hold of his hand. 'Please look at me.'

He forced his gaze to her, his expression guarded, bordering on cold.

'I am covered in dirt and blood, sitting on the filthy floor of a prison cell. I think I may have shed my Companion skin today.'

His eyes moved over her. She was a gorgeous mess all right. 'I suspect Companions are a bit like onions.'

Her eyebrows rose. 'How so?'

'You take off a layer of skin only to be met with another layer.'

Her lips twitched. 'So I am just layers of Companion skin all the way to my core?'

He knew she meant the question as a joke, but he thought about his reply. 'I honestly don't know anymore.'

Astra rose onto her knees and took hold of the bars. 'I made a mistake. I am so sorry for that mistake. I will not stand here and pretend I will not make more, because I likely will.'

Dion stared at her for the longest time before getting up on his knees also. He covered her hands with his. 'I asked you to stay.'

'I know.'

'And you left.'

She rested her forehead on the bars. 'I really wish I had not.'

He brought his head to hers. 'What if it's not enough for you?'

'It is more than enough. I know that now.'

'You might change your mind, want more.'

She pulled away to look at him. 'I already want more.'

He studied her face. 'Of course you do.'

She brought her body closer to the bars, her bloodied knees dragging on the stone floor. 'I want the entire dream you fed me—the home, the sunsets, the chickens. I want the life you breathed back into me as well as that all-consuming love that makes me run barefoot on roads and leap in front of swords.' She paused for breath. 'I want you to know that I would do it all again without hesitation.' A few tears fell, but she made no move to brush them away. 'I also want you to forgive me for leaving, for not believing in us. I want you to love and accept all of me, even the Companion layers I might never shed.'

His chest was tight, his mouth pressed into a firm line. 'Does that include your collection of half dresses?'

She laughed, forehead resting on the bars for a moment. When she lifted her face, there were fresh tears, but there was also a smile that eased the tightness inside of him. 'I left them in the wagon, though I suspect you quite liked those.'

He reached a hand through the bars and combed his fingers through the messy locks of hair falling around her face. She had never looked so unkempt, so oblivious to the fact, or more beautiful. 'You might be right.'

At that moment, a guard arrived. He paused at the top of the steps, looking awkwardly in their direction, then went to unlock the door. Dion got to his feet, pulling Astra up with him as he did so. They headed for the open door, watching one another through the bars as they walked. Astra stepped out, and Dion thanked the guard. Then they were alone again, standing face-to-face.

'Is there anything else you want?'

She lifted her chin a little. 'Yes, actually. I would like to help you protect children on all sides of the border. I am not great with a bow, but I am good with words, and they can be a very powerful weapon.'

He frowned across at her. 'You want to use your Companion powers for good?'

'Yes.'

He nodded. 'Is that it?'

'No.'

He exhaled. 'Why am I not surprised?'

'I would like to get married.'

Dion's smile faded. He searched her eyes for hints that she was joking, finding none. She was serious. He looked down at her bare feet. 'To whom?'

'Does Elenor Talsworth have a brother?'

His gaze travelled back up to meet hers. 'She does. He's not as funny as me—and he's married.'

'You say that like it is an obstacle.' Her eyes shone at him.

He reached up, hand resting along her jaw. 'Yes to everything, except Elenor Talsworth's brother.' He leaned forwards, kissing her cheek, kissing the other one, then brushing his nose over hers before kissing her open mouth. He breathed her in before pulling back to look at her. 'I'm not sure I thanked you for saving my life.'

She held on to his wrists, her eyes glassy again. 'I am not sure I thanked you for saving *mine*.'

He brought his forehead to hers, eyes closing. 'I really think we should find you some shoes.'

She nodded. 'I know where one shoe is. Fancy a walk down to the scaffold?'

'Absolutely not.' He scooped her up off the ground, gathering her in his arms. 'I'd rather carry you back to Goldmont.'

She held on to him. 'It might be too soon for another scandal.'

'That's just your Companion layers talking.'

She buried her face in his neck. 'I guess I am just going to have to trust your judgement.'

He kissed the top of her head, gathered her closer, and carried her down the stairs of the tower.

EPILOGUE

*a*stra stood with her hands on her hips, head shaking. 'How could you? And today of all days.'

Primrose got to her feet and shook out her feathers, sending a cloud of dust into the air. Astra coughed and waved a hand in front of her face.

'Everyone's ready,' Sapphira called out, walking across the lawn with Malin perched on her hip.

Astra looked down at her light blue gown, brushing delicately at the lace. 'Not everyone. Primrose decided to have a dust bath.'

Sapphira's eyes moved over Astra. 'Did you... join her?'

Astra sighed. 'Is it that bad?'

'Only by your standards. No one else will notice.'

'Very reassuring.' Astra leaned forwards, touching her nose to Malin's, making him smile. 'Shall we do this?'

The boy laughed in response.

As Astra made her way across the lush lawn of Goldmont House, she felt a lightness in her chest. Her gaze swept over the waiting guests. Eda, Hann, all the children dressed in their best, Isolda and her parents, and Prince Stamitos. Then there were those who had travelled across an ocean to be there, the people she had assumed would not come but was incredibly grateful they had. Prince Tyron, Princess Aldara, Lord Yuri and Hali, and the exiled mentor of Archdale Castle, Fedora.

Violeta had stepped into the role of mentor and was doing a good job by all accounts. Astra had asked Stamitos to bring Fedora back to Goldmont House, where she was welcomed into the big orphaned family. Astra had been surprised when the children warmed to her, as she was not known for her motherly traits. It would take some time for the mentor to shed all those layers—onion that she was.

Dion was standing with Father Agnar, who was looking very suave in his purple robes. He knew his audience. The men stopped talking when they spotted her, and Astra stopped walking. She looked around at the odd assortment of friends and could not stop the smile.

'Shall we get started?' Father Agnar asked.

Dion walked over to collect Astra, kissing her cheek and whispering into her ear, 'You look like a queen.'

Her smile grew.

'And smell a little dusty,' he finished.

Her smile faded, and she glared down at Primrose, who lingered at her feet. 'You are a very bad girl.'

Dion took her face in his hands, not caring in the slightest. 'Still want to marry me?'

She looked around at their guests; all eyes were on them. 'I would feel a bit rude backing out now.' Her mouth stretched into another smile.

He kissed her, then threaded his fingers through hers, leading her towards Father Agnar. 'That'll teach me for asking.' He glanced sideways at her. 'The dress is beautiful, by the way.'

Astra smiled at Aldara as they passed. The princess was

tucked under Tyron's arm, still the golden beauty she remembered arriving at Archdale all those years back. 'Would you consider this a full dress or half dress?' She kept her voice low so only Dion could hear.

'Somewhere in between,' Dion replied without looking at her. 'It's the perfect balance of old and new.'

She held on to his arm. 'That is what Isolda said when we were designing it.' A friendship had grown between the women over the previous months, despite Elenor Talsworth's blatant disapproval. Astra kissed Dion's arm, growing lighter by the minute. 'I love you. More than I will ever be able to put into words in front of these people.'

He pressed his lips to the top of her head. 'I know. I'm not expecting gushing confessions of love in front of a crowd.'

'Am I to expect gushing confessions of love from you?'

'I did that last night, remember?'

They reached Father Agnar, and Astra turned to Dion, who took both her hands in his. He gave them a small squeeze, his eyes smiling at her. Of course she smiled back. She could not have held it back if she wanted to.

'Our dearly beloved God,' Father Agnar began. 'Stretch out Thy hand from Thy holy dwelling place and unite Thy servant and this handmaiden.'

~

'Should you be working at your own wedding?' Hali asked, frowning as Astra placed some pies on the table.

Astra shook her head. 'It is hardly work. Besides, I made the pies, so it seems only fitting that I serve them.'

Hali's eyes widened as she poked at one of the crusts. 'You made these? But they look amazing.'

'I think Hali means it as a compliment,' Aldara said,

joining them. 'Not sure why she is surprised. You have always excelled at anything you set your mind to.'

Hali folded her arms. 'Must you win at this also?'

'We are no longer in competition,' Aldara reminded her.

'Speak for yourself.'

Astra held back a smile. 'It is the only thing I can cook. Eda rarely lets me near anything else.'

Hali relaxed a little. 'You know, I have never seen you so...'

'Happy?' Aldara offered.

Hali bit down on her lip. 'I was going to say nice, but happy works also.'

Astra glanced at Aldara, who was smiling at the ground. 'Thank you—I think.'

Clearing her throat, Hali asked, 'Are you aware that there is a chicken following you around?'

Astra handed her a bowl filled with apple pie and a scoop of fresh cream. 'Yes.' She picked up another bowl and handed it to Aldara before picking up one for herself. The three women turned and looked over at the men standing in a group a few yards away.

'I have to say,' Astra said, 'I much prefer standing here eating pie than being over there feigning interest in their conversation.'

Aldara swallowed her mouthful of food. 'I was never very convincing anyway. Tyron saw straight through me.'

'They just talk about the most boring things,' Hali said, using her spoon to investigate the inside of the pie. 'I spent much of my time at Archdale fighting the urge to shout "no one cares about your sheep".' Astra and Aldara laughed quietly, and Hali leaned towards them. 'You know, having Fedora here makes me very nervous. I keep waiting for her to walk over and tell us to put our bowls down and go socialise.'

'We *are* socialising,' Aldara said, taking another spoonful of pie and looking in the mentor's direction. Fedora was seated with Sapphira and Isolda, who was talking her ear off. 'I can see her fighting the urge to stand and start organising everybody.'

'I did catch her straightening the plates earlier,' Hali whispered.

Aldara smiled. 'This outdoor setting will be giving her heart failure. Too many unknown variables.'

'She is actually much better than when she first arrived,' Astra said.

Hali groaned. 'She would have been unbearable, taking over everything.'

'How has it been between her and Sapphira?' Aldara asked.

Hali chewed quickly, covering her mouth. 'Mmm, yes, do tell.'

Astra shrugged and continued eating. 'Sapphira was quite happy to hand over what she describes as all the "boring aspects of running the household".'

Aldara glanced in Tyron's direction, and he broke away from the group and came towards them.

'Ladies,' he said, kissing Aldara's head as he stepped up to them. He peered behind her at the pies. 'Do I get a piece?'

'Here, have mine,' Aldara said, handing him her bowl.

Hali tutted. 'You could have been a little more discreet if you did not care for it.'

Aldara tilted her head. 'It was lovely. I am just full.'

Hali leaned closer to Astra. 'Always so polite.'

'I was just telling your husband,' Tyron said, changing the subject, 'that we will have to bring the children with us next time. They miss their cousins.'

'We would love that.'

'They wanted to come this time,' Aldara said, 'but the queen mother was rather eager for time with them.'

Tyron nodded. 'Eager is an understatement.'

A maid exited the house, and all the dogs loitering around the food took off in her direction. Astra's eyes narrowed on the letter in the young maid's hand.

'Excuse me for a moment,' she said, breaking away from the group.

Dion was already walking in that direction. They met halfway, and he slung an arm over her shoulders.

'I can't stop looking over at you,' he said. 'My beautiful wife.'

Astra kissed his rough cheek.

'You're not disappointed your family didn't come?'

She glanced over her shoulder. 'My family is here. Besides, my mother sent well wishes and a gift, which is far more than I was expecting.'

They came to a stop in front of the maid, Dion thanking the girl as he took the letter from her.

'Please tell me you do not have to go to Swanton Fort on our wedding night,' Astra said.

He kissed her again before opening the letter. She watched his face as he read, his eyebrows drawing closer together.

'I am afraid to ask.'

'It's from King Linus.' Dion glanced in Stamitos's direction. The moment the prince saw his face, he excused himself and made his way over to them.

'What is the matter?' Astra asked.

Dion looked at her. 'News from Drake Castle.'

'What kind of news?'

Dion handed the letter straight to Stamitos when he reached them. The prince ran his eyes over it, then swore.

'I need to tell Tyron.'

Dion nodded. 'Of course.'

Astra watched him jog off in the direction of his brother. 'What has happened?'

Dion's expression was tense. 'Brom and his men have surrounded Drake Castle.'

'Why?'

'I don't have the details.'

Astra searched his eyes. 'It is beginning.' She looked over at Stamitos and Tyron, who were now talking in hushed voices away from the women. 'They will be worried about Queen Cora.'

Dion rubbed his forehead. 'Any sensible brother would be.' He reached out and took hold of her face. 'I'm so sorry. I need to go to Reave Castle and meet with the king.'

She gave him a small smile. 'Of course you do. You are captain of the king's army. I knew who I was marrying.'

'I love you.' He kissed her before letting go of her face. 'Please go and enjoy your friends. I'll be back as soon as I can.'

She missed him already. They were rarely apart overnight. It had been that way since her return to Goldmont six months earlier. 'I am not going anywhere.'

Another kiss. And another.

'Go.' She laughed.

A final kiss and he was gone.

The princes went with Dion to Reave Castle for updates. Lord Yuri kept the children occupied with sword skills while Fedora watched on with disapproval. Isolda and her parents left after congratulating Astra once more and making her promise she would come to dinner. Eda and Hann pottered around, cleaning up after the celebration, not letting anyone else help.

'Take this and go,' Eda said, thrusting a bottle of wine at

Astra and ushering her away from the table. 'All of you now. Off you go.'

The women filled their cups and wandered down to Astra's favourite spot. Dion and the children had built her a bench seat beneath the tall maple near the chicken palace, where she could sit and watch the sunset. The pair often sat there long after the sun had disappeared, her legs draped across his. Now the four women sat shoulder to shoulder, drinks in hand, watching the sky change colour.

'I see why you love it here,' Aldara said.

'Because I'm here?' Sapphira asked, smiling.

Hali laughed into her drink. 'Yes, that is why. Nothing to do with Captain Honey Cake.'

Astra frowned. 'Is that what you all call him?'

'That is what Hali calls him,' Aldara replied.

Sapphira took a drink. 'It always comes back to food with Hali. Do you remember when she used to refer to Lord Thanos as Lord Sweet Buns?'

'That name had very little to do with food,' Hali replied.

Aldara laughed, and Astra shook her head.

'I cannot believe the two of you are leaving tomorrow,' Astra said. 'The time has gone so fast.' She looked at Hali. 'I hope Leksi and Petra did not mind having your daughter a few days.'

Hali waved her cup. 'Not at all. The children are always moving between the two houses. Adelaide thinks the boys are her cousins.'

Sapphira leaned forwards. 'They had a boy?'

'A little Leksi cut-out,' Aldara said.

Hali nodded in agreement. 'All smiles and dimples.' She took a drink, then looked at Astra. 'Do you think you and Captain Honey Cake will have children?'

'You do not think they have enough children here?' Aldara asked.

'Fair point.'

Astra took a long drink from her cup before speaking. 'I still take the herbs. Every day, without fail.'

Aldara reached over and squeezed her hand. 'You have plenty of time if it's something you want. You only got married today.'

Astra breathed out. 'I have spent years terrified by the idea of falling pregnant. I cannot imagine feeling any other way.'

Sapphira leaned back. 'Malin's breech birth probably didn't sell you on the idea.'

Hali pressed her knees together. 'Ouch.'

'I'm tempted to start back on the herbs after that delivery,' Sapphira said.

They all laughed, and Hali shifted forwards so she could see everyone. 'I think we should raise our cups to Astra.'

'Not just to me,' Astra said. 'To all of us.'

Aldara nodded. 'All right. What shall we drink to?'

Astra looked between them. 'How about strong women and new beginnings?'

'I like it,' Sapphira said, raising her cup.

Hali smiled. 'To strong women and new beginnings.'

Cups clinked, and then the four of them settled back on the bench, watching as the final smudges of orange sky faded to grey.

ACKNOWLEDGMENTS

I would like to express my gratitude to the many people who contributed to this book. My biggest thanks goes to my readers. Without you guys, I wouldn't get to do what I love. Next, a huge thank you to my rock star husband who supports and encourages me even though my writing takes time away from him. I love you to bits. A big thank you to Joanna Walsh for your ongoing feedback and support. A big shout-out to my beta readers, who each brought a unique perspective. Thank you to Kristin and the team at Hot Tree Editing for polishing the manuscript into something beautiful, and to my proofreader Rebecca Fletcher for catching everything I missed. A round of applause for my cover designer, MiblArt, for another gorgeous cover. And finally, a huge thank you to my Launch Team for your encouragement, honest reviews, and being the final set of eyes on my work. You guys are amazing.

ALSO BY TANYA BIRD

You can find a complete list of published works at
tanyabird.com/books